Henry James

Henry James OM (15 April 1843 – 28 February 1916) was an American-British author regarded as a key transitional figure between literary realism and literary modernism, and is considered by many to be among the greatest novelists in the English language. He was the son of Henry James Sr. and the brother of renowned philosopher and psychologist William James and diarist Alice James.

He is best known for a number of novels dealing with the social and marital interplay between émigré Americans, English people, and continental Europeans. Examples of such novels include The Portrait of a Lady, The Ambassadors, and The Wings of the Dove. His later works were increasingly experimental. In describing the internal states of mind and social dynamics of his characters, James often made use of a style in which ambiguous or contradictory motives and impressions were overlaid or juxtaposed in the discussion of a character's psyche.(Source: Wikipedia)

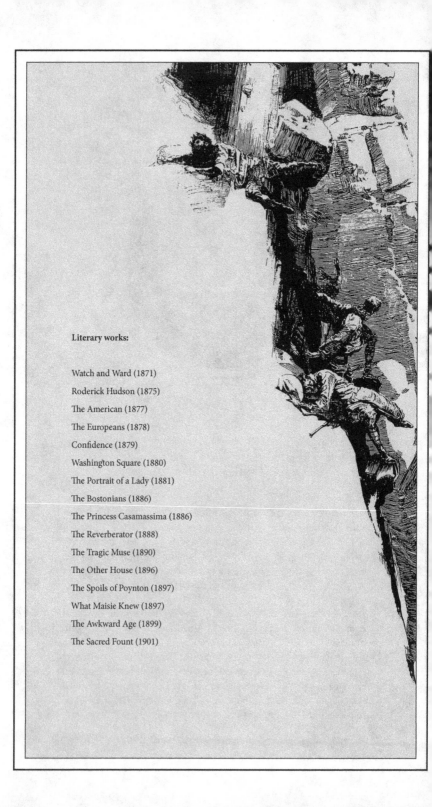

Literary works:

Watch and Ward (1871)

Roderick Hudson (1875)

The American (1877)

The Europeans (1878)

Confidence (1879)

Washington Square (1880)

The Portrait of a Lady (1881)

The Bostonians (1886)

The Princess Casamassima (1886)

The Reverberator (1888)

The Tragic Muse (1890)

The Other House (1896)

The Spoils of Poynton (1897)

What Maisie Knew (1897)

The Awkward Age (1899)

The Sacred Fount (1901)

THE
WORKS
OF
HENRY JAMES

VOL. 08 (OF 36)

GREVILLE FANE

HAWTHORNE

An Imprint of Moon Classics LLC

A Wholly Owned Subsidiary of Queenior LLC

A Melodragon Company

Copyright © 2020

First Printing: 2020

ISBN 978-1-6627-1562-4 (Paperback)

ISBN 978-1-6627-1563-1 (Hardcover)

Published by Moon Classics

www.moonclassics.com

Contents

THE
WORKS
OF
HENRY JAMES
VOL. 08 (OF 36)

GREVILLE FANE

GREVILLE FANE.

COMING in to dress for dinner, I found a telegram: "Mrs. Stormer dying; can you give us half a column for to-morrow evening? Let her off easy, but not too easy." I was late; I was in a hurry; I had very little time to think, but at a venture I dispatched a reply: "Will do what I can." It was not till I had dressed and was rolling away to dinner that, in the hansom, I bethought myself of the difficulty of the condition attached. The difficulty was not of course in letting her off easy but in qualifying that indulgence. "I simply won't qualify it," I said to myself. I didn't admire her, but I liked her, and I had known her so long that I almost felt heartless in sitting down at such an hour to a feast of indifference. I must have seemed abstracted, for the early years of my acquaintance with her came back to me. I spoke of her to the lady I had taken down, but the lady I had taken down had never heard of Greville Fane. I tried my other neighbour, who pronounced her books "too vile." I had never thought them very good, but I should let her off easier than that.

I came away early, for the express purpose of driving to ask about her. The journey took time, for she lived in the north-west district, in the neighbourhood of Primrose Hill. My apprehension that I should be too late was justified in a fuller sense than I had attached to it—I had only feared that the house would be shut up. There were lights in the windows, and the temperate tinkle of my bell brought a servant immediately to the door, but poor Mrs. Stormer had passed into a state in which the resonance of no earthly knocker was to be feared. A lady, in the hall, hovering behind the servant, came forward when she heard my voice. I recognised Lady Luard, but she had mistaken me for the doctor.

"Excuse my appearing at such an hour," I said; "it was the first possible moment after I heard."

"It's all over," Lady Luard replied. "Dearest mamma!"

She stood there under the lamp with her eyes on me; she was very tall, very stiff, very cold, and always looked as if these things, and some others beside, in her dress, her manner and even her name, were an implication that she was very admirable. I had never been able to follow the argument, but that is a detail. I expressed briefly and frankly what I felt, while the little mottled maidservant flattened herself against the wall of the narrow passage and tried to look detached without looking indifferent. It was not a moment to make a visit, and I was on the point of retreating when Lady Luard arrested me with a queer, casual, drawling "Would you—a—would you, perhaps, be *writing* something?" I felt for the instant like an interviewer, which I was not. But I pleaded guilty to this intention, on which she rejoined: "I'm so very glad—but I think my brother would like to see you." I detested her brother, but it wasn't an occasion to act this out; so I suffered myself to be inducted, to my surprise, into a small back room which I immediately recognised as the scene, during the later years, of Mrs. Stormer's imperturbable industry. Her table was there, the battered and blotted accessory to innumerable literary lapses, with its contracted space for the arms (she wrote only from the elbow down) and the confusion of scrappy, scribbled sheets which had already become literary remains. Leolin was also there, smoking a cigarette before the fire and looking impudent even in his grief, sincere as it well might have been.

To meet him, to greet him, I had to make a sharp effort; for the air that he wore to me as he stood before me was quite that of his mother's murderer. She lay silent for ever upstairs—as dead as an unsuccessful book, and his swaggering erectness was a kind of symbol of his having killed her. I wondered if he had already, with his sister, been calculating what they could get for the poor papers on the table; but I had not long to wait to learn, for in reply to the scanty words of sympathy I addressed him he puffed out: "It's miserable, miserable, yes; but she has left three books complete." His words had the oddest effect; they converted the cramped little room into a seat of trade and made the "book" wonderfully feasible. He would certainly get all that could be got for the three. Lady Luard explained to me that her husband had been with them but had had to go down to the House. To her brother she explained that I was going to write something, and to me again she made it clear that she hoped I would "do mamma justice." She added that she didn't think this had ever been done. She said to her brother: "Don't you think there are some things he ought thoroughly to understand?" and on his instantly exclaiming "Oh, thoroughly—thoroughly!" she went on, rather austerely: "I mean about mamma's birth."

"Yes, and her connections," Leolin added.

I professed every willingness, and for five minutes I listened, but it would be too much to say that I understood. I don't even now, but it is not important. My vision was of other matters than those they put before me, and while they desired there should be no mistake about their ancestors I became more and more lucid about themselves. I got away as soon as possible, and walked home through the great dusky, empty London—the best of all conditions for thought. By the time I reached my door my little article was practically composed—ready to be transferred on the morrow from the polished plate of fancy. I believe it attracted some notice, was thought "graceful" and was said to be by some one else. I had to be pointed without being lively, and it took some tact. But what I said was much less interesting than what I thought—especially during the half-hour I spent in my armchair by the fire, smoking the cigar I always light before going to bed. I went to sleep there, I believe; but I continued to moralise about Greville Fane. I am reluctant to lose that retrospect altogether, and this is a dim little memory of it, a document not to "serve." The dear woman had written a hundred stories, but none so curious as her own.

When first I knew her she had published half-a-dozen fictions, and I believe I had also perpetrated a novel. She was more than a dozen years older than I, but she was a person who always acknowledged her relativity. It was not so very long ago, but in London, amid the big waves of the present, even a near horizon gets hidden. I met her at some dinner and took her down, rather flattered at offering my arm to a celebrity. She didn't look like one, with her matronly, mild, inanimate face, but I supposed her greatness would come out in her conversation. I gave it all the opportunities I could, but I was not disappointed when I found her only a dull, kind woman. This was why I liked her—she rested me so from literature. To myself literature was an irritation, a torment; but Greville Fane slumbered in the intellectual part of it

15

like a Creole in a hammock. She was not a woman of genius, but her faculty was so special, so much a gift out of hand, that I have often wondered why she fell below that distinction. This was doubtless because the transaction, in her case, had remained incomplete; genius always pays for the gift, feels the debt, and she was placidly unconscious of obligation. She could invent stories by the yard, but she couldn't write a page of English. She went down to her grave without suspecting that though she had contributed volumes to the diversion of her contemporaries she had not contributed a sentence to the language. This had not prevented bushels of criticism from being heaped upon her head; she was worth a couple of columns any day to the weekly papers, in which it was shown that her pictures of life were dreadful but her style really charming. She asked me to come and see her, and I went. She lived then in Montpellier Square; which helped me to see how dissociated her imagination was from her character.

An industrious widow, devoted to her daily stint, to meeting the butcher and baker and making a home for her son and daughter, from the moment she took her pen in her hand she became a creature of passion. She thought the English novel deplorably wanting in that element, and the task she had cut out for herself was to supply the deficiency. Passion in high life was the general formula of this work, for her imagination was at home only in the most exalted circles. She adored, in truth, the aristocracy, and they constituted for her the romance of the world or, what is more to the point, the prime material of fiction. Their beauty and luxury, their loves and revenges, their temptations and surrenders, their immoralities and diamonds were as familiar to her as the blots on her writing-table. She was not a belated producer of the old fashionable novel, she had a cleverness and a modernness of her own, she had freshened up the fly-blown tinsel. She turned off plots by the hundred and—so far as her flying quill could convey her—was perpetually going abroad. Her types, her illustrations, her tone were nothing if not cosmopolitan. She recognised nothing less provincial than European society, and her fine folk knew each other and made love to each other from Doncaster to Bucharest. She had an idea that she resembled Balzac, and her favourite historical characters were Lucien de Rubempré and the Vidame de Pamiers. I must add that when I once asked her who the latter personage was

16

she was unable to tell me. She was very brave and healthy and cheerful, very abundant and innocent and wicked. She was clever and vulgar and snobbish, and never so intensely British as when she was particularly foreign.

This combination of qualities had brought her early success, and I remember having heard with wonder and envy of what she "got," in those days, for a novel. The revelation gave me a pang: it was such a proof that, practising a totally different style, I should never make my fortune. And yet when, as I knew her better she told me her real tariff and I saw how rumour had quadrupled it, I liked her enough to be sorry. After a while I discovered too that if she got less it was not that *I* was to get any more. My failure never had what Mrs. Stormer would have called the banality of being relative—it was always admirably absolute. She lived at ease however in those days—ease is exactly the word, though she produced three novels a year. She scorned me when I spoke of difficulty—it was the only thing that made her angry. If I hinted that a work of art required a tremendous licking into shape she thought it a pretension and a *pose*. She never recognised the "torment of form"; the furthest she went was to introduce into one of her books (in satire her hand was heavy) a young poet who was always talking about it. I couldn't quite understand her irritation on this score, for she had nothing at stake in the matter. She had a shrewd perception that form, in prose at least, never recommended any one to the public we were condemned to address, and therefore she lost nothing (putting her private humiliation aside) by not having any. She made no pretence of producing works of art, but had comfortable tea-drinking hours in which she freely confessed herself a common pastrycook, dealing in such tarts and puddings as would bring customers to the shop. She put in plenty of sugar and of cochineal, or whatever it is that gives these articles a rich and attractive colour. She had a serene superiority to observation and opportunity which constituted an inexpugnable strength and would enable her to go on indefinitely. It is only real success that wanes, it is only solid things that melt. Greville Fane's ignorance of life was a resource still more unfailing than the most approved receipt. On her saying once that the day would come when she should have written herself out I answered: "Ah, you look into fairyland, and the fairies love you, and *they* never change. Fairyland is always there; it always was from the beginning of time, and it always will be to the end. They've given you the key and you can always open the door. With me it's different; I try, in my clumsy way, to be in some direct relation to life." "Oh, bother your direct relation to life!" she used to reply, for she was always annoyed by the phrase—which would not in the least prevent her from using it when she wished to try for style. With no more prejudices than an old sausage-mill, she would give forth again with patient punctuality any poor verbal scrap that had been dropped into her. I cheered her with saying that the dark day, at the end, would be for the like of *me*; inasmuch as, going in our small way by experience and observation, we depended not on a revelation, but on a little tiresome process. Observation depended on opportunity, and where should we be when opportunity failed?

One day she told me that as the novelist's life was so delightful and during the good years at least such a comfortable support (she had these staggering optimisms) she meant to train up her boy to follow it. She took the ingenious view that it was a profession like another and that therefore everything was to be gained by beginning young and serving an apprenticeship. Moreover the education would be less expensive than any other special course, inasmuch as she could administer it herself. She didn't profess to keep a school, but she could at least teach her own child. It was not that she was so very clever, but (she confessed to me as if she were afraid I would laugh at her) that *he* was. I didn't laugh at her for that, for I thought the boy sharp—I had seen him at sundry times. He was well grown and good-looking and unabashed, and both he and his sister made me wonder about their defunct papa, concerning whom the little I knew was that he had been a clergyman. I explained them to myself by suppositions and imputations possibly unjust to the departed; so little were they—superficially at least—the children of their mother. There used to be, on an easel in her drawing-room, an enlarged photograph of her husband, done by some horrible posthumous "process" and draped, as to its florid frame, with a silken scarf, which testified to the candour of Greville Fane's bad taste. It made him look like an unsuccessful tragedian; but it was not a thing to trust. He may have been a successful comedian. Of the two children the girl was the elder, and struck me in all her younger years as singularly colourless. She was only very long, like an undecipherable letter.

It was not till Mrs. Stormer came back from a protracted residence abroad that Ethel (which was this young lady's name) began to produce the effect, which was afterwards remarkable in her, of a certain kind of high resolution. She made one apprehend that she meant to do something for herself. She was long-necked and near-sighted and striking, and I thought I had never seen sweet seventeen in a form so hard and high and dry. She was cold and affected and ambitious, and she carried an eyeglass with a long handle, which she put up whenever she wanted not to see. She had come out, as the phrase is, immensely; and yet I felt as if she were surrounded with a spiked iron railing. What she meant to do for herself was to marry, and it was the only thing, I think, that she meant to do for any one else; yet who would be inspired to clamber over that bristling barrier? What flower of tenderness or of intimacy would such an adventurer conceive as his reward?

This was for Sir Baldwin Luard to say; but he naturally never confided to me the secret. He was a joyless, jokeless young man, with the air of having other secrets as well, and a determination to get on politically that was indicated by his never having been known to commit himself—as regards any proposition whatever—beyond an exclamatory "Oh!" His wife and he must have conversed mainly in prim ejaculations, but they understood sufficiently that they were kindred spirits. I remember being angry with Greville Fane when she announced these nuptials to me as magnificent; I remember asking her what splendour there was in the union of the daughter of a woman of genius with an irredeemable mediocrity. "Oh! he's awfully clever," she said; but she blushed for the maternal fib. What she meant was that though Sir Baldwin's estates were not vast (he had a dreary house in South Kensington and a still drearier "Hall" somewhere in Essex, which was let), the connection was a "smarter" one than a child of hers could have aspired to form. In spite of the social bravery of her novels she took a very humble and dingy view of herself, so that of all her productions "my daughter Lady Luard" was quite the one she was proudest of. That personage thought her mother very vulgar and was distressed and perplexed by the occasional license of her pen, but had a complicated attitude in regard to this indirect connection with literature. So far as it was lucrative her ladyship approved of it, and could compound with the inferiority of the pursuit by doing practical justice to some of its advantages. I had reason to know (my reason was simply that poor Mrs. Stormer told me) that she suffered the inky fingers to press an occasional bank-note into her palm. On the other hand she deplored the "peculiar style" to which Greville Fane had devoted herself, and wondered where an author who had the convenience of so lady-like a daughter could have picked up such views about the best society. "She might know better, with Leolin and me," Lady Luard had been known to remark; but it appeared that some of Greville Fane's superstitions were incurable. She didn't live in Lady Luard's society, and the best was not good enough for her—she must make it still better.

I could see that this necessity grew upon her during the years she spent abroad, when I had glimpses of her in the shifting sojourns that lay in the path of my annual ramble. She betook herself from Germany to Switzerland and from Switzerland to Italy; she favoured cheap places and set up her desk in the smaller capitals. I took a look at her whenever I could, and I always asked how Leolin was getting on. She gave me beautiful accounts of him, and whenever it was possible the boy was produced for my edification. I had entered from the first into the joke of his career—I pretended to regard him as a consecrated child. It had been a joke for Mrs. Stormer at first, but the boy himself had been shrewd enough to make the matter serious. If his mother accepted the principle that the intending novelist cannot begin too early to see life, Leolin was not interested in hanging back from the application of it. He was eager to qualify himself, and took to cigarettes at ten, on the highest literary grounds. His poor mother gazed at him with extravagant envy and, like Desdemona, wished heaven had made *her* such a man. She explained to me more than once that in her profession she had found her sex a dreadful drawback. She loved the story of Madame George Sand's early rebellion against this hindrance, and believed that if she had worn trousers she could have written as well as that lady. Leolin had for the career at least the qualification of trousers, and as he grew older he recognised its importance by laying in an immense assortment. He grew up in gorgeous apparel, which was his way of interpreting his mother's system. Whenever I met her I found her still under the impression that she was carrying this system out and that Leolin's training was bearing fruit. She was giving him experience, she was giving him impressions, she was putting a *gagnepain* into his hand. It was another name for spoiling him with the best conscience in the world. The queerest pictures come back to me of this period of the good lady's life and of the extraordinarily virtuous, muddled, bewildering tenor of it. She had an idea that she was seeing foreign manners as well as her petticoats would allow; but, in reality she was not seeing anything, least of all fortunately how much she was laughed at. She drove her whimsical pen at Dresden and at Florence, and produced in all places and at all times the same romantic and ridiculous fictions. She carried about her box of properties and fished out promptly the familiar, tarnished old puppets. She believed in them when others couldn't, and as they were like nothing that was to be seen under the sun it was impossible to prove by comparison that they were wrong. You can't compare birds and fishes; you could only feel that, as Greville Fane's characters had the fine plumage of the former species, human beings must be of the latter.

It would have been droll if it had not been so exemplary to see her tracing the loves of the duchesses beside the innocent cribs of her children. The immoral and the maternal lived together in her diligent days on the most comfortable terms, and she stopped curling the mustaches of her Guardsmen to pat the heads of her babes. She was haunted by solemn spinsters who came to tea from continental *pensions*, and by unsophisticated Americans who told her she was just loved in *their* country. "I had rather be just paid there," she usually replied; for this tribute of transatlantic opinion was the only thing that galled her. The Americans went away thinking her coarse; though as the author of so many beautiful love-stories she was disappointing to most of these pilgrims, who had not expected to find a shy, stout, ruddy lady in a cap like a crumbled pyramid. She wrote about the affections and the impossibility of controlling them, but she talked of the price of *pension* and the convenience of an English chemist. She devoted much thought and many thousands of francs to the education of her daughter, who spent three years at a very superior school at Dresden, receiving wonderful instruction in sciences, arts and tongues, and who, taking a different line from Leolin, was to be brought up wholly as a *femme du monde*. The girl was musical and philological; she made a specialty of languages and learned enough about them to be inspired with a great contempt for her mother's artless accents. Greville Fane's French and Italian were droll; the imitative faculty had been denied her, and she had an unequalled gift, especially pen in hand, of squeezing big mistakes into small opportunities. She knew it, but she didn't care; correctness was the virtue in the world that, like her heroes and heroines, she valued least. Ethel, who had perceived in her pages some remarkable lapses, undertook at one time to revise her proofs; but I remember her telling me a year after the girl had left school that this function had been very briefly exercised. "She can't read me," said Mrs. Stormer; "I offend her taste. She tells me that at Dresden— at school—I was never allowed." The good lady seemed surprised at this, having the best conscience in the world about her lucubrations. She had never meant to fly in the face of anything, and considered that she grovelled before the Rhadamanthus of the English literary tribunal, the celebrated and awful Young Person. I assured her, as a joke, that she was frightfully indecent (she hadn't in fact that reality any more than any other) my purpose being solely to prevent her from guessing that her daughter had dropped her not because she was immoral but because she was vulgar. I used to figure her children closeted together and asking each other while they exchanged a gaze of dismay: "Why should she *be* so—and so *fearfully* so—when she has the advantage of our society? Shouldn't *we* have taught her better?" Then I imagined their recognising with a blush and a shrug that she was unteachable, irreformable. Indeed she was, poor lady; but it is never fair to read by the light of taste things that were not written by it. Greville Fane had, in the topsy-turvy, a serene good faith that ought to have been safe from allusion, like a stutter or a *faux pas*.

She didn't make her son ashamed of the profession to which he was destined, however; she only made him ashamed of the way she herself exercised it. But he bore his humiliation much better than his sister, for he was ready to take for granted that he should one day restore the balance. He was a canny and far-seeing youth, with appetites and aspirations, and he had not a scruple in his composition. His mother's theory of the happy knack he could pick up deprived him of the wholesome discipline required to prevent young idlers from becoming cads. He had, abroad, a casual tutor and a snatch or two of a Swiss school, but no consecutive study, no prospect of a university or a degree. It may be imagined with what zeal, as the years went on, he entered into the pleasantry of there being no manual so important to him as the massive book of life. It was an expensive volume to peruse, but Mrs. Stormer was willing to lay out a sum in what she would have called her *premiers frais*. Ethel disapproved—she thought this education far too unconventional for an English gentleman. Her voice was for Eton and Oxford, or for any public school (she would have resigned herself) with the army to follow. But Leolin never was afraid of his sister, and they visibly disliked, though they sometimes agreed to assist, each other. They could combine to work the oracle—to keep their mother at her desk.

When she came back to England, telling me she had got all the continent could give her, Leolin was a broad-shouldered, red-faced young man, with an immense wardrobe and an extraordinary assurance of manner. She was fondly obstinate about her having taken the right course with him, and proud of all that he knew and had seen. He was now quite ready to begin, and a little while later she told me he *had* begun. He had written something tremendously clever, and it was coming out in the *Cheapside*. I believe it came out; I had no time to look for it; I never heard anything about it. I took for granted that if this contribution had passed through his mother's hands it had practically become a specimen of her own genius, and it was interesting to consider Mrs. Stormer's future in the light of her having to write her son's novels as well as her own. This was not the way she looked at it herself; she took the charming ground that he would help her to write hers. She used to tell me that he supplied passages of the greatest value to her own work—all sorts of technical things, about hunting and yachting and wine—that she couldn't be expected to get very straight. It was all so much practice for him and so much alleviation for her. I was unable to identify these pages, for I had long since ceased to "keep up" with Greville Fane; but I was quite able to believe that the wine-question had been put, by Leolin's good offices, on a better footing, for the dear lady used to mix her drinks (she was perpetually serving the most splendid suppers) in the queerest fashion. I could see that he was willing enough to accept a commission to look after that department. It occurred to me indeed, when Mrs. Stormer settled in England again, that by making a shrewd use of both her children she might be able to rejuvenate her style. Ethel had come back to gratify her young ambition, and if she couldn't take her mother into society she would at least go into it herself. Silently, stiffly, almost grimly, this young lady held up her head, clenched her long teeth, squared her lean elbows and made her way up the staircases she had elected. The only communication she ever made to me, the only effusion of confidence with which she ever honoured me, was when she said: "I don't want to know the people mamma knows; I mean to know others." I took due note of the remark, for I was not one of the "others." I couldn't trace therefore the steps of her process; I could only admire it at a distance and congratulate her mother on the results. The results were that Ethel went to "big" parties and got people to take her. Some of them were people she had met abroad, and others were people whom the people she had met abroad had met. They ministered alike to Miss Ethel's convenience, and I wondered how she extracted so many favours without the expenditure of a smile. Her smile was the dimmest thing in the world, diluted lemonade, without sugar, and she had arrived precociously at social wisdom, recognising that if she was neither pretty enough nor rich enough nor clever enough, she could at least in her muscular youth be rude enough. Therefore if she was able to tell her mother what really took place in the mansions of the great, give her notes to work from, the quill could be driven at home to better purpose and precisely at a moment when it would have to be more active than ever. But if she did tell, it would appear that poor Mrs. Stormer didn't believe. As regards many points this was not a wonder; at any rate I heard nothing of Greville Fane's having developed a new manner. She had only one manner from start to finish, as Leolin would have said.

She was tired at last, but she mentioned to me that she couldn't afford to pause. She continued to speak of Leolin's work as the great hope of their future (she had saved no money) though the young man wore to my sense an aspect more and more professional if you like, but less and less literary. At the end of a couple of years there was something monstrous in the impudence with which he played his part in the comedy. When I wondered how she could play *her* part I had to perceive that her good faith was complete and that what kept it so was simply her extravagant fondness. She loved the young impostor with a simple, blind, benighted love, and of all the heroes of romance who had passed before her eyes he was by far the most brilliant.

He was at any rate the most real—she could touch him, pay for him, suffer for him, worship him. He made her think of her princes and dukes, and when she wished to fix these figures in her mind's eye she thought of her boy. She had often told me she was carried away by her own creations, and she was certainly carried away by Leolin. He vivified, by potentialities at least, the whole question of youth and passion. She held, not unjustly, that the sincere novelist should feel the whole flood of life; she acknowledged with regret that she had not had time to feel it herself, and it was a joy to her that the deficiency might be supplied by the sight of the way it was rushing through this magnificent young man. She exhorted him, I suppose, to let it rush; she wrung her own flaccid little sponge into the torrent. I knew not what passed between them in her hours of tuition, but I gathered that she mainly impressed on him that the great thing was to live, because that gave you material. He asked nothing better; he collected material, and the formula served as a universal pretext. You had only to look at him to see that, with his rings and breastpins, his cross-barred jackets, his early *embonpoint*, his eyes that looked like imitation jewels, his various indications of a dense, full-blown temperament, his idea of life was singularly vulgar; but he was not so far wrong as that his response to his mother's expectations was not in a high degree practical. If she had imposed a profession on him from his tenderest years it was exactly a profession that he followed. The two were not quite the same, inasmuch as *his* was simply to live at her expense; but at least she couldn't say that he hadn't taken a line. If she insisted on believing in him he offered himself to the sacrifice. My impression is that her secret dream was that he should have a *liaison* with a countess, and he persuaded her without difficulty that he had one. I don't know what countesses are capable of, but I have a clear notion of what Leolin was.

He didn't persuade his sister, who despised him—she wished to work her mother in her own way, and I asked myself why the girl's judgment of him didn't make me like her better. It was because it didn't save her after all from a mute agreement with him to go halves. There were moments when I couldn't help looking hard into his atrocious young eyes, challenging him to confess his fantastic fraud and give it up. Not a little tacit conversation passed between us in this way, but he had always the best of it. If I said: "Oh, come now, with *me* you needn't keep it up; plead guilty, and I'll let you off," he wore the most ingenuous, the most candid expression, in the depths of which I could read: "Oh, yes, I know it exasperates you—that's just why I do it." He took the line of earnest inquiry, talked about Balzac and Flaubert, asked me if I thought Dickens *did* exaggerate and Thackeray *ought* to be called a pessimist. Once he came to see me, at his mother's suggestion he declared, on purpose to ask me how far, in my opinion, in the English novel, one really might venture to "go." He was not resigned to the usual pruderies—he suffered under them already. He struck out the brilliant idea that nobody knew how far we might go, for nobody had ever tried. Did I think *he* might safely try—would it injure his mother if he did? He would rather disgrace himself by his timidities than injure his mother, but certainly some one ought to try. Wouldn't *I* try—couldn't I be prevailed upon to look at it as a duty? Surely the ultimate point ought to be fixed—he was worried, haunted by the question. He patronised me unblushingly, made me feel like a foolish amateur, a helpless novice, inquired into my habits of work and conveyed to me that I was utterly *vieux jeu* and had not had the advantage of an early training. I had not been brought up from the germ, I knew nothing of life—didn't go at it on *his* system. He had dipped into French feuilletons and picked up plenty of phrases, and he made a much better show in talk than his poor mother, who never had time to read anything and could only be vivid with her pen. If I didn't kick him downstairs it was because he would have alighted on her at the bottom.

When she went to live at Primrose Hill I called upon her and found her weary and wasted. It had waned a good deal, the elation caused the year before by Ethel's marriage; the foam on the cup had subsided and there was a bitterness in the draught.

She had had to take a cheaper house and she had to work still harder to pay even for that. Sir Baldwin was obliged to be close; his charges were fearful, and the dream of her living with her daughter (a vision she had never mentioned to me) must be renounced. "I would have helped with things, and I could have lived perfectly in one room," she said; "I would have paid for everything, and—after all—I'm some one, ain't I? But I don't fit in, and Ethel tells me there are tiresome people she *must* receive. I can help them from here, no doubt, better than from there. She told me once, you know, what she thinks of my picture of life. 'Mamma, your picture of life is preposterous!' No doubt it is, but she's vexed with me for letting my prices go down; and I had to write three novels to pay for all her marriage cost me. I did it very well—I mean the outfit and the wedding; but that's why I'm here. At any rate she doesn't want a dingy old woman in her house. I should give it an atmosphere of literary glory, but literary glory is only the eminence of nobodies. Besides, she doubts my glory—she knows I'm glorious only at Peckham and Hackney. She doesn't want her friends to ask if I've never known nice people. She can't tell them I've never been in society. She tried to teach me better once, but I couldn't learn. It would seem too as if Peckham and Hackney had had enough of me; for (don't tell any one!) I've had to take less for my last than I ever took for anything." I asked her how little this had been, not from curiosity, but in order to upbraid her, more disinterestedly than Lady Luard had done, for such concessions. She answered "I'm ashamed to tell you," and then she began to cry.

I had never seen her break down, and I was proportionately moved; she sobbed, like a frightened child, over the extinction of her vogue and the exhaustion of her vein. Her little workroom seemed indeed a barren place to grow flowers, and I wondered, in the after years (for she continued to produce and publish) by what desperate and heroic process she dragged them out of the soil. I remember asking her on that occasion what had become of Leolin, and how much longer she intended to allow him to amuse himself at her cost. She rejoined with spirit, wiping her eyes, that he was down at Brighton hard at work—he was in the midst of a novel—and that he *felt* life so, in all its misery and mystery, that it was cruel to speak of such experiences as a pleasure. "He goes beneath the surface," she said, "and he *forces* himself to look at things from which he would rather turn away. Do you call that amusing yourself? You should see his face sometimes! And he does it for me as much as for himself. He tells me everything—he comes home to me with his *trouvailles*. We are artists together, and to the artist all things are pure. I've often heard you say so yourself." The novel that Leolin was engaged in at Brighton was never published, but a friend of mine and of Mrs. Stormer's who was staying there happened to mention to me later that he had seen the young apprentice to fiction driving, in a dogcart, a young lady with a very pink face. When I suggested that she was perhaps a woman of title with whom he was conscientiously flirting my informant replied: "She is indeed, but do you know what her title is?" He pronounced it—it was familiar and descriptive—but I won't reproduce it here. I don't know whether Leolin mentioned it to his mother: she would have needed all the purity of the artist to forgive him. I hated so to come across him that in the very last years I went rarely to see her, though I knew that she had come pretty well to the end of her rope. I didn't want her to tell me that she had fairly to give her books away—I didn't want to see her cry. She kept it up amazingly, and every few months, at my club, I saw three new volumes, in green, in crimson, in blue, on the book-table that groaned with light literature. Once I met her at the Academy soirée, where you meet people you thought were dead, and she vouchsafed the information, as if she owed it to me in candour, that Leolin had been obliged to recognise insuperable difficulties in the question of *form*, he was so fastidious; so that she had now arrived at a definite understanding with him (it was such a comfort) that *she* would do the form if he would bring home the substance. That was now his position—he foraged for her in the great world at a salary. "He's my 'devil,' don't you see? as if I were a great lawyer: he gets up the case and I argue it." She mentioned further that in addition to his salary he was paid by the piece: he got so much for a striking character, so much for a pretty name, so much for a plot, so much for an incident, and had so much promised him if he would invent a new crime.

"He *has* invented one," I said, "and he's paid every day of his life."

"What is it?" she asked, looking hard at the picture of the year; "Baby's Tub," near which we happened to be standing.

I hesitated a moment. "I myself will write a little story about it, and then you'll see."

But she never saw; she had never seen anything, and she passed away with her fine blindness unimpaired. Her son published every scrap of scribbled paper that could be extracted from her table-drawers, and his sister quarrelled with him mortally about the proceeds, which showed that she only wanted a pretext, for they cannot have been great. I don't know what Leolin lives upon, unless it be on a queer lady many years older than himself, whom he lately married. The last time I met him he said to me with his infuriating smile: "Don't you think we can go a little further still—just a little?" *He* really goes too far.

HAWTHORNE

CHAPTER I. EARLY YEARS.

It will be necessary, for several reasons, to give this short sketch the form rather of a critical essay than of a biography. The data for a life of Nathaniel Hawthorne are the reverse of copious, and even if they were abundant they would serve but in a limited measure the purpose of the biographer. Hawthorne's career was probably as tranquil and uneventful a one as ever fell to the lot of a man of letters; it was almost strikingly deficient in incident, in what may be called the dramatic quality. Few men of equal genius and of equal eminence can have led on the whole a simpler life. His six volumes of Note-Books illustrate this simplicity; they are a sort of monument to an unagitated fortune. Hawthorne's career had few vicissitudes or variations; it was passed for the most part in a small and homogeneous society, in a provincial, rural community; it had few perceptible points of contact with what is called the world, with public events, with the manners of his time, even with the life of his neighbours. Its literary incidents are not numerous. He produced, in quantity, but little. His works consist of four novels and the fragment of another, five volumes of short tales, a collection of sketches, and a couple of story-books for children. And yet some account of the man and the writer is well worth giving. Whatever may have been Hawthorne's private lot, he has the importance of being the most beautiful and most eminent representative of a literature. The importance of the literature may be questioned, but at any rate, in the field of letters, Hawthorne is the most valuable example of the American genius. That genius has not, as a whole, been literary; but Hawthorne was on his limited scale a master of expression. He is the writer to whom his countrymen most confidently point when they wish to make a claim to have enriched the mother-tongue, and, judging from present appearances, he will long occupy this honourable position. If there is something very fortunate for him in the way that he borrows an added relief from the absence of competitors in his own line and from the general flatness of the literary field that surrounds him, there is also, to a spectator, something almost touching in his situation. He was so modest and delicate a genius that we may fancy him appealing from the lonely honour of a representative attitude—perceiving a painful incongruity between his imponderable literary baggage and the large conditions of American life. Hawthorne on the one side is so subtle and slender and unpretending, and the American world on the other is so vast and various and substantial, that it might seem to the author of *The Scarlet Letter* and the *Mosses from an Old Manse*, that we render him a poor service in contrasting his proportions with those of a great civilization. But our author must accept the awkward as well as the graceful side of his fame; for he has the advantage of pointing a valuable moral. This moral is that the flower of art blooms only where the soil is deep, that it takes a great deal of history to produce a little literature, that it needs a complex social machinery to set a writer in motion. American civilization has hitherto had other things to do than to produce flowers, and before giving birth to writers it has wisely occupied itself with providing something for them to write about. Three or four beautiful talents of trans-Atlantic growth are the sum of what the world usually recognises, and in this modest nosegay the genius of Hawthorne is admitted to have the rarest and sweetest fragrance.

His very simplicity has been in his favour; it has helped him to appear complete and homogeneous. To talk of his being national would be to force the note and make a mistake of proportion; but he is, in spite of the absence of the realistic quality, intensely and vividly local. Out of the soil of New England he sprang—in a crevice of that immitigable granite he sprouted and bloomed. Half of the interest that he possesses for an American reader with any turn for analysis must reside in his latent New England savour; and I think it no more than just to say that whatever entertainment he may yield to those who know him at a distance, it is an almost indispensable condition of properly appreciating him to have received a personal impression of the manners, the morals, indeed of the very climate, of the great region of which the remarkable city of Boston is the metropolis. The cold, bright air of New England seems to blow through his pages, and these, in the opinion of many people, are the medium in which it is most agreeable to make the acquaintance of that tonic atmosphere. As to whether it is worth while to seek to know something of New England in order to extract a more intimate quality from *The House of Seven Gables* and *The Blithedale Romance*, I need not pronounce; but it is certain that a considerable observation of the society to which these productions were more directly addressed is a capital preparation for enjoying them. I have alluded to the absence in Hawthorne of that quality of realism which is now so much in fashion, an absence in regard to which there will of course be more to say; and yet I think I am not fanciful in saying that he testifies to the sentiments of the society in which he flourished almost as pertinently (proportions observed) as Balzac and some of his descendants—MM. Flaubert and Zola—testify to the manners and morals of the French people. He was not a man with a literary theory; he was guiltless of a system, and I am not sure that he had ever heard of Realism, this remarkable compound having (although it was invented some time earlier) come into general use only since his death. He had certainly not proposed to himself to give an account of the social idiosyncrasies of his fellow-citizens, for his touch on such points is always light and vague, he has none of the apparatus of an historian, and his shadowy style of portraiture never suggests a rigid standard of accuracy. Nevertheless he virtually offers the most vivid reflection of New England life that has found its way into literature. His value in this respect is not diminished by the fact that he has not attempted to portray the usual Yankee of comedy, and that he has been almost culpably indifferent to his opportunities for commemorating the variations of colloquial English that may be observed in the New World. His characters do not express themselves in the dialect of the *Biglow Papers*—their language indeed is apt to be too elegant, too delicate. They are not portraits of actual types, and in their phraseology there is nothing imitative. But none the less, Hawthorne's work savours thoroughly of the local soil—it is redolent of the social system in which he had his being.

This could hardly fail to be the case, when the man himself was so deeply rooted in the soil. Hawthorne sprang from the primitive New England stock; he had a very definite and conspicuous pedigree. He was born at Salem, Massachusetts, on the 4th of July, 1804, and his birthday was the great American festival, the anniversary of the Declaration of national Independence.[1] Hawthorne was in his disposition an unqualified and unflinching American; he found occasion to give us the measure of the fact during the seven years that he spent in Europe toward the close of his life; and this was no more than proper on the part of a man who had enjoyed the honour of coming into the world on the day on which of all the days in the year the great Republic enjoys her acutest fit of self-consciousness. Moreover, a person who has been ushered into life by the ringing of bells and the booming of cannon (unless indeed he be frightened straight out of it again by the uproar of his awakening) receives by this very fact an injunction to do something great, something that will justify such striking natal accompaniments. Hawthorne was by race of the clearest Puritan strain. His earliest American ancestors (who wrote the name "Hathorne"—the shape in which it was transmitted to Nathaniel, who inserted the *w*,) was the younger son of a Wiltshire family, whose residence, according to a note of our author's in 1837, was "Wigcastle, Wigton." Hawthorne, in the note in question, mentions the gentleman who was at that time the head of the family; but it does not appear that he at any period renewed acquaintance with his English kinsfolk. Major William Hathorne came out to Massachusetts in the early years of the Puritan settlement; in 1635 or 1636, according to the note to which I have just alluded; in 1630 according to information presumably more accurate. He was one of the band of companions of the virtuous and exemplary John Winthrop, the almost life-long royal Governor of the young colony, and the brightest and most amiable figure in the early Puritan annals. How amiable William Hathorne may have been I know not, but he was evidently of the stuff of which the citizens of the Commonwealth were best advised to be made. He was a sturdy fighting man, doing solid execution upon both the inward and outward enemies of the State. The latter were the savages, the former the Quakers; the energy expended by the early Puritans in resistance to the tomahawk not weakening their disposition to deal with spiritual dangers. They employed the same—or almost the same—weapons in both directions; the flintlock and the halberd against the Indians, and the cat-o'-nine-tails against the heretics. One of the longest, though by no means one of the most successful, of Hawthorne's shorter tales (*The Gentle Boy*) deals with this pitiful persecution of the least aggressive of all schismatic bodies. William Hathorne, who had been made a magistrate of the town of Salem, where a grant of land had been offered him as an inducement to residence, figures in New England history as having given orders that "Anne Coleman and four of her friends" should be whipped through Salem, Boston, and Dedham. This Anne Coleman, I suppose, is the woman alluded to in that fine passage in the Introduction to *The Scarlet Letter*, in which Hawthorne pays a qualified tribute to the founder of the American branch of his race:—

"The figure of that first ancestor, invested by family tradition with a dim and dusky grandeur, was present to my boyish imagination as far back as I can remember. It still haunts me, and induces a sort of home-feeling with the past, which I scarcely claim in reference to the present, phase of the town. I seem to have a stronger claim to a residence here on account of this grave, bearded, sable-cloaked and steeple-crowned progenitor—who came so early, with his Bible and his sword, and trod the unworn street with such a stately port, and make so large a figure as a man of war and peace—a stronger claim than for myself, whose name is seldom heard and my face hardly known. He was a soldier, legislator, judge; he was a ruler in the church; he had all the Puritanic traits, both good and evil. He was likewise a bitter persecutor, as witness the Quakers, who have remembered him in their histories, and relate an incident of his hard severity towards a woman of their sect which will last longer, it is to be feared, than any of his better deeds, though these were many."

FOOTNOTE

[1]It is proper that before I go further I should acknowledge my large obligations to the only biography of our author, of any considerable length, that has been written—the little volume

entitled *A Study of Hawthorne*, by Mr. George Parsons Lathrop, the son-in-law of the subject of the work. (Boston, 1876.) To this ingenious and sympathetic sketch, in which the author has taken great pains to collect the more interesting facts of Hawthorne's life, I am greatly indebted. Mr. Lathrop's work is not pitched in the key which many another writer would have chosen, and his tone is not to my sense the truly critical one; but without the help afforded by his elaborate essay the present little volume could not have been prepared.

William Hathorne died in 1681; but those hard qualities that his descendant speaks of were reproduced in his son John, who bore the title of Colonel, and who was connected, too intimately for his honour, with that deplorable episode of New England history, the persecution of-the so-called Witches of Salem. John Hathorne is introduced into the little drama entitled *The Salem Farms* in Longfellow's *New England Tragedies*. I know not whether he had the compensating merits of his father, but our author speaks of him, in the continuation of the passage I have just quoted, as having made himself so conspicuous in the martyrdom of the witches, that their blood may be said to have left a stain upon him. "So deep a stain, indeed," Hawthorne adds, characteristically, "that his old dry bones in the Charter Street burial-ground must still retain it, if they have not crumbled utterly to dust." Readers of *The House of the Seven Gables* will remember that the story concerns itself with a family which is supposed to be overshadowed by a curse launched against one of its earlier members by a poor man occupying a lowlier place in the world, whom this ill-advised ancestor had been the means of bringing to justice for the crime of witchcraft. Hawthorne apparently found the idea of the history of the Pyncheons in his own family annals. His witch-judging ancestor was reported to have incurred a malediction from one of his victims, in consequence of which the prosperity of the race faded utterly away. "I know not," the passage I have already quoted goes on, "whether these ancestors of mine bethought themselves to repent and ask pardon of Heaven for their cruelties, or whether they are now groaning under the heavy consequences of them in another state of being. At all events, I, the present writer, hereby take shame upon myself for their sakes, and pray that any curse incurred by them—as I have heard, and as the dreary and unprosperous condition of the race for some time back would argue to exist—may be now and henceforth removed." The two first American Hathornes had been people of importance and responsibility; but with the third generation the family lapsed into an obscurity from which it emerged in the very person of the writer who begs so gracefully for a turn in its affairs. It is very true, Hawthorne proceeds, in the Introduction to *The Scarlet Letter*, that from the original point of view such lustre as he might have contrived to confer upon the name would have appeared more than questionable.

"Either of these stern and black-browed Puritans would have thought it quite a sufficient retribution for his sins that after so long a lapse of years the old trunk of the family tree, with so much venerable moss upon it, should have borne, as its topmost bough, an idler like myself. No aim that I have ever cherished would they recognise as laudable; no success of mine, if my life, beyond its domestic scope, had ever been brightened by success, would they deem otherwise than worthless, if not positively disgraceful. 'What is he?' murmurs one grey shadow of my forefathers to the other. 'A writer of story-books! What kind of a business in life, what manner of glorifying God, or being serviceable to mankind in his day and generation, may that be? Why, the degenerate fellow might as well have been a fiddler!' Such are the compliments bandied between my great grandsires and myself across the gulf of time! And yet, let them scorn me as they will, strong traits of their nature have intertwined themselves with mine."

In this last observation we may imagine that there was not a little truth. Poet and novelist as Hawthorne was, sceptic and dreamer and little of a man of action, late-coming fruit of a tree which might seem to have lost the power to bloom, he was morally, in an appreciative degree, a chip of the old block. His forefathers had crossed the Atlantic for conscience' sake, and it was the idea of the urgent conscience that haunted the imagination of their so-called degenerate successor. The Puritan strain in his blood ran clear—there are passages in his Diaries, kept during his residence in Europe, which might almost have been written by the grimmest of the old Salem worthies. To him as to them, the consciousness of *sin* was the most importunate fact of life, and if they had undertaken to write little tales, this baleful substantive, with its attendant adjective, could hardly have been more frequent in their pages than in those of their fanciful descendant. Hawthorne had moreover in his composition contemplator and dreamer as he was, an element of simplicity and rigidity, a something plain and masculine and sensible, which might have kept his black-browed grandsires on better terms with him than he admits to be possible. However little they might have appreciated the artist, they would have approved of the man. The play of Hawthorne's intellect was light and capricious, but the man himself was firm and rational. The imagination was profane, but the temper was not degenerate.

The "dreary and unprosperous condition" that he speaks of in regard to the fortunes of his family is an allusion to the fact that several generations followed each other on the soil in which they had been planted, that during the eighteenth century a succession of Hathornes trod the simple streets of Salem without ever conferring any especial lustre upon the town or receiving, presumably, any great delight from it. A hundred years of Salem would perhaps be rather a dead-weight for any family to carry, and we venture to imagine that the Hathornes were dull and depressed. They did what they could, however, to improve their situation; they trod the Salem streets as little as possible. They went to sea, and made long voyages; seamanship became the regular profession of the family. Hawthorne has said it in charming language. "From father to son, for above a hundred years, they followed the sea; a grey-headed shipmaster, in each generation, retiring from the quarter-deck to the homestead, while a boy of fourteen took the hereditary place before the mast, confronting the salt spray and the gale which had blustered against his sire and grandsire. The boy also, in due time, passed from the forecastle to the cabin, spent a tempestuous manhood, and returned from his world-wanderings to grow old and die and mingle his dust with the natal earth." Our author's grandfather, Daniel Hathorne, is mentioned by Mr. Lathrop, his biographer and son-in-law, as a hardy privateer during the war of Independence. His father, from whom he was named, was also a shipmaster, and he died in foreign lands, in the exercise of his profession. He was carried off by a fever, at Surinam, in 1808. He left three children, of whom Nathaniel was the only boy. The boy's mother, who had been a Miss Manning, came of a New England stock almost as long-established as that of her husband; she is described by our author's biographer as a woman of remarkable beauty, and by an authority whom he quotes, as being "a minute observer of religious festivals," of "feasts, fasts, new-moons, and Sabbaths." Of feasts the poor lady in her Puritanic home can have had but a very limited number to celebrate; but of new-moons, she may be supposed to have enjoyed the usual, and of Sabbaths even more than the usual, proportion.

In quiet provincial Salem, Nathaniel Hawthorne passed the greater part of his boyhood, as well as many years of his later life. Mr. Lathrop has much to say about the ancient picturesqueness of the place, and about the mystic influences it would project upon such a mind and character as Hawthorne's. These things are always relative, and in appreciating them everything depends upon the point of view. Mr. Lathrop writes for American readers, who in such a matter as this are very easy to please. Americans have as a general thing a hungry passion for the picturesque, and they are so fond of local colour that they contrive to perceive it in localities in which the amateurs of other countries would detect only the most neutral tints. History, as yet, has left in the United States but so thin and impalpable a deposit that we very soon touch the hard substratum of nature; and nature herself, in the western world, has the peculiarity of seeming rather crude and immature. The very air looks new and young; the light of the sun seems fresh and innocent, as if it knew as yet but few of the secrets of the world and none of the weariness of shining; the vegetation has the appearance of not having reached its majority. A large juvenility is stamped upon the face of things, and in the vividness of the present, the past, which died so young and had time to produce so little, attracts but scanty attention. I doubt whether English observers would discover any very striking trace of it in the ancient town of Salem. Still, with all respect to a York and a Shrewsbury, to a Toledo and a Verona, Salem has a physiognomy in which the past plays a more important part than the present. It is of course a very recent past; but one must remember that the dead of yesterday are not more alive than those of a century ago. I know not of what picturesqueness Hawthorne was conscious in his respectable birthplace; I suspect his perception of it was less keen than his biographer assumes it to have been; but he must have felt at least that of whatever complexity of earlier life there had been in the country, the elm-shadowed streets of Salem were a recognisable memento. He has made considerable mention of the place, here and there, in his tales; but he has nowhere dilated upon it very lovingly, and it is noteworthy that in *The House of the Seven Gables*, the only one of his novels of which the scene is laid in it, he has by no means availed himself of the opportunity to give a description of it. He had of course a filial fondness for it—a deep-seated sense of connection with it; but he must have spent some very dreary years there, and the two feelings, the mingled tenderness and rancour, are visible in the Introduction to *The Scarlet Letter*.

"The old town of Salem," he writes,—"my native place, though I have dwelt much away from it, both in boyhood and in maturer years—possesses, or did possess, a hold on my affections, the force of which I have never realized during my seasons of actual residence here. Indeed, so far as the physical aspect is concerned, with its flat, unvaried surface, covered chiefly with wooden houses, few or none of which pretend to architectural beauty; its irregularity, which is neither picturesque nor quaint, but only tame; its long and lazy street, lounging wearisomely through the whole extent of the peninsula, with Gallows Hill and New Guinea at one end, and a view of the almshouse at the other—such being the features of my native town it would be quite as reasonable to form a sentimental attachment to a disarranged chequer-board."

But he goes on to say that he has never divested himself of the sense of intensely belonging to it—that the spell of the continuity of his life with that of his predecessors has never been broken. "It is no matter that the place is joyless for him; that he is weary of the old wooden houses, the mud and the dust, the dead level of site and sentiment, the chill east wind, and the chilliest of social atmospheres;—all these and whatever faults besides he may see or imagine, are nothing to the purpose. The spell survives, and just as powerfully as if the natal spot were an earthly paradise." There is a very American quality in this perpetual consciousness of a spell on Hawthorne's part; it is only in a country where newness and change and brevity of tenure are the common substance of life, that the fact of one's ancestors having lived for a hundred and seventy years in a single spot would become an element of one's morality. It is only an imaginative American that would feel urged to keep reverting to this circumstance, to keep analysing and cunningly considering it.

The Salem of to-day has, as New England towns go, a physiognomy of its own, and in spite of Hawthorne's analogy of the disarranged draught-board, it is a decidedly agreeable one. The spreading elms in its streets, the proportion of large, square, honourable-looking houses, suggesting an easy, copious material life, the little gardens, the grassy waysides, the open windows, the air of space and salubrity and decency, and above all the intimation of larger antecedents—these things compose a picture which has little of the element that painters call depth of tone, but which is not without something that they would admit to be style. To English eyes the oldest and most honourable of the smaller American towns must seem in a manner primitive and rustic; the shabby, straggling, village-quality appears marked in them, and their social tone is not unnaturally inferred to bear the village stamp. Village-like they are, and it would be no gross incivility to describe them as large, respectable, prosperous, democratic villages. But even a village, in a great and vigorous democracy, where there are no overshadowing squires, where the "county" has no social existence, where the villagers are conscious of no superincumbent strata of gentility, piled upwards into vague regions of privilege—even a village is not an institution to accept of more or less graceful patronage; it thinks extremely well of itself, and is absolute in its own regard. Salem is a sea-port, but it is a sea-port deserted and decayed. It belongs to that rather melancholy group of old coast-towns, scattered along the great sea-face of New England, and of which the list is completed by the names of Portsmouth, Plymouth, New Bedford, Newburyport, Newport—superannuated centres of the traffic with foreign lands, which have seen their trade carried away from them by the greater cities. As Hawthorne says, their ventures have gone "to swell, needlessly and imperceptibly, the mighty flood of commerce at New York or Boston." Salem, at the beginning of the present century, played a great part in the Eastern trade; it was the residence of enterprising shipowners who despatched their vessels to Indian and Chinese seas. It was a place of large fortunes, many of which have remained, though the activity that produced them has passed away. These successful traders constituted what Hawthorne calls "the aristocratic class." He alludes in one of his slighter sketches (*The Sister Years*) to the sway of this class and the "moral influence of wealth" having been more marked in Salem than in any other New England town. The sway, we may believe, was on the whole gently exercised, and the moral influence of wealth was not exerted in the cause of immorality. Hawthorne was probably but imperfectly conscious of an advantage which familiarity had made stale— the fact that he lived in the most democratic and most virtuous of modern communities. Of the virtue it is but civil to suppose that his own family had a liberal share; but not much of the wealth, apparently, came into their way. Hawthorne was not born to a patrimony, and his income, later in life, never exceeded very modest proportions.

Of his childish years there appears to be nothing very definite to relate, though his biographer devotes a good many graceful pages to them. There is a considerable sameness in the behaviour of small boys, and it is probable that if we were acquainted with the details of our author's infantine career we should find it to be made up of the same pleasures and pains as that of many ingenuous lads for whom fame has had nothing in keeping.

The absence of precocious symptoms of genius is on the whole more striking in the lives of men who have distinguished themselves than their juvenile promise; though it must be added that Mr. Lathrop has made out, as he was almost in duty bound to do, a very good case in favour of Hawthorne's having been an interesting child. He was not at any time what would be called a sociable man, and there is therefore nothing unexpected in the fact that he was fond of long walks in which he was not known to have had a companion. "Juvenile literature" was but scantily known at that time, and the enormous and extraordinary contribution made by the United States to this department of human happiness was locked in the bosom of futurity. The young Hawthorne, therefore, like many of his contemporaries, was constrained to amuse himself, for want of anything better, with the *Pilgrim's Progress* and the *Faery Queen*. A boy may have worse company than Bunyan and Spenser, and it is very probable that in his childish rambles our author may have had associates of whom there could be no record. When he was nine years old he met with an accident at school which threatened for a while to have serious results. He was struck on the foot by a ball and so severely lamed that he was kept at home for a long time, and had not completely recovered before his twelfth year. His school, it is to be supposed, was the common day-school of New England—the primary factor in that extraordinarily pervasive system of instruction in the plainer branches of learning, which forms one of the principal ornaments of American life. In 1818, when he was fourteen years old, he was taken by his mother to live in the house of an uncle, her brother, who was established in the town of Raymond, near Lake Sebago, in the State of Maine. The immense State of Maine, in the year 1818, must have had an even more magnificently natural character than it possesses at the present day, and the uncle's dwelling, in consequence of being in a little smarter style than the primitive structures that surrounded it, was known by the villagers as Manning's Folly. Mr. Lathrop pronounces this region to be of a "weird and woodsy" character; and Hawthorne, later in life, spoke of it to a friend as the place where "I first got my cursed habits of solitude." The outlook, indeed, for an embryonic novelist, would not seem to have been cheerful; the social dreariness of a small New England community lost amid the forests of Maine, at the beginning of the present century, must have been consummate. But for a boy with a relish for solitude there were many natural resources, and we can understand that Hawthorne should in after years have spoken very tenderly of this episode. "I lived in Maine like a bird of the air, so perfect was the freedom I enjoyed." During the long summer days he roamed, gun in hand, through the great woods, and during the moonlight nights of winter, says his biographer, quoting another informant, "he would skate until midnight, all alone, upon Sebago Lake, with the deep shadows of the icy hills on either hand."

In 1819 he was sent back to Salem to school, and in the following year he wrote to his mother, who had remained at Raymond (the boy had found a home at Salem with another uncle), "I have left school and have begun to fit for college under Benjm. L. Oliver, Lawyer. So you are in danger of having one learned man in your family.... I get my lessons at home and recite them to him (Mr. Oliver) at seven o'clock in the morning.... Shall you want me to be a Minister, Doctor, or Lawyer? A Minister I will not be." He adds, at the close of this epistle—"O how I wish I was again with you, with nothing to do but to go a-gunning! But the happiest days of my life are gone." In 1821, in his seventeenth year, he entered Bowdoin College, at Brunswick, Maine. This institution was in the year 1821—a quarter of a century after its foundation—a highly honourable, but not a very elaborately organized, nor a particularly impressive, seat of learning. I say it was not impressive, but I immediately remember that impressions depend upon the minds receiving them; and that to a group of simple New England lads, upwards of sixty years ago, the halls and groves of Bowdoin, neither dense nor lofty though they can have been, may have seemed replete with Academic stateliness. It was a homely, simple, frugal, "country college," of the old-fashioned American stamp; exerting within its limits a civilizing influence, working, amid the forests and the lakes, the log-houses and the clearings, toward the amenities and humanities and other collegiate graces, and offering a very sufficient education to the future lawyers, merchants, clergymen, politicians, and editors, of the very active and knowledge-loving community that supported it. It did more than this—it numbered poets and statesmen among its undergraduates, and on the roll-call of its sons it has several distinguished names. Among Hawthorne's fellow-students was Henry Wadsworth Longfellow, who divides with our author the honour of being the most distinguished of American men of letters. I know not whether Mr. Longfellow was especially intimate with Hawthorne at this period (they were very good friends later in life), but with two of his companions he formed a friendship which lasted always. One of these was Franklin Pierce, who was destined to fill what Hawthorne calls "the most august position in the world." Pierce was elected President of the United States in 1852. The other was Horatio Bridge, who afterwards served with distinction in the Navy, and to whom the charming prefatory letter of the collection of tales published under the name of *The Snow Image*, is addressed. "If anybody is responsible at this day for my being an author it is yourself. I know not whence your faith came; but while we were lads together at a country college—gathering blueberries in study-hours under those tall Academic pines; or watching the great logs as they tumbled along the current of the Androscoggin; or shooting pigeons and grey squirrels in the woods; or bat-fowling in the summer twilight; or catching trout in that shadowy little stream which, I suppose, is still wandering river-ward through the forest—though you and I will never cast a line in it again—two idle lads, in short (as we need not fear to acknowledge now), doing a hundred things the Faculty never heard of, or else it had been worse for us—still it was your prognostic of your friend's destiny that he was to be a writer of fiction." That is a very pretty picture, but it is a picture of happy urchins at school, rather than of undergraduates "panting," as Macaulay says, "for one and twenty." Poor Hawthorne was indeed thousands of miles away from Oxford and Cambridge; that touch about the blueberries and the logs on the Androscoggin tells the whole story, and strikes the note, as it were, of his circumstances. But if the pleasures at Bowdoin were not expensive, so neither were the penalties. The amount of Hawthorne's collegiate bill for one term was less than 4*l.*, and of this sum more than 9*s.* was made up of fines. The fines, however, were not heavy. Mr. Lathrop prints a letter addressed by the President to "Mrs. Elizabeth C. Hathorne," requesting her co-operation with the officers of this college, "in the attempt to induce your son faithfully to observe the laws of this institution." He has just been fined fifty cents for playing cards for money during the preceding term. "Perhaps he might not have gamed," the Professor adds, "were it not for the influence of a student whom we have dismissed from college." The biographer quotes a letter from Hawthorne to one of his sisters, in which the writer says, in allusion to this remark, that it is a great mistake to think that he has been led away by the wicked ones. "I was fully as willing to play as the person he suspects of having enticed me, and would have been influenced by no one. I have a great mind to commence playing again, merely to show him that I scorn to be seduced by another into anything wrong." There is something in these few words that accords with the impression that the observant reader of Hawthorne gathers of the personal character that underlay his duskily-sportive imagination—an impression of simple manliness and transparent honesty.

He appears to have been a fair scholar, but not a brilliant one; and it is very probable that as the standard of scholarship at Bowdoin was not high, he graduated none the less comfortably on this account. Mr. Lathrop is able to testify to the fact, by no means a surprising one, that he wrote verses at college, though the few stanzas that the biographer quotes are not such as to make us especially regret that his rhyming mood was a transient one.

"The ocean hath its silent caves,

Deep, quiet and alone.

Though there be fury on the waves,

Beneath them there is none."

That quatrain may suffice to decorate our page. And in connection with his college days I may mention his first novel, a short romance entitled *Fanshawe*, which was published in Boston in 1828, three years after he graduated. It was probably also written after that event, but the scene of the tale is laid at Bowdoin (which figures under an altered name), and Hawthorne's attitude with regard to the book, even shortly after it was published, was such as to assign it to this boyish period. It was issued anonymously, but he so repented of his venture that he annihilated the edition, of which, according to Mr. Lathrop, "not half a dozen copies are now known to be extant." I have seen none of these rare volumes, and I know nothing of *Fanshawe* but what the writer just quoted relates. It is the story of a young lady who goes in rather an odd fashion to reside at "Harley College" (equivalent of Bowdoin), under the care and guardianship of Dr. Melmoth, the President of the institution, a venerable, amiable, unworldly, and henpecked, scholar. Here she becomes very naturally an object of interest to two of the students; in regard to whom I cannot do better than quote Mr. Lathrop. One of these young men "is Edward Wolcott, a wealthy, handsome, generous, healthy young fellow from one of the sea-port towns; and the other Fanshawe, the hero, who is a poor but ambitious recluse, already passing into a decline through overmuch devotion to books and meditation. Fanshawe, though the deeper nature of the two, and intensely moved by his new passion, perceiving that a union between himself and Ellen could not be a happy one, resigns the hope of it from the beginning. But circumstances bring him into intimate relation with her. The real action of the book, after the preliminaries, takes up only some three days, and turns upon the attempt of a man named Butler to entice Ellen away under his protection, then marry her, and secure the fortune to which she is heiress. This scheme is partly frustrated by circumstances, and Butler's purpose towards Ellen thus becomes a much more sinister one. From this she is rescued by Fanshawe, and knowing that he loves her, but is concealing his passion, she gives him the opportunity and the right to claim her hand. For a moment the rush of desire and hope is so great that he hesitates; then he refuses to take advantage of her generosity, and parts with her for a last time. Ellen becomes engaged to Wolcott, who had won her heart from the first; and Fanshawe, sinking into rapid consumption, dies before his class graduates." The story must have had a good deal of innocent lightness; and it is a proof of how little the world of observation lay open to Hawthorne, at this time, that he should have had no other choice than to make his little drama go forward between the rather naked walls of Bowdoin, where the presence of his heroine was an essential incongruity. He was twenty-four years old, but the "world," in its social sense, had not disclosed itself to him. He had, however, already, at moments, a very pretty writer's touch, as witness this passage, quoted by Mr. Lathrop, and which is worth transcribing. The heroine has gone off with the nefarious Butler, and the good Dr. Melmoth starts in pursuit of her, attended by young Wolcott.

"'Alas, youth, these are strange times,' observed the President, 'when a doctor of divinity and an undergraduate set forth, like a knight-errant and his squire, in search of a stray damsel. Methinks I am an epitome of the church militant, or a new species of polemical divinity. Pray Heaven, however, there be no such encounter in store for us; for I utterly forgot to provide myself with weapons.'

"'I took some thought for that matter, reverend knight,' replied Edward, whose imagination was highly tickled by Dr. Melmoth's chivalrous comparison.

"'Aye, I see that you have girded on a sword,' said the divine. 'But wherewith shall I defend myself? my hand being empty except of this golden-headed staff, the gift of Mr. Langton.'

"'One of these, if you will accept it,' answered Edward, exhibiting a brace of pistols, 'will serve to begin the conflict before you join the battle hand to hand.'

"'Nay, I shall find little safety in meddling with that deadly instrument, since I know not accurately from which end proceeds the bullet,' said Dr. Melmoth. 'But were it not better, since we are so well provided with artillery, to betake ourselves, in the event of an encounter, to some stone wall or other place of strength?'

"'If I may presume to advise,' said the squire, 'you, as being most valiant and experienced, should ride forward, lance in hand (your long staff serving for a lance), while I annoy the enemy from afar.'

"'Like Teucer, behind the shield of Ajax,' interrupted Dr. Melmoth, 'or David with his stone and sling. No, no, young man; I have left unfinished in my study a learned treatise, important not only to the present age, but to posterity, for whose sake I must take heed to my safety. But, lo! who rides yonder?'"

On leaving college Hawthorne had gone back to live at Salem.

CHAPTER II. EARLY MANHOOD.

The twelve years that followed were not the happiest or most brilliant phase of Hawthorne's life; they strike me indeed as having had an altogether peculiar dreariness. They had their uses; they were the period of incubation of the admirable compositions which eventually brought him reputation and prosperity. But of their actual aridity the young man must have had a painful consciousness; he never lost the impression of it. Mr. Lathrop quotes a phrase to this effect from one of his letters, late in life. "I am disposed to thank God for the gloom and chill of my early life, in the hope that my share of adversity came then, when I bore it alone." And the same writer alludes to a touching passage in the English Note-Books, which I shall quote entire:—

"I think I have been happier this Christmas (1854) than ever before—by my own fireside, and with my wife and children about me—more content to enjoy what I have, less anxious for anything beyond it, in this life. My early life was perhaps a good preparation for the declining half of life; it having been such a blank that any thereafter would compare favourably with it. For a long, long while, I have occasionally been visited with a singular dream; and I have an impression that I have dreamed it ever since I have been in England. It is, that I am still at college, or, sometimes, even, at school—and there is a sense that I have been there unconscionably long, and have quite failed to make such progress as my contemporaries have done; and I seem to meet some of them with a feeling of shame and depression that broods over me as I think of it, even when awake. This dream, recurring all through these twenty or thirty years, must be one of the effects of that heavy seclusion in which I shut myself up for twelve years after leaving college, when everybody moved onward and left me behind. How strange that it should come now, when I may call myself famous and prosperous!—when I am happy too."

The allusion here is to a state of solitude which was the young man's positive choice at the time—or into which he drifted at least under the pressure of his natural shyness and reserve. He was not expansive, he was not addicted to experiments and adventures of intercourse, he was not, personally, in a word, what is called sociable. The general impression of this silence-loving and shade-seeking side of his character is doubtless exaggerated, and, in so far as it points to him as a sombre and sinister figure, is almost ludicrously at fault. He was silent, diffident, more inclined to hesitate, to watch and wait and meditate, than to produce himself, and fonder, on almost any occasion, of being absent than of being present. This quality betrays itself in all his writings. There is in all of them something cold and light and thin, something belonging to the imagination alone, which indicates a man but little disposed to multiply his relations, his points of contact, with society. If we read the six volumes of Note-Books with an eye to the evidence of this unsocial side of his life, we find it in sufficient abundance. But we find at the same time that there was nothing unamiable or invidious in his shyness, and above all that there was nothing preponderantly gloomy. The qualities to which the Note-Books most testify are, on the whole, his serenity and amenity of mind. They reveal these characteristics indeed in an almost phenomenal degree. The serenity, the simplicity, seem in certain portions almost child-like; of brilliant gaiety, of high spirits, there is little; but the placidity and evenness of temper, the cheerful and contented view of the things he notes, never belie themselves. I know not what else he may have written in this copious record, and what passages of gloom and melancholy may have been suppressed; but as his Diaries stand, they offer in a remarkable degree the reflection of a mind whose development was not in the direction of sadness. A very clever French critic, whose fancy is often more lively than his observation is deep, M. Emile Montégut, writing in the *Revue des Deux Mondes*, in the year 1860, invents for our author the appellation of "Un Romancier Pessimiste." Superficially speaking, perhaps, the title is a happy one; but only superficially. Pessimism consists in having morbid and bitter views and theories about human nature; not in indulging in shadowy fancies and conceits. There is nothing whatever to show that Hawthorne had any such doctrines or convictions; certainly, the note of depression, of despair, of the disposition to undervalue the human race, is never sounded in his Diaries. These volumes contain the record of very few convictions or theories of any kind; they move with curious evenness, with a charming, graceful flow, on a level which lies above that of a man's philosophy. They adhere with such persistence to this upper level that they prompt the reader to believe that Hawthorne had no appreciable philosophy at all—no general views that were, in the least uncomfortable. They are the exhibition of an unperplexed intellect. I said just now that the development of Hawthorne's mind was not towards sadness; and I should be inclined to go still further, and say that his mind proper—his mind in so far as it was a repository of opinions and articles of faith—had no development that it is of especial importance to look into. What had a development was his imagination—that delicate and penetrating imagination which was always at play, always entertaining itself, always engaged in a game of hide and seek in the region in which it seemed to him, that the game could best be played—among the shadows and substructions, the dark-based pillars and supports, of our moral nature. Beneath this movement and ripple of his imagination—as free and spontaneous as that of the sea surface—lay directly his personal affections. These were solid and strong, but, according to my impression, they had the place very much to themselves.

His innocent reserve, then, and his exaggerated, but by no means cynical, relish for solitude, imposed themselves upon him, in a great measure, with a persistency which helped to make the time a tolerably arid one—so arid a one indeed that we have seen that in the light of later happiness he pronounced it a blank. But in truth, if these were dull years, it was not all Hawthorne's fault. His situation was intrinsically poor—poor with a poverty that one almost hesitates to look into. When we think of what the conditions of intellectual life, of taste, must have been in a small New England town fifty years ago; and when we think of a young man of beautiful genius, with a love of literature and romance, of the picturesque, of style and form and colour, trying to make a career for himself in the midst of them, compassion for the young man becomes our dominant sentiment, and we see the large dry village picture in perhaps almost too hard a light. It seems to me then that it was possibly a blessing for Hawthorne that he was not expansive and inquisitive, that he lived much to himself and asked but little of his *milieu*. If he had been exacting and ambitious, if his appetite had been large and his knowledge various, he would probably have found the bounds of Salem intolerably narrow. But his culture had been of a simple sort—there was little of any other sort to be obtained in America in those days, and though he was doubtless haunted by visions of more suggestive opportunities, we may safely assume that he was not to his own perception the object of compassion that he appears to a critic who judges him after half a century's civilization has filtered into the twilight of that earlier time. If New England was socially a very small place in those days, Salem was a still smaller one; and if the American tone at large was intensely provincial, that of New England was not greatly helped by having the best of it. The state of things was extremely natural, and there could be now no greater mistake than to speak of it with a redundancy of irony. American life had begun to constitute itself from the foundations; it had begun to *be*, simply; it was at an immeasurable distance from having begun to enjoy. I imagine there was no appreciable group of people in New England at that time proposing to itself to enjoy life; this was not an undertaking for which any provision had been made, or to which any encouragement was offered. Hawthorne must have vaguely entertained some such design upon destiny; but he must have felt that his success would have to depend wholly upon his own ingenuity. I say he must have proposed to himself to enjoy, simply because he proposed to be an artist, and because this enters inevitably into the artist's scheme. There are a thousand ways of enjoying life, and that of the artist is one of the most innocent. But for all that, it connects itself with the idea of pleasure. He proposes to give pleasure, and to give it he must first get it. Where he gets it will depend upon circumstances, and circumstances were not encouraging to Hawthorne.

He was poor, he was solitary, and he undertook to devote himself to literature in a community in which the interest in literature was as yet of the smallest. It is not too much to say that even to the present day it is a considerable discomfort in the United States not to be "in business." The young man who attempts to launch himself in a career that does not belong to the so-called practical order; the young man who has not, in a word, an office in the business-quarter of the town, with his name painted on the door, has but a limited place in the social system, finds no particular bough to perch upon. He is not looked at askance, he is not regarded as an idler; literature and the arts have always been held in extreme honour in the American world, and those who practise them are received on easier terms than in other countries. If the tone of the American world is in some respects provincial, it is in none more so than in this matter of the exaggerated homage rendered to authorship. The gentleman or the lady who has written a book is in many circles the object of an admiration too indiscriminating to operate as an encouragement to good writing. There is no reason to suppose that this was less the case fifty years ago; but fifty years ago, greatly more than now, the literary man must have lacked the comfort and inspiration of belonging to a class. The best things come, as a general thing, from the talents that are members of a group; every man works better when he has companions working in the same line, and yielding the stimulus of suggestion, comparison, emulation. Great things of course have been done by solitary workers; but they have usually been done with double the pains they would have cost if they had been produced in more genial circumstances. The solitary worker loses the profit of example and discussion; he is apt to make awkward experiments; he is in the nature of the case more or less of an empiric. The empiric may, as I say, be treated by the world as an expert; but the drawbacks and discomforts of empiricism remain to him, and are in fact increased by the suspicion that is mingled with his gratitude, of a want in the public taste of a sense of the proportions of things. Poor Hawthorne, beginning to write subtle short tales at Salem, was empirical enough; he was one of, at most, some dozen Americans who had taken up literature as a profession. The profession in the United States is still very young, and of diminutive stature; but in the year 1830 its head could hardly have been seen above ground. It strikes the observer of to-day that Hawthorne showed great courage in entering a field in which the honours and emoluments were so scanty as the profits of authorship must have been at that time. I have said that in the United States at present authorship is a pedestal, and literature is the fashion; but Hawthorne's history is a proof that it was possible, fifty years ago, to write a great many little masterpieces without becoming known. He begins the preface to the *Twice-Told Tales* by remarking that he was "for many years the obscurest man of letters in America." When once this work obtained recognition, the recognition left little to be desired. Hawthorne never, I believe, made large sums of money by his writings, and the early profits of these charming sketches could not have been considerable; for many of them, indeed, as they appeared in journals and magazines, he had never been paid at all; but the honour, when once it dawned—and it dawned tolerably early in the author's career—was never thereafter wanting. Hawthorne's countrymen are solidly proud of him, and the tone of Mr. Lathrop's *Study* is in itself sufficient evidence of the manner in which an American story-teller may in some cases look to have his eulogy pronounced.

Hawthorne's early attempt to support himself by his pen appears to have been deliberate; we hear nothing of those experiments in counting-houses or lawyers' offices, of which a permanent invocation to the Muse is often the inconsequent sequel. He began to write, and to try and dispose of his writings; and he remained at Salem apparently only because his family, his mother and his two sisters, lived there. His mother had a house, of which during the twelve years that elapsed until 1838, he appears to have been an inmate. Mr. Lathrop learned from his surviving sister that after publishing *Fanshawe* he produced a group of short stories entitled *Seven Tales of my Native Land*, and that this lady retained a very favourable recollection of the work, which her brother had given her to read. But it never saw the light; his attempts to get it published were unsuccessful, and at last, in a fit of irritation and despair, the young author burned the manuscript.

There is probably something autobiographic in the striking little tale of *The Devil in Manuscript*. "They have been offered to seventeen publishers," says the hero of that sketch in regard to a pile of his own lucubrations.

"It would make you stare to read their answers.... One man publishes nothing but school-books; another has five novels already under examination;... another gentleman is just giving up business, on purpose, I verily believe, to avoid publishing my book. In short, of all the seventeen booksellers, only one has vouchsafed even to read my tales; and he—a literary dabbler himself, I should judge—has the impertinence to criticise them, proposing what he calls vast improvements, and concluding, after a general sentence of condemnation, with the definitive assurance that he will not be concerned on any terms.... But there does seem to be one righteous man among these seventeen unrighteous ones, and he tells me, fairly, that no American publisher will meddle with an American work—seldom if by a known writer, and never if by a new one— unless at the writer's risk."

But though the *Seven Tales* were not printed, Hawthorne, proceeded to write others that were; the two collections of the *Twice-Told Tales*, and the *Snow Image*, are gathered from a series of contributions to the local journals and the annuals of that day. To make these three volumes, he picked out the things he thought the best. "Some very small part," he says of what remains, "might yet be rummaged out (but it would not be worth the trouble), among the dingy pages of fifteen or twenty-years-old periodicals, or within the shabby morocco covers of faded *Souvenirs*." These three volumes represent no large amount of literary labour for so long a period, and the author admits that there is little to show "for the thought and industry of that portion of his life." He attributes the paucity of his productions to a "total lack of sympathy at the age when his mind would naturally have been most effervescent." "He had no incitement to literary effort in a reasonable prospect of reputation or profit; nothing but the pleasure itself of composition, an enjoyment not at all amiss in its way, and perhaps essential to the merit of the work in hand, but which in the long run will hardly keep the chill out of a writer's heart, or the numbness out of his fingers." These words occur in the preface attached in 1851 to the second edition of the *Twice-Told Tales*; *à propos* of which I may say that there is always a charm in Hawthorne's prefaces which makes one grateful for a pretext to quote from them. At this time *The Scarlet Letter* had just made his fame, and the short tales were certain of a large welcome; but the account he gives of the failure of the earlier edition to produce a sensation (it had been published in two volumes, at four years apart), may appear to contradict my assertion that, though he was not recognised immediately, he was recognised betimes. In 1850, when *The Scarlet Letter* appeared, Hawthorne was forty-six years old, and this may certainly seem a long-delayed popularity. On the other hand, it must be remembered that he had not appealed to the world with any great energy. *The Twice-Told Tales*, charming as they are, do not constitute a very massive literary pedestal. As soon as the author, resorting to severer measures, put forth *The Scarlet Letter*, the public ear was touched and charmed, and after that it was held to the end. "Well it might have been!" the reader will exclaim. "But what a grievous pity that the dulness of this same organ should have operated so long as a deterrent, and by making Hawthorne wait till he was nearly fifty to publish his first novel, have abbreviated by so much his productive career!" The truth is, he cannot have been in any very high degree ambitious; he was not an abundant producer, and there was manifestly a strain of generous indolence in his composition. There was a loveable want of eagerness about him. Let the encouragement offered have been what it might, he had waited till he was lapsing from middle-life to strike his first noticeable blow; and during the last ten years of his career he put forth but two complete works, and the fragment of a third.

It is very true, however, that during this early period he seems to have been very glad to do whatever came to his hand. Certain of his tales found their way into one of the annuals of the time, a publication endowed with the brilliant title of *The Boston Token and Atlantic Souvenir*. The editor of this graceful repository was S. G. Goodrich, a gentleman who, I suppose, may be called one of the pioneers of American periodical literature. He is better known to the world as Mr. Peter Parley, a name under which he produced a multitude of popular school-books, story-books, and other attempts to vulgarize human knowledge and adapt it to the infant mind. This enterprising purveyor of literary wares appears, incongruously enough, to have been Hawthorne's earliest protector, if protection is the proper word for the treatment that the young author received from him. Mr. Goodrich induced him in 1836 to go to Boston to edit a periodical in which he was interested, *The American Magazine of Useful and Entertaining Knowledge*. I have never seen the work in question, but Hawthorne's biographer gives a sorry account of it. It was managed by the so-called Bewick Company, which "took its name from Thomas Bewick, the English restorer of the art of wood-engraving, and the magazine was to do his memory honour by his admirable illustrations. But in fact it never did any one honour, nor brought any one profit. It was a penny popular affair, containing condensed information about innumerable subjects, no fiction, and little poetry. The woodcuts were of the crudest and most frightful sort. It passed through the hands of several editors and several publishers. Hawthorne was engaged at a salary of five hundred dollars a year; but it appears that he got next to nothing, and did not stay in the position long." Hawthorne wrote from Boston in the winter of 1836: "I came here trusting to Goodrich's positive promise to pay me forty-five dollars as soon as I arrived; and he has kept promising from one day to another, till I do not see that he means to pay at all. I have now broke off all intercourse with him, and never think of going near him.... I don't feel at all obliged to him about the editorship, for he is a stockholder and director in the Bewick Company ... and I defy them to get another to do for a thousand dollars, what I do for five hundred."—"I make nothing," he says in another letter, "of writing a history or biography before dinner." Goodrich proposed to him to write a *Universal History* for the use of schools, offering him a hundred dollars for his share in the work. Hawthorne accepted the offer and took a hand—I know not how large a one—in the job. His biographer has been able to identify a single phrase as our author's. He is speaking of George IV: "Even when he was quite a young man this King cared as much about dress as any young coxcomb. He had a great deal of taste in such matters, and it is a pity that he was a King, for he might otherwise have made an excellent tailor." The *Universal History* had a great vogue and passed through hundreds of editions; but it does not appear that Hawthorne ever received more than his hundred dollars. The writer of these pages vividly remembers making its acquaintance at an early stage of his education—a very fat, stumpy-looking book, bound in boards covered with green paper, and having in the text very small woodcuts, of the most primitive sort. He associates it to this day with the names of Sesostris and Semiramis whenever he encounters them, there having been, he supposes, some account of the conquests of these potentates that would impress itself upon the imagination of a child. At the end of four months, Hawthorne had received but twenty dollars—four pounds—for his editorship of the *American Magazine*.

There is something pitiful in this episode, and something really touching in the sight of a delicate and superior genius obliged to concern himself with such paltry undertakings. The simple fact was that for a man attempting at that time in America to live by his pen, there were no larger openings; and to live at all Hawthorne had, as the phrase is, to make himself small. This cost him less, moreover, than it would have cost a more copious and strenuous genius, for his modesty was evidently extreme, and I doubt whether he had any very ardent consciousness of rare talent. He went back to Salem, and from this tranquil standpoint, in the spring of 1837, he watched the first volume of his *Twice-Told Tales* come into the world. He had by this time been living some ten years of his manhood in Salem, and an American commentator may be excused for feeling the desire to construct, from the very scanty material that offers itself, a slight picture of his life there. I have quoted his own allusions to its dulness and blankness, but I confess that these observations serve rather to quicken than to depress my curiosity. A biographer has of necessity a relish for detail; his business is to multiply points of characterisation. Mr. Lathrop tells us that our author "had little communication with even the members of his family. Frequently his meals were brought and left at his locked door, and it was not often that the four inmates of the old Herbert Street mansion met in family circle. He never read his stories aloud to his mother and sisters.... It was the custom in this household for the several members to remain very much by themselves; the three ladies were perhaps nearly as rigorous recluses as himself, and, speaking of the isolation which reigned among them, Hawthorne once said, 'We do not even *live* at our house!'" It is added that he was not in the habit of going to church. This is not a lively picture, nor is that other sketch of his daily habits much more exhilarating, in which Mr. Lathrop affirms that though the statement that for several years "he never saw the sun" is entirely an error, yet it is true that he stirred little abroad all day and "seldom chose to walk in the town except at night." In the dusky hours he took walks of many miles along the coast, or else wandered about the sleeping streets of Salem. These were his pastimes, and these were apparently his most intimate occasions of contact with life. Life, on such occasions, was not very exuberant, as any one will reflect who has been acquainted with the physiognomy of a small New England town after nine o'clock in the evening. Hawthorne, however, was an inveterate observer of small things, and he found a field for fancy among the most trivial accidents. There could be no better example of this happy faculty than the little paper entitled "Night Sketches," included among the *Twice-Told Tales*. This small dissertation is about nothing at all, and to call attention to it is almost to overrate its importance. This fact is equally true, indeed, of a great many of its companions, which give even the most appreciative critic a singular feeling of his own indiscretion—almost of his own cruelty. They are so light, so slight, so tenderly trivial, that simply to mention them is to put them in a false position. The author's claim for them is barely audible, even to the most acute listener. They are things to take or to leave—to enjoy, but not to talk about. Not to read them would be to do them an injustice (to read them is essentially to relish them), but to bring the machinery of criticism to bear upon them would be to do them a still greater wrong. I must remember, however, that to carry this principle too far would be to endanger the general validity of the present little work—a consummation which it can only be my desire to avert. Therefore it is that I think it permissible to remark that in Hawthorne, the whole class of little descriptive effusions directed upon common things, to which these just-mentioned Night Sketches belong, have a greater charm than there is any warrant for in their substance. The charm is made up of the spontaneity, the personal quality, of the fancy that plays through them, its mingled simplicity and subtlety, its purity and its *bonhomie*. The Night Sketches are simply the light, familiar record of a walk under an umbrella, at the end of a long, dull, rainy day, through the sloppy, ill-paved streets of a country town, where the rare gas-lamps twinkle in the large puddles, and the blue jars in the druggist's window shine through the vulgar drizzle. One would say that the inspiration of such a theme could have had no great force, and such doubtless was the case; but out of the Salem puddles, nevertheless, springs, flower-like, a charming and natural piece of prose.

I have said that Hawthorne was an observer of small things, and indeed he appears to have thought nothing too trivial to be suggestive. His Note-Books give us the measure of his perception of common and casual things, and of his habit of converting them into *memoranda*. These Note-Books, by the way—this seems as good a place as any other to say it—are a very singular series of volumes; I doubt whether there is anything exactly corresponding to them in the whole body of literature. They were published—in six volumes, issued at intervals—some years after Hawthorne's death, and no person attempting to write an account of the romancer could afford to regret that they should have been given to the world. There is a point of view from which this may be regretted; but the attitude of the biographer is to desire as many documents as possible. I am thankful, then, as a biographer, for the Note-Books, but I am obliged to confess that, though I have just re-read them carefully, I am still at a loss to perceive how they came to be written—what was Hawthorne's purpose in carrying on for so many years this minute and often trivial chronicle. For a person desiring information about him at any cost, it is valuable; it sheds a vivid light upon his character, his habits, the nature of his mind. But we find ourselves wondering what was its value to Hawthorne himself. It is in a very partial degree a register of impressions, and in a still smaller sense a record of emotions. Outward objects play much the larger part in it; opinions, convictions, ideas pure and simple, are almost absent. He rarely takes his Note-Book into his confidence or commits to its pages any reflections that might be adapted for publicity; the simplest way to describe the tone of these extremely objective journals is to say that they read like a series of very pleasant, though rather dullish and decidedly formal, letters, addressed to himself by a man who, having suspicions that they might be opened in the post, should have determined to insert nothing compromising. They contain much that is too futile for things intended for publicity; whereas, on the other hand, as a receptacle of private impressions and opinions, they are curiously cold and empty. They widen, as I have said, our glimpse of Hawthorne's mind (I do not say that they elevate our estimate of it), but they do so by what they fail to contain, as much as by what we find in them. Our business for the moment, however, is not with the light that they throw upon his intellect, but with the information they offer about his habits and his social circumstances.

I know not at what age he began to keep a diary; the first entries in the American volumes are of the summer of 1835. There is a phrase in the preface to his novel of *Transformation*, which must have lingered in the minds of many Americans who have tried to write novels and to lay the scene of them in the western world. "No author, without a trial, can conceive of the difficulty of writing a romance about a country where there is no shadow, no antiquity, no mystery, no picturesque and gloomy wrong, nor anything but a commonplace prosperity, in broad and simple daylight, as is happily the case with my dear native land." The perusal of Hawthorne's American Note-Books operates as a practical commentary upon this somewhat ominous text. It does so at least to my own mind; it would be too much perhaps to say that the effect would be the same for the usual English reader. An American reads between the lines—he completes the suggestions—he constructs a picture. I think I am not guilty of any gross injustice in saying that the picture he constructs from Hawthorne's American diaries, though by no means without charms of its own, is not, on the whole, an interesting one. It is characterised by an extraordinary blankness—a curious paleness of colour and paucity of detail. Hawthorne, as I have said, has a large and healthy appetite for detail, and one is therefore the more struck with the lightness of the diet to which his observation was condemned. For myself, as I turn the pages of his journals, I seem to see the image of the crude and simple society in which he lived. I use these epithets, of course, not invidiously, but descriptively; if one desire to enter as closely as possible into Hawthorne's situation, one must endeavour to reproduce his circumstances. We are struck with the large number of elements that were absent from them, and the coldness, the thinness, the blankness, to repeat my epithet, present themselves so vividly that our foremost feeling is that of compassion for a romancer looking for subjects in such a field. It takes so many things, as Hawthorne must have felt later in life, when he made the acquaintance of the denser, richer, warmer-European spectacle—it takes such an accumulation of history and custom, such a complexity of manners and types, to form a fund of suggestion for a novelist. If Hawthorne had been a young Englishman, or a young Frenchman of the same degree of genius, the same cast of mind, the same habits, his consciousness of the world around him would have been a very different affair; however obscure, however reserved, his own personal life, his sense of the life of his fellow-mortals would have been almost infinitely more various. The negative side of the spectacle on which Hawthorne looked out, in his contemplative saunterings and reveries, might, indeed, with a little ingenuity, be made almost ludicrous; one might enumerate the items of high civilization, as it exists in other countries, which are absent from the texture of American life, until it should become a wonder to know what was left. No State, in the European sense of the word, and indeed barely a specific national name. No sovereign, no court, no personal loyalty, no aristocracy, no church, no clergy, no army, no diplomatic service, no country gentlemen, no palaces, no castles, nor manors, nor old country-houses, nor parsonages, nor thatched cottages nor ivied ruins; no cathedrals, nor abbeys, nor little Norman churches; no great Universities nor public schools—no Oxford, nor Eton, nor Harrow; no literature, no novels, no museums, no pictures, no political society, no sporting class—no Epsom nor Ascot! Some such list as that might be drawn up of the absent things in American life—especially in the American life of forty years ago, the effect of which, upon an English or a French imagination, would probably as a general thing be appalling. The natural remark, in the almost lurid light of such an indictment, would be that if these things are left out, everything is left out. The American knows that a good deal remains; what it is that remains— that is his secret, his joke, as one may say. It would be cruel, in this terrible denudation, to deny him the consolation of his national gift, that "American humour" of which of late years we have heard so much.

But in helping us to measure what remains, our author's Diaries, as I have already intimated, would give comfort rather to persons who might have taken the alarm from the brief sketch I have just attempted of what I have called the negative side of the American social situation, than to those reminding themselves of its fine compensations. Hawthorne's entries are to a great degree accounts of walks in the country, drives in stage-coaches, people he met in taverns. The minuteness of the things that attract his attention and that he deems worthy of being commemorated is frequently extreme, and from this fact we get the impression of a general vacancy in the field of vision. "Sunday evening, going by the jail, the setting sun kindled up the windows most cheerfully; as if there were a bright, comfortable light within its darksome stone wall." "I went yesterday with Monsieur S—— to pick raspberries. He fell through an old log-bridge, thrown over a hollow; looking back, only his head and shoulders appeared through the rotten logs and among the bushes.—A shower coming on, the rapid running of a little barefooted boy, coming up unheard, and dashing swiftly past us, and showing us the soles of his naked feet as he ran adown the path and up the opposite side." In another place he devotes a page to a description of a dog whom he saw running round after its tail; in still another he remarks, in a paragraph by itself—"The aromatic odor of peat-smoke, in the sunny autumnal air is very pleasant." The reader says to himself that when a man turned thirty gives a place in his mind—and his inkstand—to such trifles as these, it is because nothing else of superior importance demands admission. Everything in the Notes indicates a simple, democratic, thinly-composed society; there is no evidence of the writer finding himself in any variety or intimacy of relations with any one or with anything. We find a good deal of warrant for believing that if we add that statement of Mr. Lathrop's about his meals being left at the door of his room, to rural rambles of which an impression of the temporary phases of the local apple-crop were the usual, and an encounter with an organ-grinder, or an eccentric dog, the rarer, outcome, we construct a rough image of our author's daily life during the several years that preceded his marriage. He appears to have read a good deal, and that he must have been familiar with the sources of good English we see from his charming, expressive, slightly self-conscious, cultivated, but not too cultivated, style. Yet neither in these early volumes of his Note-Books, nor in the later, is there any mention of his reading. There are no literary judgments or impressions—there is almost no allusion to works or to authors. The allusions to individuals of any kind are indeed much less numerous than one might have expected; there is little psychology, little description of manners. We are told by Mr. Lathrop that there existed at Salem during the early part of Hawthorne's life "a strong circle of wealthy families," which "maintained rigorously the distinctions of class," and whose "entertainments were splendid, their manners magnificent." This is a rather pictorial way of saying that there were a number of people in the place—the commercial and professional aristocracy, as it were—who lived in high comfort and respectability, and who, in their small provincial way, doubtless had pretensions to be exclusive. Into this delectable company Mr. Lathrop intimates that his hero was free to penetrate. It is easy to believe it, and it would be difficult to perceive why the privilege should have been denied to a young man of genius and culture, who was very good-looking (Hawthorne must have been in these days, judging by his appearance later in life, a strikingly handsome fellow), and whose American pedigree was virtually as long as the longest they could show. But in fact Hawthorne appears to have ignored the good society of his native place almost completely; no echo of its conversation is to be found in his tales or his journals. Such an echo would possibly not have been especially melodious, and if we regret the shyness and stiffness, the reserve, the timidity, the suspicion, or whatever it was, that kept him from knowing what there was to be known, it is not because we have any very definite assurance that his gains would have been great. Still, since a beautiful writer was growing up in Salem, it is a pity that he should not have given himself a chance to commemorate some of the types that flourished in the richest soil of the place. Like almost all people who possess in a strong degree the storytelling faculty, Hawthorne had a democratic strain in his composition and a relish for the commoner stuff of human nature. Thoroughly American in all ways, he was in none more so than in the vagueness of his sense of social distinctions and his readiness to forget them if a moral or intellectual sensation were to be gained by it. He liked to fraternise with plain people, to take them on their own terms, and put himself if possible into their shoes. His Note-Books, and even his tales, are full of evidence of this easy and natural feeling about all his unconventional fellow-mortals—this imaginative interest and contemplative curiosity—and it sometimes takes the most charming and graceful forms. Commingled as it is with his own subtlety and delicacy, his complete exemption from vulgarity, it is one of the points in his character which his reader comes most to appreciate—that reader I mean for whom he is not as for some few, a dusky and malarious genius.

But even if he had had, personally, as many pretensions as he had few, he must in the nature of things have been more or less of a consenting democrat, for democracy was the very key-stone of the simple social structure in which he played his part. The air of his journals and his tales alike are full of the genuine democratic feeling. This feeling has by no means passed out of New England life; it still flourishes in perfection in the great stock of the people, especially in rural communities; but it is probable that at the present hour a writer of Hawthorne's general fastidiousness would not express it quite so artlessly. "A shrewd gentlewoman, who kept a tavern in the town," he says, in *Chippings with a Chisel*, "was anxious to obtain two or three gravestones for the deceased members of her family, and to pay for these solemn commodities by taking the sculptor to board." This image of a gentlewoman keeping a tavern and looking out for boarders, seems, from the point of view to which I allude, not at all incongruous. It will be observed that the lady in question was shrewd; it was probable that she was substantially educated, and of reputable life, and it is certain that she was energetic. These qualities would make it natural to Hawthorne to speak of her as a gentlewoman; the natural tendency in societies where the sense of equality prevails, being to take for granted the high level rather than the low. Perhaps the most striking example of the democratic sentiment in all our author's tales, however, is the figure of Uncle Venner, in *The House of the Seven Gables*. Uncle Venner is a poor old man in a brimless hat and patched trousers, who picks up a precarious subsistence by rendering, for a compensation, in the houses and gardens of the good people of Salem, those services that are known in New England as "chores." He carries parcels, splits firewood, digs potatoes, collects refuse for the maintenance of his pigs, and looks forward with philosophic equanimity to the time when he shall end his days in the almshouse. But in spite of the very modest place that he occupies in the social scale, he is received on a footing of familiarity in the household of the far-descended Miss Pyncheon; and when this ancient lady and her companions take the air in the garden of a summer evening, he steps into the estimable circle and mingles the smoke of his pipe with their refined conversation. This obviously is rather imaginative—Uncle Venner is a creation with a purpose. He is an original, a natural moralist, a philosopher; and Hawthorne, who knew perfectly what he was about in introducing him—Hawthorne always knew perfectly what he was about—wished to give in his person an example of humorous resignation and of a life reduced to the simplest and homeliest elements, as opposed to the fantastic pretensions of the antiquated heroine of the story. He wished to strike a certain exclusively human and personal note. He knew that for this purpose he was taking a licence; but the point is that he felt he was not indulging in any extravagant violation of reality. Giving in a letter, about 1830, an account of a little journey he was making in Connecticut, he says, of the end of a seventeen miles' stage, that "in the evening, however, I went to a Bible-class with a very polite and agreeable gentleman, whom I afterwards discovered to be a strolling tailor of very questionable habits."

Hawthorne appears on various occasions to have absented himself from Salem, and to have wandered somewhat through the New England States. But the only one of these episodes of which there is a considerable account in the Note-Books is a visit that he paid in the summer of 1837 to his old college-mate, Horatio Bridge, who was living upon his father's property in Maine, in company with an eccentric young Frenchman, a teacher of his native tongue, who was looking for pupils among the northern forests. I have said that there was less psychology in Hawthorne's Journals than might have been looked for; but there is nevertheless a certain amount of it, and nowhere more than in a number of pages relating to this remarkable "Monsieur S." (Hawthorne, intimate as he apparently became with him, always calls him "Monsieur," just as throughout all his Diaries he invariably speaks of all his friends, even the most familiar, as "Mr." He confers the prefix upon the unconventional Thoreau, his fellow-woodsman at Concord, and upon the emancipated brethren at Brook Farm.) These pages are completely occupied with Monsieur S., who was evidently a man of character, with the full complement of his national vivacity. There is an elaborate effort to analyse the poor young Frenchman's disposition, something conscientious and painstaking, respectful, explicit, almost solemn. These passages are very curious as a reminder of the absence of the off-hand element in the manner in which many Americans, and many New Englanders especially, make up their minds about people whom they meet. This, in turn, is a reminder of something that may be called the importance of the individual in the American world; which is a result of the newness and youthfulness of society and of the absence of keen competition. The individual counts for more, as it were, and, thanks to the absence of a variety of social types and of settled heads under which he may be easily and conveniently pigeon-holed, he is to a certain extent a wonder and a mystery. An Englishman, a Frenchman—a Frenchman above all—judges quickly, easily, from his own social standpoint, and makes an end of it. He has not that rather chilly and isolated sense of moral responsibility which is apt to visit a New Englander in such processes; and he has the advantage that his standards are fixed by the general consent of the society in which he lives. A Frenchman, in this respect, is particularly happy and comfortable, happy and comfortable to a degree which I think is hardly to be over-estimated; his standards being the most definite in the world, the most easily and promptly appealed to, and the most identical with what happens to be the practice of the French genius itself. The Englishman is not-quite so well off, but he is better off than his poor interrogative and tentative cousin beyond the seas. He is blessed with a healthy mistrust of analysis, and hair-splitting is the occupation he most despises. There is always a little of the Dr. Johnson in him, and Dr. Johnson would have had woefully little patience with that tendency to weigh moonbeams which in Hawthorne was almost as much a quality of race as of genius; albeit that Hawthorne has paid to Boswell's hero (in the chapter on "Lichfield and Uttoxeter," in his volume on England), a tribute of the finest appreciation. American intellectual standards are vague, and Hawthorne's countrymen are apt to hold the scales with a rather uncertain hand and a somewhat agitated conscience.

CHAPTER III. EARLY WRITINGS.

The second volume of the *Twice-Told Tales* was published in 1845, in Boston; and at this time a good many of the stories which were afterwards collected into the *Mosses from an Old Manse* had already appeared, chiefly in *The Democratic Review*, a sufficiently flourishing periodical of that period. In mentioning these things I anticipate; but I touch upon the year 1845 in order to speak of the two collections of *Twice-Told Tales* at once. During the same year Hawthorne edited an interesting volume, the *Journals of an African Cruiser*, by his friend Bridge, who had gone into the Navy and seen something of distant waters. His biographer mentions that even then Hawthorne's name was thought to bespeak attention for a book, and he insists on this fact in contradiction to the idea that his productions had hitherto been as little noticed as his own declaration that he remained "for a good many years the obscurest man of letters in America," might lead one, and has led many people, to suppose. "In this dismal chamber FAME was won," he writes in Salem in 1836. And we find in the Note-Books (1840), this singularly beautiful and touching passage:—

"Here I sit in my old accustomed chamber, where I used to sit in days gone by.... Here I have written many tales—many that have been burned to ashes, many that have doubtless deserved the same fate. This claims to be called a haunted chamber, for thousands upon thousands of visions have appeared to me in it; and some few of them have become visible to the world. If ever I should have a biographer, he ought to make great mention of this chamber in my memoirs, because so much of my lonely youth was wasted here, and here my mind and character were formed; and here I have been glad and hopeful, and here I have been despondent. And here I sat a long, long time, waiting patiently for the world to know me, and sometimes wondering why it did not know me sooner, or whether it would ever know me at all—at least till I were in my grave. And sometimes it seems to me as if I were already in the grave, with only life enough to be chilled and benumbed. But oftener I was happy—at least as happy as I then knew how to be, or was aware of the possibility of being. By and by the world found me out in my lonely chamber and called me forth—not indeed with a loud roar of acclamation, but rather with a still small voice—and forth I went, but found nothing in the world I thought preferable to my solitude till now.... And now I begin to understand why I was imprisoned so many years in this lonely chamber, and why I could never break through the viewless bolts and bars; for if I had sooner made my escape into the world, I should have grown hard and rough, and been covered with earthly dust, and my heart might have become callous by rude encounters with the multitude.... But living in solitude till the fulness of time was come, I still kept the dew of my youth and the freshness of my heart.... I used to think that I could imagine all passions, all feelings, and states of the heart and mind; but how little did I know!... Indeed, we are but shadows; we are not endowed with real life, and all that seems most real about us is but the thinnest substance of a dream—till the heart be touched. That touch creates us—then we begin to be—thereby we are beings of reality and inheritors of eternity."

There is something exquisite in the soft philosophy of this little retrospect, and it helps us to appreciate it to know that the writer had at this time just become engaged to be married to a charming and accomplished person, with whom his union, which took place two years later, was complete and full of happiness. But I quote it more particularly for the evidence it affords that, already in 1840, Hawthorne could speak of the world finding him out and calling him forth, as of an event tolerably well in the past. He had sent the first of the *Twice-Told* series to his old college friend, Longfellow, who had already laid, solidly, the foundation of his great poetic reputation, and at the time of his sending it had written him a letter from which it will be to our purpose to quote a few lines:—

"You tell me you have met with troubles and changes. I know not what these may have been; but I can assure you that trouble is the next best thing to enjoyment, and that there is no fate in the world so horrible as to have no share in either its joys or sorrows. For the last ten years I have not lived, but only dreamed of living. It may be true that there may have been some unsubstantial pleasures here in the shade, which I might have missed in the sunshine, but you cannot conceive how utterly devoid of satisfaction all my retrospects are. I have laid up no treasure of pleasant remembrances against old age; but there is some comfort in thinking that future years may be more varied, and therefore more tolerable, than the past. You give me more credit than I deserve in supposing that I have led a studious life. I have indeed turned over a good many books, but in so desultory a way that it cannot be called study, nor has it left me the fruits of study.... I have another great difficulty in the lack of materials; for I have seen so little of the world that I have nothing but thin air to concoct my stories of, and it is not easy to give a life-like semblance to such shadowy stuff. Sometimes, through a peephole, I have caught a glimpse of the real world, and the two or three articles in which I have portrayed these glimpses please me better than the others."

It is more particularly for the sake of the concluding lines that I have quoted this passage; for evidently no portrait of Hawthorne at this period is at all exact which, fails to insist upon the constant struggle which must have gone on between his shyness and his desire to know something of life; between what may be called his evasive and his inquisitive tendencies. I suppose it is no injustice to Hawthorne to say that on the whole his shyness always prevailed; and yet, obviously, the struggle was constantly there. He says of his *Twice-Told Tales*, in the preface, "They are not the talk of a secluded man with his own mind and heart (had it been so they could hardly have failed to be more deeply and permanently valuable,) but his attempts, and very imperfectly successful ones, to open an intercourse with the world." We are speaking here of small things, it must be remembered—of little attempts, little sketches, a little world. But everything is relative, and this smallness of scale must not render less apparent the interesting character of Hawthorne's efforts. As for the *Twice-Told Tales* themselves, they are an old story now; every one knows them a little, and those who admire them particularly have read them a great many times. The writer of this sketch belongs to the latter class, and he has been trying to forget his familiarity with them, and ask himself what impression they would have made upon him at the time they appeared, in the first bloom of their freshness, and before the particular Hawthorne-quality, as it may be called, had become an established, a recognised and valued, fact. Certainly, I am inclined to think, if one had encountered these delicate, dusky flowers in the blossomless garden of American journalism, one would have plucked them with a very tender hand; one would have felt that here was something essentially fresh and new; here, in no extraordinary force or abundance, but in a degree distinctly appreciable, was an original element in literature. When I think of it, I almost envy Hawthorne's earliest readers; the sensation of opening upon *The Great Carbuncle, The Seven Vagabonds,* or *The Threefold Destiny* in an American annual of forty years ago, must have been highly agreeable.

Among these shorter things (it is better to speak of the whole collection, including the *Snow Image,* and the *Mosses from an Old Manse* at once) there are three sorts of tales, each one of which has an original stamp. There are, to begin with, the stories of fantasy and allegory—those among which the three I have just mentioned would be numbered, and which on the whole, are the most original. This is the group to which such little masterpieces as *Malvin's Burial, Rappacini's Daughter,* and *Young Goodman Brown* also belong—these two last perhaps representing the highest point that Hawthorne reached in this direction. Then there are the little tales of New England history, which are scarcely less admirable, and of which *The Grey Champion, The Maypole of Merry Mount,* and the four beautiful *Legends of the Province House,* as they are called, are the most successful specimens. Lastly come the slender sketches of actual scenes and of the objects and manners about him, by means of which, more particularly, he endeavoured "to open an intercourse with the world," and which, in spite of their slenderness, have an infinite grace and charm. Among these things *A Rill from the Town Pump*, *The Village Uncle*, *The Toll-Gatherer's Day*, the *Chippings with a Chisel*, may most naturally be mentioned. As we turn over these volumes we feel that the pieces that spring most directly from his fancy, constitute, as I have said (putting his four novels aside), his most substantial claim to our attention. It would be a mistake to insist too much upon them; Hawthorne was himself the first to recognise that. "These fitful sketches," he says in the preface to the *Mosses from an Old Manse*, "with so little of external life about them, yet claiming no profundity of purpose—so reserved even while they sometimes seem so frank—often but half in earnest, and never, even when most so, expressing satisfactorily the thoughts which they profess to image—such trifles, I truly feel, afford no solid basis for a literary reputation." This is very becomingly uttered; but it may be said, partly in answer to it, and partly in confirmation, that the valuable element in these things was not what Hawthorne put into them consciously, but what passed into them without his being able to measure it—the element of simple genius, the quality of imagination. This is the real charm of Hawthorne's writing—this purity and spontaneity and naturalness of fancy. For the rest, it is interesting to see how it borrowed a particular colour from the other faculties that lay near it—how the imagination, in this capital son of the old Puritans, reflected the hue of the more purely moral part, of the dusky, overshadowed conscience. The conscience, by no fault of its own, in every genuine offshoot of that sombre lineage, lay under the shadow of the sense of *sin*. This darkening cloud was no essential part of the nature of the individual; it stood fixed in the general moral heaven, under which he grew up and looked at life. It projected from above, from outside, a black patch over his spirit, and it was for him to do what he could with the black patch. There were all sorts of possible ways of dealing with it; they depended upon the personal temperament. Some natures would let it lie as it fell, and contrive to be tolerably comfortable beneath it. Others would groan and sweat and suffer; but the dusky blight would remain, and their lives would be lives of misery. Here and there an individual, irritated beyond endurance, would throw it off in anger, plunging probably into what would be deemed deeper abysses of depravity. Hawthorne's way was the best, for he contrived, by an exquisite process, best known to himself, to transmute this heavy moral burden into the very substance of the imagination, to make it evaporate in the light and charming fumes of artistic production. But Hawthorne, of course, was exceptionally fortunate; he had his genius to help him. Nothing is more curious and interesting than this almost exclusively *imported* character of the sense of sin in Hawthorne's mind; it seems to exist there merely for an artistic or literary purpose. He had ample cognizance of the Puritan conscience; it was his natural heritage; it was reproduced in him; looking into his soul, he found it there. But his relation to it was only, as one may say, intellectual; it was not moral and theological. He played with it and used it as a pigment; he treated it, as the metaphysicians say, objectively. He was not discomposed, disturbed, haunted by it, in the manner of its usual and regular victims, who had not the little postern door of fancy to slip through, to the other side of the wall. It was, indeed, to his imaginative vision, the great fact of man's nature; the light element that had been mingled with his own composition always clung to this rugged prominence of moral responsibility, like the mist that hovers about the mountain. It was a necessary condition for a man of Hawthorne's stock that if his imagination should take licence to amuse itself, it should at least select this grim precinct of the Puritan morality for its play-ground. He speaks of the dark disapproval with which his old ancestors, in the case of their coming to life, would see him trifling himself away as a story-teller. But how far more darkly would they have frowned could they have understood that he had converted the very principle of their own being into one of his toys!

It will be seen that I am far from being struck with the justice of that view of the author of the *Twice-Told Tales*, which is so happily expressed by the French critic to whom I alluded at an earlier stage of this essay. To speak of Hawthorne, as M. Emile Montégut does, as a *romancier pessimiste*, seems to me very much beside the mark. He is no more a pessimist than an optimist, though he is certainly not much of either. He does not pretend to conclude, or to have a philosophy of human nature; indeed, I should even say that at bottom he does not take human nature as hard as he may seem to do. "His bitterness," says M. Montégut, "is without abatement, and his bad opinion of man is without compensation.... His little tales have the air of confessions which the soul makes to itself; they are so many little slaps which the author applies to our face." This, it seems to me, is to exaggerate almost immeasurably the reach of Hawthorne's relish of gloomy subjects. What pleased him in such subjects was their picturesqueness, their rich duskiness of colour, their chiaroscuro; but they were not the expression of a hopeless, or even of a predominantly melancholy, feeling about the human soul. Such at least is my own impression. He is to a considerable degree ironical—this is part of his charm—part even, one may say, of his brightness; but he is neither bitter nor cynical—he is rarely even what I should call tragical. There have certainly been story-tellers of a gayer and lighter spirit; there have been observers more humorous, more hilarious—though on the whole Hawthorne's observation has a smile in it oftener than may at first appear; but there has rarely been an observer more serene, less agitated by what he sees and less disposed to call things deeply into question. As I have already intimated, his Note-Books are full of this simple and almost child-like serenity. That dusky pre-occupation with the misery of human life and the wickedness of the human heart which such a critic as M. Emile Montégut talks about, is totally absent from them; and if we may suppose a person to have read these Diaries before looking into the tales, we may be sure that such a reader would be greatly surprised to hear the author described as a disappointed, disdainful genius. "This marked love of cases of conscience," says M. Montégut, "this taciturn, scornful cast of mind, this habit of seeing sin everywhere and hell always gaping open, this dusky gaze bent always upon a damned world and a nature draped in mourning, these lonely conversations of the imagination with the conscience, this pitiless analysis resulting from a perpetual examination of one's self, and from the tortures of a heart closed before men and open to God—all these elements of the Puritan character have passed into Mr. Hawthorne, or to speak more justly, have *filtered* into him, through a long succession of generations." This is a very pretty and very vivid account of Hawthorne, superficially considered; and it is just such a view of the case as would commend itself most easily and most naturally to a hasty critic. It is all true indeed, with a difference;

Hawthorne was all that M. Montégut says, *minus* the conviction. The old Puritan moral sense, the consciousness of sin and hell, of the fearful nature of our responsibilities and the savage character of our Taskmaster—these things had been lodged in the mind of a man of Fancy, whose fancy had straightway begun to take liberties and play tricks with them—to judge them (Heaven forgive him!) from the poetic and æsthetic point of view, the point of view of entertainment and irony. This absence of conviction makes the difference; but the difference is great.

Hawthorne was a man of fancy, and I suppose that in speaking of him it is inevitable that we should feel ourselves confronted with the familiar problem of the difference between the fancy and the imagination. Of the larger and more potent faculty he certainly possessed a liberal share; no one can read *The House of the Seven Gables* without feeling it to be a deeply imaginative work. But I am often struck, especially in the shorter tales, of which I am now chiefly speaking, with a kind of small ingenuity, a taste for conceits and analogies, which bears more particularly what is called the fanciful stamp. The finer of the shorter tales are redolent of a rich imagination.

"Had Goodman Brown fallen asleep in the forest and only dreamed a wild dream of witch-meeting? Be it so, if you will; but, alas, it was a dream of evil omen for young Goodman Brown! a stern, a sad, a darkly meditative, a distrustful, if not a desperate, man, did he become from the night of that fearful dream. On the Sabbath-day, when the congregation were singing a holy psalm, he could not listen, because an anthem of sin rushed loudly upon his ear and drowned all the blessed strain. When the minister spoke from the pulpit, with power and fervid eloquence, and with his hand on the open Bible of the sacred truth of our religion, and of saint-like lives and triumphant deaths, and of future bliss or misery unutterable, then did Goodman Brown grow pale, dreading lest the roof should thunder down upon the gray blasphemer and his hearers. Often, awaking suddenly at midnight, he shrank from the bosom of Faith; and at morning or eventide, when the family knelt down at prayer, he scowled and muttered to himself, and gazed sternly at his wife, and turned away. And when he had lived long, and was borne to his grave a hoary corpse, followed by Faith, an aged woman, and children, and grandchildren, a goodly procession, besides neighbours not a few, they carved no hopeful verse upon his tombstone, for his dying hour was gloom."

There is imagination in that, and in many another passage that I might quote; but as a general thing I should characterise the more metaphysical of our author's short stories as graceful and felicitous conceits. They seem to me to be qualified in this manner by the very fact that they belong to the province of allegory. Hawthorne, in his metaphysical moods, is nothing if not allegorical, and allegory, to my sense, is quite one of the lighter exercises of the imagination. Many excellent judges, I know, have a great stomach for it; they delight in symbols and correspondences, in seeing a story told as if it were another and a very different story. I frankly confess that I have as a general thing but little enjoyment of it and that it has never seemed to me to be, as it were, a first-rate literary form. It has produced assuredly some first-rate works; and Hawthorne in his younger years had been a great reader and devotee of Bunyan and Spenser, the great masters of allegory. But it is apt to spoil two good things—a story and a moral, a meaning and a form; and the taste for it is responsible for a large part of the forcible-feeble writing that has been inflicted upon the world. The only cases in which it is endurable is when it is extremely spontaneous, when the analogy presents itself with eager promptitude. When it shows signs of having been groped and fumbled for, the needful illusion is of course absent and the failure complete. Then the machinery alone is visible, and the end to which it operates becomes a matter of indifference. There was but little literary criticism in the United States at the time Hawthorne's earlier works were published; but among the reviewers Edgar Poe perhaps held the scales the highest. He at any rate rattled them loudest, and pretended, more than any one else, to conduct the weighing-process on scientific principles. Very remarkable was this process of Edgar

Poe's, and very extraordinary were his principles; but he had the advantage of being a man of genius, and his intelligence was frequently great. His collection of critical sketches of the American writers flourishing in what M. Taine would call his *milieu* and *moment*, is very curious and interesting reading, and it has one quality which ought to keep it from ever being completely forgotten. It is probably the most complete and exquisite specimen of *provincialism* ever prepared for the edification of men. Poe's judgments are pretentious, spiteful, vulgar; but they contain a great deal of sense and discrimination as well, and here and there, sometimes at frequent intervals, we find a phrase of happy insight imbedded in a patch of the most fatuous pedantry. He wrote a chapter upon Hawthorne, and spoke of him on the whole very kindly; and his estimate is of sufficient value to make it noticeable that he should express lively disapproval of the large part allotted to allegory in his tales—in defence of which, he says, "however, or for whatever object employed, there is scarcely one respectable word to be said.... The deepest emotion," he goes on, "aroused within us by the happiest allegory *as* allegory, is a very, *very* imperfectly satisfied sense of the writer's ingenuity in overcoming a difficulty we should have preferred his not having attempted to overcome.... One thing is clear, that if allegory ever establishes a fact, it is by dint of overturning a fiction;" and Poe has furthermore the courage to remark that the *Pilgrim's Progress* is a "ludicrously overrated book." Certainly, as a general thing, we are struck with the ingenuity and felicity of Hawthorne's analogies and correspondences; the idea appears to have made itself at home in them easily. Nothing could be better in this respect than *The Snow-Image* (a little masterpiece), or *The Great Carbuncle*, or *Doctor Heidegger's Experiment*, or *Rappacini's Daughter*. But in such things as *The Birth-Mark* and *The Bosom-Serpent*, we are struck with something stiff and mechanical, slightly incongruous, as if the kernel had not assimilated its envelope. But these are matters of light impression, and there would be a want of tact in pretending to discriminate too closely among things which all, in one way or another, have a charm. The charm—the great charm—is that they are glimpses of a great field, of the whole deep mystery of man's soul and conscience. They are moral, and their interest is moral; they deal with something more than the mere accidents and conventionalities, the surface occurrences of life. The fine thing in Hawthorne is that he cared for the deeper psychology, and that, in his way, he tried to become familiar with it. This natural, yet fanciful familiarity with it, this air, on the author's part, of being a confirmed *habitué* of a region of mysteries and subtleties, constitutes the originality of his tales. And then they have the further merit of seeming, for what they are, to spring up so freely and lightly. The author has all the ease, indeed, of a regular dweller in the moral, psychological realm; he goes to and fro in it, as a man who knows his way. His tread is a light and modest one, but he keeps the key in his pocket.

His little historical stories all seem to me admirable; they are so good that you may re-read them many times. They are not numerous, and they are very short; but they are full of a vivid and delightful sense of the New England past; they have, moreover, the distinction, little tales of a dozen and fifteen pages as they are, of being the only successful attempts at historical fiction that have been made in the United States. Hawthorne was at home in the early New England history; he had thumbed its records and he had breathed its air, in whatever odd receptacles this somewhat pungent compound still lurked. He was fond of it, and he was proud of it, as any New Englander must be, measuring the part of that handful of half-starved fanatics who formed his earliest precursors, in laying the foundations of a mighty empire. Hungry for the picturesque as he always was, and not finding any very copious provision of it around him, he turned back into the two preceding centuries, with the earnest determination that the primitive annals of Massachusetts should at least *appear* picturesque. His fancy, which was always alive, played a little with the somewhat meagre and angular facts of the colonial period and forthwith converted a great many of them into impressive legends and pictures. There is a little infusion of colour, a little vagueness about certain details, but it is very gracefully and discreetly done, and realities are kept in view sufficiently to make us feel that if we are reading romance, it is romance that rather supplements than contradicts history. The early annals of New England were not fertile in legend, but Hawthorne laid his hands upon everything that would serve his purpose, and in two or three cases his version of the story has a great deal of beauty. *The Grey Champion* is a sketch of less than eight pages, but the little figures stand up in the tale as stoutly, at the least, as if they were propped up on half-a-dozen chapters by a dryer annalist, and the whole thing has the merit of those cabinet pictures in which the artist has been able to make his persons look the size of life. Hawthorne, to say it again, was not in the least a realist—he was not to my mind enough of one; but there is no genuine lover of the good city of Boston but will feel grateful to him for his courage in attempting to recount the "traditions" of Washington Street, the main thoroughfare of the Puritan capital. The four *Legends of the Province House* are certain shadowy stories which he professes to have gathered in an ancient tavern lurking behind the modern shop-fronts of this part of the city. The Province House disappeared some years ago, but while it stood it was pointed to as the residence of the Royal Governors of Massachusetts before the Revolution. I have no recollection of it, but it cannot have been, even from Hawthorne's account of it, which is as pictorial as he ventures to make it, a very imposing piece of antiquity. The writer's charming touch, however, throws a rich brown tone over its rather shallow venerableness; and we are beguiled into believing, for instance, at the close of *Howe's Masquerade* (a story of a strange occurrence at an entertainment given by Sir William Howe, the last of the Royal Governors, during the siege of Boston by Washington), that "superstition, among other legends of this mansion, repeats the wondrous tale that on the anniversary night of Britain's discomfiture the ghosts of the ancient governors of Massachusetts still glide through the Province House. And last of all comes a figure shrouded in a military cloak, tossing his clenched hands into the air and stamping his iron-shod boots upon the freestone steps, with a semblance of feverish despair, but without the sound of a foot-tramp." Hawthorne had, as regards the two earlier centuries of New England life, that faculty which is called now-a-days the historic consciousness. He never sought to exhibit it on a large scale; he exhibited it indeed on a scale so minute that we must not linger too much upon it. His vision of the past was filled with definite images—images none the less definite that they were concerned with events as shadowy as this dramatic passing away of the last of King George's representatives in his long loyal but finally alienated colony.

I have said that Hawthorne had become engaged in about his thirty-fifth-year; but he was not married until 1842. Before this event took place he passed through two episodes which (putting his falling in love aside) were much the most important things that had yet happened to him. They interrupted the painful monotony of his life, and brought the affairs of men within his personal experience. One of these was moreover in itself a curious and interesting chapter of observation, and it fructified, in Hawthorne's memory, in one of his best productions. How urgently he needed at this time to be drawn within the circle of social accidents, a little anecdote related by Mr. Lathrop in connection with his first acquaintance with the young lady he was to marry, may serve as an example. This young lady became known to him through her sister, who had first approached him as an admirer of the *Twice-Told Tales* (as to the authorship of which she had been so much in the dark as to have attributed it first, conjecturally, to one of the two Miss Hathornes); and the two Miss Peabodys, desiring to see more of the charming writer, caused him to be invited to a species of *conversazione* at the house of one of their friends, at which they themselves took care to be punctual. Several other ladies, however, were as punctual as they, and Hawthorne presently arriving, and seeing a bevy of admirers where he had expected but three or four, fell into a state of agitation, which is vividly described by his biographer. He "stood perfectly motionless, but with the look of a sylvan creature on the point of fleeing away.... He was stricken with dismay; his face lost colour and took on a warm paleness ... his agitation was very great; he stood by a table and, taking up some small object that lay upon it, he found his hand trembling so that he was obliged to lay it down." It was desirable, certainly, that something should occur to break the spell of a diffidence that might justly be called morbid. There is another little sentence dropped by Mr. Lathrop in relation to this period of Hawthorne's life, which appears to me worth quoting, though I am by no means sure that it will seem so to the reader. It has a very simple and innocent air, but to a person not without an impression of the early days of "culture" in New England, it will be pregnant with historic meaning. The elder Miss Peabody, who afterwards was Hawthorne's sister-in-law and who acquired later in life a very honourable American fame as a woman of benevolence, of learning, and of literary accomplishment, had invited the Miss Hathornes to come to her house for the evening, and to bring with them their brother, whom she wished to thank for his beautiful tales. "Entirely to her surprise," says Mr. Lathrop, completing thereby his picture of the attitude of this remarkable family toward society—"entirely to her surprise they came. She herself opened the door, and there, before her, between his sisters, stood a splendidly handsome youth, tall and strong, with no appearance whatever of timidity, but instead, an almost fierce determination making his face stern. This was his resource for carrying off the extreme inward tremor which he really felt. His hostess brought out Flaxman's designs for Dante, just received from Professor Felton, of Harvard, and the party made an evening's entertainment out of them." This last sentence is the one I allude to; and were it not for fear of appearing too fanciful I should say that these few words were, to the initiated mind, an unconscious expression of the lonely frigidity which characterised most attempts at social recreation in the New England world some forty years ago. There was at that time a great desire for culture, a great interest in knowledge, in art, in æsthetics, together with a very scanty supply of the materials for such pursuits. Small things were made to do large service; and there is something even touching in the solemnity of consideration that was bestowed by the emancipated New England conscience upon little wandering books and prints, little echoes and rumours of observation and experience. There flourished at that time in Boston a very remarkable and interesting woman, of whom we shall have more to say, Miss Margaret Fuller by name. This lady was the apostle of culture, of intellectual curiosity, and in the peculiarly interesting account of her life, published in 1852 by Emerson and two other of her friends, there are pages of her letters and diaries which narrate her visits to the Boston Athenæum and the emotions aroused in her mind by turning over portfolios of engravings. These emotions were ardent and passionate—could hardly have been more so had she been prostrate with contemplation in the Sistine Chapel or in one of the chambers of the Pitti Palace. The only analogy I can recall to this earnestness of interest in great works of art at a distance from them, is furnished by the great Goethe's elaborate study of plaster-casts and pencil-drawings at Weimar. I mention Margaret Fuller here because a glimpse of her state of mind—her vivacity of desire and poverty of knowledge—helps to define the situation. The situation lives for a moment in those few words of Mr. Lathrop's. The initiated mind, as I have ventured to call it, has a vision of a little unadorned parlour, with the snow-drifts of a Massachusetts winter piled up about its windows, and a group of sensitive and serious people, modest votaries of opportunity, fixing their eyes upon a bookful of Flaxman's attenuated outlines.

At the beginning of the year 1839 he received, through political interest, an appointment as weigher and gauger in the Boston Custom-house. Mr. Van Buren then occupied the Presidency, and it appears that the Democratic party, whose successful candidate he had been, rather took credit for the patronage it had bestowed upon literary men. Hawthorne was a Democrat, and apparently a zealous one; even in later years, after the Whigs had vivified their principles by the adoption of the Republican platform, and by taking up an honest attitude on the question of slavery, his political faith never wavered. His Democratic sympathies were eminently natural, and there would have been an incongruity in his belonging to the other party. He was not only by conviction, but personally and by association, a Democrat. When in later years he found himself in contact with European civilisation, he appears to have become conscious of a good deal of latent radicalism in his disposition; he was oppressed with the burden of antiquity in Europe, and he found himself sighing for lightness and freshness and facility of change. But these things are relative to the point of view, and in his own country Hawthorne cast his lot with the party of conservatism, the party opposed to change and freshness. The people who found something musty and mouldy in his literary productions would have regarded this quite as a matter of course; but we are not obliged to use invidious epithets in describing his political preferences. The sentiment that attached him to the Democracy was a subtle and honourable one, and the author of an attempt to sketch a portrait of him, should be the last to complain of this adjustment of his sympathies. It falls much more smoothly into his reader's conception of him than any other would do; and if he had had the perversity to be a Republican, I am afraid our ingenuity would have been considerably taxed in devising a proper explanation of the circumstance. At any rate, the Democrats gave him a small post in the Boston Custom-house, to which an annual salary of $1,200 was attached, and Hawthorne appears at first to have joyously welcomed the gift. The duties of the office were not very congruous to the genius of a man of fancy; but it had the advantage that it broke the spell of his cursed solitude, as he called it, drew him away from Salem, and threw him, comparatively speaking, into the world. The first volume of the American Note-Books contains some extracts from letters written during his tenure of this modest office, which indicate sufficiently that his occupations cannot have been intrinsically gratifying.

"I have been measuring coal all day," he writes, during the winter of 1840, "on board of a black little British schooner, in a dismal dock at the north end of the city. Most of the time I paced the deck to keep myself warm; for the wind (north-east, I believe) blew up through the dock as if it had been the pipe of a pair of bellows. The vessel lying deep between two wharves, there was no more delightful prospect, on the right hand and on the left, than the posts and timbers, half immersed in the water and covered with ice, which the rising and falling of successive tides had left upon them, so that they looked like immense icicles. Across the water, however, not more than half a mile off, appeared the Bunker's Hill Monument, and what interested me considerably more, a church-steeple, with the dial of a clock upon it, whereby I was enabled to measure the march of the weary hours. Sometimes I descended into the dirty little cabin of the schooner, and warmed myself by a red-hot stove, among biscuit-barrels, pots and kettles, sea-chests, and innumerable lumber of all sorts—my olfactories meanwhile being greatly refreshed with the odour of a pipe, which the captain, or some one of his crew, was smoking. But at last came the sunset, with delicate clouds, and a purple light upon the islands; and I blessed it, because it was the signal of my release."

A worse man than Hawthorne would have measured coal quite as well, and of all the dismal tasks to which an unremunerated imagination has ever had to accommodate itself, I remember none more sordid than the business depicted in the foregoing lines. "I pray," he writes some weeks later, "that in one year more I may find some way of escaping from this unblest Custom-house; for it is a very grievous thraldom. I do detest all offices; all, at least, that are held on a political tenure, and I want nothing to do with politicians. Their hearts wither away and die out of their bodies. Their consciences are turned to india-rubber, or to some substance as black as that and which will stretch as much. One thing, if no more, I have gained by my Custom-house experience—to know a politician. It is a knowledge which no previous thought or power of sympathy could have taught me; because the animal, or the machine rather, is not in nature." A few days later he goes on in the same strain:—

"I do not think it is the doom laid upon me of murdering so many of the brightest hours of the day at the Custom-house that makes such havoc with my wits, for here I am again trying to write worthily ... yet with a sense as if all the noblest part of man had been left out of my composition, or had decayed out of it since my nature was given to my own keeping.... Never comes any bird of Paradise into that dismal region. A salt or even a coal-ship is ten million times preferable; for there the sky is above me, and the fresh breeze around me, and my thoughts having hardly anything to do with my occupation, are as free as air. Nevertheless ... it is only once in a while that the image and desire of a better and happier life makes me feel the iron of my chain; for after all a human spirit may find no insufficiency of food for it, even in the Custom-house. And with such materials as these I do think and feel and learn things that are worth knowing, and which I should not know unless I had learned them there; so that the present position of my life shall not be quite left out of the sum of my real existence.... It is good for me, on many accounts, that my life has had this passage in it. I know much more than I did a year ago. I have a stronger sense of power to act as a man among men. I have gained worldly wisdom, and wisdom also that is not altogether of this world. And when I quit this earthy career where I am now buried, nothing will cling to me that ought to be left behind. Men will not perceive, I trust, by my look or the tenor of my thoughts and feelings, that I have been a Custom-house officer."

He says, writing shortly afterwards, that "when I shall be free again, I will enjoy all things with the fresh simplicity of a child of five years old. I shall grow young again, made all over anew. I will go forth and stand in a summer shower, and all the worldly dust that has collected on me shall be washed away at once, and my heart will be like a bank of fresh flowers for the weary to rest upon."

This forecast of his destiny was sufficiently exact. A year later, in April 1841, he went to take up his abode in the socialistic community of Brook Farm. Here he found himself among fields and flowers and other natural products—as well as among many products that could not very justly be called natural. He was exposed to summer showers in plenty; and his personal associations were as different as possible from, those he had encountered in fiscal circles. He made acquaintance with Transcendentalism and the Transcendentalists.

CHAPTER IV. BROOK FARM AND CONCORD.

The history of the little industrial and intellectual association which formed itself at this time in one of the suburbs of Boston has not, to my knowledge, been written; though it is assuredly a curious and interesting chapter in the domestic annals of New England. It would of course be easy to overrate the importance of this ingenious attempt of a few speculative persons to improve the outlook of mankind. The experiment came and went very rapidly and quietly, leaving very few traces behind it. It became simply a charming personal reminiscence for the small number of amiable enthusiasts who had had a hand in it. There were degrees of enthusiasm, and I suppose there were degrees of amiability; but a certain generous brightness of hope and freshness of conviction pervaded the whole undertaking and rendered it, morally speaking, important to an extent of which any heed that the world in general ever gave to it is an insufficient measure. Of course it would be a great mistake to represent the episode of Brook Farm as directly related to the manners and morals of the New England world in general—and in especial to those of the prosperous, opulent, comfortable part of it. The thing was the experiment of a coterie—it was unusual, unfashionable, unsuccessful. It was, as would then have been said, an amusement of the Transcendentalists—a harmless effusion of Radicalism. The Transcendentalists were not, after all, very numerous; and the Radicals were by no means of the vivid tinge of those of our own day. I have said that the Brook Farm community left no traces behind it that the world in general can appreciate; I should rather say that the only trace is a short novel, of which the principal merits reside in its qualities of difference from the affair itself. *The Blithedale Romance* is the main result of Brook Farm; but *The Blithedale Romance* was very properly never recognised by the Brook Farmers as an accurate portrait of their little colony.

Nevertheless, in a society as to which the more frequent complaint is that it is monotonous, that it lacks variety of incident and of type, the episode, our own business with which is simply that it was the cause of Hawthorne's writing an admirable tale, might be welcomed as a picturesque variation. At the same time, if we do not exaggerate its proportions, it may seem to contain a fund of illustration as to that phase of human life with which our author's own history mingled itself. The most graceful account of the origin of Brook Farm is probably to be found in these words of one of the biographers of Margaret Fuller: "In Boston and its vicinity, several friends, for whose character Margaret felt the highest-honour, were earnestly considering the possibility of making such industrial, social, and educational arrangements as would simplify economies, combine leisure for study with healthful and honest toil, avert unjust collisions of caste, equalise refinements, awaken generous affections, diffuse courtesy, and sweeten and sanctify life as a whole." The reader will perceive that this was a liberal scheme, and that if the experiment failed, the greater was the pity. The writer goes on to say that a gentleman, who afterwards distinguished himself in literature (he had begun by being a clergyman), "convinced by his experience in a faithful ministry that the need was urgent for a thorough application of the professed principles of Fraternity to actual relations, was about staking his all of fortune, reputation, and influence, in an attempt to organize a joint-stock company at Brook Farm." As Margaret Fuller passes for having suggested to Hawthorne the figure of Zenobia in *The Blithedale Romance*, and as she is probably, with one exception, the person connected with the affair who, after Hawthorne, offered most of what is called a personality to the world, I may venture to quote a few more passages from her Memoirs—a curious, in some points of view almost a grotesque, and yet, on the whole, as I have said, an extremely interesting book. It was a strange history and a strange destiny, that of this brilliant, restless, and unhappy woman—this ardent New Englander, this impassioned Yankee, who occupied so large a place in the thoughts, the lives, the affections, of an intelligent and appreciative society, and yet left behind her nothing but the memory of a memory. Her function, her reputation, were singular, and not altogether reassuring: she was a talker, she was *the* talker, she was the genius of talk. She had a magnificent, though by no means an unmitigated, egotism; and in some of her utterances it is difficult to say whether pride or humility prevails—as for instance when she writes that she feels "that there is plenty of room in the Universe for my faults, and as if I could not spend time in thinking of them when so many things interest me more." She has left the same sort of reputation as a great actress. Some of her writing has extreme beauty, almost all of it has a real interest, but her value, her activity, her sway (I am not sure that one can say her charm), were personal and practical. She went to Europe, expanded to new desires and interests, and, very poor herself, married an impoverished Italian nobleman. Then, with her husband and child, she embarked to return to her own country, and was lost at sea in a terrible storm, within sight of its coasts. Her tragical death combined with many of the elements of her life to convert her memory into a sort of legend, so that the people who had known her well, grew at last to be envied by later comers. Hawthorne does not appear to have been intimate with her; on the contrary, I find such an entry as this in the American Note-Books in 1841: "I was invited to dine at Mr. Bancroft's yesterday, with Miss Margaret Fuller; but Providence had given me some business to do; for which I was very thankful!" It is true that, later, the lady is the subject of one or two allusions of a gentler cast. One of them indeed is so pretty as to be worth quoting:—

"After leaving the book at Mr. Emerson's, I returned through the woods, and, entering Sleepy Hollow, I perceived a lady reclining near the path which bends along its verge. It was Margaret herself. She had been there the whole afternoon, meditating or reading, for she had a book in her hand with some strange title which I did not understand and have forgotten. She said that nobody had broken her solitude, and was just giving utterance to a theory that no inhabitant of Concord ever visited Sleepy Hollow, when we saw a group of people entering the sacred precincts. Most of them followed a path which led them away from us; but an old man passed near us, and smiled to see Margaret reclining on the ground and me standing by her side. He made some remark upon the beauty of the afternoon, and withdrew himself into the shadow of the wood. Then we talked about autumn, and about the pleasures of being lost in the woods, and about the crows, whose voices Margaret had heard; and about the experiences of early childhood, whose influence remains upon the character after the recollection of them has passed away; and about the sight of mountains from a distance, and the view from their summits; and about other matters of high and low philosophy."

It is safe to assume that Hawthorne could not on the whole have had a high relish for the very positive personality of this accomplished and argumentative woman, in whose intellect high noon seemed ever to reign, as twilight did in his own. He must have been struck with the glare of her understanding, and, mentally speaking, have scowled and blinked a good deal in conversation with her. But it is tolerably manifest, nevertheless, that she was, in his imagination, the starting-point of the figure of Zenobia; and Zenobia is, to my sense, his only very definite attempt at the representation of a character. The portrait is full of alteration and embellishment; but it has a greater reality, a greater abundance of detail, than any of his other figures, and the reality was a memory of the lady whom he had encountered in the Roxbury pastoral or among the wood-walks of Concord, with strange books in her hand and eloquent discourse on her lips. *The Blithedale Romance* was written just after her unhappy death, when the reverberation of her talk would lose much of its harshness. In fact, however, very much the same qualities that made Hawthorne a Democrat in polities—his contemplative turn and absence of a keen perception of abuses, his taste for old ideals, and loitering paces, and muffled tones—would operate to keep him out of active sympathy with a woman of the so-called progressive type. We may be sure that in women his taste was conservative.

It seems odd, as his biographer says, "that the least gregarious of men should have been drawn into a socialistic community;" but although it is apparent that Hawthorne went to Brook Farm without any great Transcendental fervour, yet he had various good reasons for casting his lot in this would-be happy family. He was as yet unable to marry, but he naturally wished to do so as speedily as possible, and there was a prospect that Brook Farm would prove an economical residence. And then it is only fair to believe that Hawthorne was interested in the experiment, and that though he was not a Transcendentalist, an Abolitionist, or a Fourierite, as his companions were in some degree or other likely to be, he was willing, as a generous and unoccupied young man, to lend a hand in any reasonable scheme for helping people to live together on better terms than the common. The Brook Farm scheme was, as such things go, a reasonable one; it was devised and carried out by shrewd and sober-minded New Englanders, who were careful to place economy first and idealism afterwards, and who were not afflicted with a Gallic passion for completeness of theory. There were no formulas, doctrines, dogmas; there was no interference whatever with private life or individual habits, and not the faintest adumbration of a rearrangement of that difficult business known as the relations of the sexes. The relations of the sexes were neither more nor less than what they usually are in American life, excellent; and in such particulars the scheme was thoroughly conservative and irreproachable. Its main characteristic was that each individual concerned in it should do a part of the work necessary for keeping the whole machine going. He could choose his work and he could live as he liked; it was hoped, but it was by no means demanded, that he would make himself agreeable, like a gentleman invited to a dinner-party. Allowing, however, for everything that was a concession to worldly traditions and to the laxity of man's nature, there must have been in the enterprise a good deal of a certain freshness and purity of spirit, of a certain noble credulity and faith in the perfectibility of man, which it would have been easier to find in Boston in the year 1840, than in London five-and-thirty years later. If that was the era of Transcendentalism, Transcendentalism could only have sprouted in the soil peculiar to the general locality of which I speak—the soil of the old New England morality, gently raked and refreshed by an imported culture. The Transcendentalists read a great deal of French and German, made themselves intimate with George Sand and Goethe, and many other writers; but the strong and deep New England conscience accompanied them on all their intellectual excursions, and there never was a so-called "movement" that embodied itself, on the whole, in fewer eccentricities of conduct, or that borrowed a smaller licence in private deportment. Henry Thoreau, a delightful writer, went to live in the woods; but Henry Thoreau was essentially a sylvan personage and would not have been, however the fashion of his time might have turned, a man about town. The brothers and sisters at Brook Farm ploughed the fields and milked the cows; but I think that an observer from another clime and society would have been much more struck with their spirit of conformity than with their *déréglements*. Their ardour was a moral ardour, and the lightest breath of scandal never rested upon them, or upon any phase of Transcendentalism.

A biographer of Hawthorne might well regret that his hero had not been more mixed up with the reforming and free-thinking class, so that he might find a pretext for writing a chapter upon the state of Boston society forty years ago. A needful warrant for such regret should be, properly, that the biographer's own personal reminiscences should stretch back to that period and to the persons who animated it. This would be a guarantee of fulness of knowledge and, presumably, of kindness of tone. It is difficult to see, indeed, how the generation of which Hawthorne has given us, in *Blithedale*, a few portraits, should not at this time of day be spoken of very tenderly and sympathetically. If irony enter into the allusion, it should be of the lightest and gentlest. Certainly, for a brief and imperfect chronicler of these things, a writer just touching them as he passes, and who has not the advantage of having been a contemporary, there is only one possible tone. The compiler of these pages, though his recollections date only from a later period, has a memory of a certain number of persons who had been intimately connected, as Hawthorne was not, with the agitations of that interesting time. Something of its interest adhered to them still—something of its aroma clung to their garments; there was something about them which seemed to say that when they were young and enthusiastic, they had been initiated into moral mysteries, they had played at a wonderful game. Their usual mark (it is true I can think of exceptions) was that they seemed excellently good. They appeared unstained by the world, unfamiliar with worldly desires and standards, and with those various forms of human depravity which flourish in some high phases of civilisation; inclined to simple and democratic ways, destitute of pretensions and affectations, of jealousies, of cynicism, of snobbishness. This little epoch of fermentation has three or four drawbacks for the critic—drawbacks, however, that may be overlooked by a person for whom it has an interest of association. It bore, intellectually, the stamp of provincialism; it was a beginning without a fruition, a dawn without a noon; and it produced, with a single exception, no great talents. It produced a great deal of writing, but (always putting Hawthorne aside, as a contemporary but not a sharer) only one writer in whom the world at large has interested itself. The situation was summed up and transfigured in the admirable and exquisite Emerson. He expressed all that it contained, and a good deal more, doubtless, besides; he was the man of genius of the moment; he was the Transcendentalist *par excellence*. Emerson expressed, before all things, as was extremely natural at the hour and in the place, the value and importance of the individual, the duty of making the most of one's self, of living by one's own personal light and carrying out one's own disposition. He reflected with beautiful irony upon the exquisite impudence of those institutions which claim to have appropriated the truth and to dole it out, in proportionate morsels, in exchange for a subscription. He talked about the beauty and dignity of life, and about every one who is born into the world being born to the whole, having an interest and a stake in the whole. He said "all that is clearly due to-day is not to lie," and a great many other things which it would be still easier to present in a ridiculous light. He insisted upon sincerity and independence and spontaneity, upon acting in harmony with one's nature, and not conforming and compromising for the sake of being more comfortable. He urged that a man should await his call, his finding the thing to do which he should really believe in doing, and not be urged by the world's opinion to do simply the world's work. "If no call should come for years, for centuries, then I know that the want of the Universe is the attestation of faith by my abstinence.... If I cannot work, at least I need not lie." The doctrine of the supremacy of the individual to himself, of his originality and, as regards his own character, *unique* quality, must have had a great charm for people living in a society in which introspection, thanks to the want of other entertainment, played almost the part of a social resource.

In the United States, in those days, there were no great things to look out at (save forests and rivers); life was not in the least spectacular; society was not brilliant; the country was given up to a great material prosperity, a homely *bourgeois* activity, a diffusion of primary education and the common luxuries. There was therefore, among the cultivated classes, much relish for the utterances of a writer who would help one to take a picturesque view of one's internal possibilities, and to find in the landscape of the soul all sorts of fine sunrise and moonlight effects. "Meantime, while the doors of the temple stand open, night and day, before every man, and the oracles of this truth cease never, it is guarded by one stern condition; this, namely—it is an intuition. It cannot be received at second hand. Truly speaking, it is not instruction but provocation that I can receive from another soul." To make one's self so much more interesting would help to make life interesting, and life was probably, to many of this aspiring congregation, a dream of freedom and fortitude. There were faulty parts in the Emersonian philosophy; but the general tone was magnificent; and I can easily believe that, coming when it did and where it did, it should have been drunk in by a great many fine moral appetites with a sense of intoxication. One envies, even, I will not say the illusions, of that keenly sentient period, but the convictions and interests— the moral passion. One certainly envies the privilege of having heard the finest of Emerson's orations poured forth in their early newness. They were the most poetical, the most beautiful productions of the American mind, and they were thoroughly local and national. They had a music and a magic, and when one remembers the remarkable charm of the speaker, the beautiful modulation of his utterance, one regrets in especial that one might not have been present on a certain occasion which made a sensation, an era—the delivery of an address to the Divinity School of Harvard University, on a summer evening in 1838. In the light, fresh American air, unthickened and undarkened by customs and institutions established, these things, as the phrase is, told.

Hawthorne appears, like his own Miles Coverdale, to have arrived at Brook Farm in the midst of one of those April snow-storms which, during the New England spring, occasionally diversify the inaction of the vernal process. Miles Coverdale, in *The Blithedale Romance*, is evidently as much Hawthorne as he is any one else in particular. He is indeed not very markedly any one, unless it be the spectator, the observer; his chief identity lies in his success in looking at things objectively and spinning uncommunicated fancies about them. This indeed was the part that Hawthorne played socially in the little community at West Roxbury. His biographer describes him as sitting "silently, hour after hour, in the broad old-fashioned hall of the house, where he could listen almost unseen to the chat and merriment of the young people, himself almost always holding a book before him, but seldom turning the leaves." He put his hand to the plough and supported himself and the community, as they were all supposed to do, by his labour; but he contributed little to the hum of voices. Some of his companions, either then or afterwards, took, I believe, rather a gruesome view of his want of articulate enthusiasm, and accused him of coming to the place as a sort of intellectual vampire, for purely psychological purposes. He sat in a corner, they declared, and watched the inmates when they were off their guard, analysing their characters, and dissecting the amiable ardour, the magnanimous illusions, which he was too cold-blooded to share. In so far as this account of Hawthorne's attitude was a complaint, it was a singularly childish one. If he was at Brook Farm without being of it, this is a very fortunate circumstance from the point of view of posterity, who would have preserved but a slender memory of the affair if our author's fine novel had not kept the topic open. The complaint is indeed almost so ungrateful a one as to make us regret that the author's fellow-communists came off so easily. They certainly would not have done so if the author of *Blithedale* had been more of a satirist. Certainly, if Hawthorne was an observer, he was a very harmless one; and when one thinks of the queer specimens of the reforming genus with which he must have been surrounded, one almost wishes that, for our entertainment, he had given his old companions something to complain of in earnest. There is no satire whatever in the *Romance*; the quality is almost conspicuous by its absence. Of portraits there are only two; there is no sketching of odd figures—no reproduction of strange types of radicalism; the human background is left vague. Hawthorne was not a satirist, and if at Brook Farm he was, according to his habit, a good deal of a mild sceptic, his scepticism was exercised much more in the interest of fancy than in that of reality.

There must have been something pleasantly bucolic and pastoral in the habits of the place during the fine New England summer; but we have no retrospective envy of the denizens of Brook Farm in that other season which, as Hawthorne somewhere says, leaves in those regions, "so large a blank—so melancholy a deathspot—in lives so brief that they ought to be all summer-time." "Of a summer night, when the moon was full," says Mr. Lathrop, "they lit no lamps, but sat grouped in the light and shadow, while sundry of the younger men sang old ballads, or joined Tom Moore's songs to operatic airs. On other nights there would be an original essay or poem read aloud, or else a play of Shakspeare, with the parts distributed to different members; and these amusements failing, some interesting discussion was likely to take their place. Occasionally, in the dramatic season, large delegations from the farm would drive into Boston, in carriages and waggons, to the opera or the play. Sometimes, too, the young women sang as they washed the dishes in the Hive; and the youthful yeomen of the society came in and helped them with their work. The men wore blouses of a checked or plaided stuff, belted at the waist, with a broad collar folding down about the throat, and rough straw hats; the women, usually, simple calico gowns and hats." All this sounds delightfully Arcadian and innocent, and it is certain that there was something peculiar to the clime and race in some of the features of such a life; in the free, frank, and stainless companionship of young men and maidens, in the mixture of manual labour and intellectual flights—dish-washing and æsthetics, wood-chopping and philosophy. Wordsworth's "plain living and high thinking" were made actual. Some passages in Margaret Fuller's journals throw plenty of light on this. (It must be premised that she was at Brook Farm as an occasional visitor; not as a labourer in the Hive.)

"All Saturday I was off in the woods. In the evening we had a general conversation, opened by me, upon Education, in its largest sense, and on what we can do for ourselves and others. I took my usual ground:—The aim is perfection; patience the road. Our lives should be considered as a tendency, an approximation only.... Mr. R. spoke admirably on the nature of loyalty. The people showed a good deal of the *sans-culotte* tendency in their manners, throwing themselves on the floor, yawning, and going out when they had heard enough. Yet as the majority differ with me, to begin with— that being the reason this subject was chosen—they showed on the whole more interest and deference than I had expected. As I am accustomed to deference, however, and need it for the boldness and animation which my part requires, I did not speak with as much force as usual.... Sunday.—A glorious day; the woods full of perfume; I was out all the morning. In the afternoon Mrs. R. and I had a talk. I said my position would be too uncertain here, as I could not work. —— said 'they would all like to work for a person of genius.' ... 'Yes,' I told her; 'but where would be my repose when they were always to be judging whether I was worth it or not?.... Each day you must prove yourself anew.' ... We talked of the principles of the community. I said I had not a right to come, because all the confidence I had in it was as an *experiment* worth trying, and that it was part of the great wave of inspired thought.... We had valuable discussion on these points. All Monday morning in the woods again. Afternoon, out with the drawing party; I felt the evils of the want of conventional refinement, in the impudence with which one of the girls treated me. She has since thought of it with regret, I notice; and by every day's observation of me will see that she ought not to have done it. In the evening a husking in the barn ... a most picturesque scene.... I stayed and helped about half an hour, and then took a long walk beneath the stars. Wednesday.... In the evening a conversation on Impulse.... I defended nature, as I always do;—the spirit ascending through, not superseding, nature. But in the scale of Sense, Intellect, Spirit, I advocated the claims of Intellect, because those present were rather disposed to postpone them. On the nature of Beauty we had good talk. —— seemed in a much more reverent humour than the other night, and enjoyed the large plans of the universe which were unrolled.... Saturday,—Well, good-bye, Brook Farm. I know more about this place than I did when I came; but the only way to be qualified for a judge of such an experiment would be to become an active, though unimpassioned, associate in trying it.... The girl who was so rude to me stood waiting, with a timid air, to bid me good-bye."

The young girl in question cannot have been Hawthorne's charming Priscilla; nor yet another young lady, of a most humble spirit, who communicated to Margaret's biographers her recollections of this remarkable woman's visits to Brook Farm; concluding with the assurance that "after a while she seemed to lose sight of my more prominent and disagreeable peculiarities, and treated me with affectionate regard."

Hawthorne's farewell to the place appears to have been accompanied with some reflections of a cast similar to those indicated by Miss Fuller; in so far at least as we may attribute to Hawthorne himself some of the observations that he fathers upon Miles Coverdale. His biographer justly quotes two or three sentences from *The Blithedale Romance*, as striking the note of the author's feeling about the place. "No sagacious man," says Coverdale, "will long retain his sagacity if he live exclusively among reformers and progressive people, without periodically returning to the settled system of things, to correct himself by a new observation from that old standpoint." And he remarks elsewhere that "it struck me as rather odd that one of the first questions raised, after our separation from the greedy, struggling, self-seeking world, should relate to the possibility of getting the advantage over the outside barbarians in their own field of labour. But to tell the truth, I very soon became sensible that, as regarded society at large, we stood in a position of new hostility rather than new brotherhood." He was doubtless oppressed by the "sultry heat of society," as he calls it in one of the jottings in the Note-Books. "What would a man do if he were compelled to live always in the sultry heat of society, and could never bathe himself in cool solitude?" His biographer relates that one of the other Brook Farmers, wandering afield one summer's day, discovered Hawthorne stretched at his length upon a grassy hillside, with his hat pulled over his face, and every appearance, in his attitude, of the desire to escape detection. On his asking him whether he had any particular reason for this shyness of posture—"Too much of a party up there!"

Hawthorne contented himself with replying, with a nod in the direction of the Hive. He had nevertheless for a time looked forward to remaining indefinitely in the community; he meant to marry as soon as possible and bring his wife there to live. Some sixty pages of the second volume of the American Note-Books are occupied with extracts from his letters to his future wife and from his journal (which appears however at this time to have been only intermittent), consisting almost exclusively of descriptions of the simple scenery of the neighbourhood, and of the state of the woods and fields and weather. Hawthorne's fondness for all the common things of nature was deep and constant, and there is always something charming in his verbal touch, as we may call it, when he talks to himself about them. "Oh," he breaks out, of an October afternoon, "the beauty of grassy slopes, and the hollow ways of paths winding between hills, and the intervals between the road and wood-lots, where Summer lingers and sits down, strewing dandelions of gold and blue asters as her parting gifts and memorials!" He was but a single summer at Brook Farm; the rest of his residence had the winter-quality.

But if he returned to solitude, it was henceforth to be as the French say, a *solitude à deux.* He was married in July 1842, and betook himself immediately to the ancient village of Concord, near Boston, where he occupied the so-called Manse which has given the title to one of his collections of tales, and upon which this work, in turn, has conferred a permanent distinction. I use the epithets "ancient" and "near" in the foregoing sentence, according to the American measurement of time and distance. Concord is some twenty miles from Boston, and even to day, upwards of forty years after the date of Hawthorne's removal thither, it is a very fresh and well-preserved looking town. It had already a local history when, a hundred years ago, the larger current of human affairs flowed for a moment around it. Concord has the honour of being the first spot in which blood was shed in the war of the Revolution; here occurred the first exchange of musket-shots between the King's troops and the American insurgents. Here, as Emerson says in the little hymn which he contributed in 1836 to the dedication of a small monument commemorating this circumstance—

"Here once the embattled farmers stood,

And fired the shot heard round the world."

The battle was a small one, and the farmers were not destined individually to emerge from obscurity; but the memory of these things has kept the reputation of Concord green, and it has been watered, moreover, so to speak, by the life-long presence there of one of the most honoured of American men of letters—the poet from whom I just quoted two lines. Concord is indeed in itself decidedly verdant, and is an excellent specimen of a New England village of the riper sort. At the time of Hawthorne's first going there it must have been an even better specimen than to-day—more homogeneous, more indigenous, more absolutely democratic. Forty years ago the tide of foreign immigration had scarcely begun to break upon the rural strongholds of the New England race; it had at most begun to splash them with the salt Hibernian spray. It is very possible, however, that at this period there was not an Irishman in Concord; the place would have been a village community operating in excellent conditions. Such a village community was not the least honourable item in the sum of New England civilisation. Its spreading elms and plain white houses, its generous summers and ponderous winters, its immediate background of promiscuous field and forest, would have been part of the composition. For the rest, there were the selectmen and the town-meetings, the town-schools and the self-governing spirit, the rigid morality, the friendly and familiar manners, the perfect competence of the little society to manage its affairs itself. In the delightful introduction to the *Mosses*, Hawthorne has given an account of his dwelling, of his simple occupations and recreations, and of some of the characteristics of the place. The Manse is a large, square wooden house, to the surface of which—even in the dry New England air, so unfriendly to mosses and lichens and weather-stains, and the other elements of a picturesque complexion—a hundred and fifty years of exposure have imparted a kind of tone, standing just above the slow-flowing Concord river, and approached by a short avenue of overarching trees. It had been the dwelling-place of generations of Presbyterian ministers, ancestors of the celebrated Emerson, who had himself spent his early manhood and written some of his most beautiful essays there. "He used," as Hawthorne says, "to watch the Assyrian dawn, and Paphian sunset and moonrise, from the summit of our eastern hill." From its clerical occupants the place had inherited a mild mustiness of theological association—a vague reverberation of old Calvinistic sermons, which served to deepen its extra-mundane and somnolent quality. The three years that Hawthorne passed here were, I should suppose, among the happiest of his life. The future was indeed not in any special manner assured; but the present was sufficiently genial. In the American Note-Books there is a charming passage (too long to quote) descriptive of the entertainment the new couple found in renovating and re-furnishing the old parsonage, which, at the time of their going into it, was given up to ghosts and cobwebs. Of the little drawing-room, which had been most completely reclaimed, he writes that "the shade of our departed host will never haunt it; for its aspect has been as completely changed as the scenery of a theatre. Probably the ghost gave one peep into it, uttered a groan, and vanished for ever." This departed host was a certain Doctor Ripley, a venerable scholar, who left behind him a reputation of learning and sanctity which was reproduced in one of the ladies of his family, long the most distinguished woman in the little Concord circle. Doctor Ripley's predecessor had been, I believe, the last of the line of the Emerson ministers—an old gentleman who, in the earlier years of his pastorate, stood at the window of his study (the same in which Hawthorne handled a more irresponsible quill) watching, with his hands under his long coat-tails, the progress of Concord fight. It is not by any means related, however, I should add, that he waited for the conclusion to make up his mind which was the righteous cause.

Hawthorne had a little society (as much, we may infer, as he desired), and it was excellent in quality. But the pages in the Note-Books which relate to his life at the Manse, and the introduction to the *Mosses*, make more of his relations with vegetable nature, and of his customary contemplation of the incidents of wood-path and way-side, than of the human elements of the scene; though these also are gracefully touched upon. These pages treat largely of the pleasures of a kitchen-garden, of the beauty of summer-squashes, and of the mysteries of apple-raising. With the wholesome aroma of apples (as is indeed almost necessarily the case in any realistic record of New England rural life) they are especially pervaded; and with many other homely and domestic emanations; all of which derive a sweetness from the medium of our author's colloquial style. Hawthorne was silent with his lips; but he talked with his pen. The tone of his writing is often that of charming talk—ingenious, fanciful, slow-flowing, with all the lightness of gossip, and none of its vulgarity. In the preface to the tales written at the Manse he talks of many things and just touches upon some of the members of his circle—especially upon that odd genius, his fellow-villager, Henry Thoreau. I said a little way back that the New England Transcendental movement had suffered in the estimation of the world at large from not having (putting Emerson aside) produced any superior talents. But any reference to it would be ungenerous which should omit to pay a tribute in passing to the author of *Walden*. Whatever question there may be of his talent, there can be none, I think, of his genius. It was a slim and crooked one; but it was eminently personal. He was imperfect, unfinished, inartistic; he was worse than provincial—he was parochial; it is only at his best that he is readable. But at his best he has an extreme natural charm, and he must always be mentioned after those Americans—Emerson, Hawthorne, Longfellow, Lowell, Motley—who have written originally. He was Emerson's independent moral man made flesh—living for the ages, and not for Saturday and Sunday; for the Universe, and not for Concord. In fact, however, Thoreau lived for Concord very effectually, and by his remarkable genius for the observation of the phenomena of woods and streams, of plants and trees, and beasts and fishes, and for flinging a kind of spiritual interest over these things, he did more than he perhaps intended toward consolidating the fame of his accidental human sojourn. He was as shy and ungregarious as Hawthorne; but he and the latter appear to have been sociably disposed towards each other, and there are some charming touches in the preface to the *Mosses* in regard to the hours they spent in boating together on the large, quiet Concord river. Thoreau was a great voyager, in a canoe which he had constructed himself, and which he eventually made over to Hawthorne, and as expert in the use of the paddle as the Red men who had once haunted the same silent stream. The most frequent of Hawthorne's companions on these excursions appears, however, to have been a local celebrity—as well as Thoreau a high Transcendentalist—Mr. Ellery Channing, whom I may mention, since he is mentioned very explicitly in the preface to the *Mosses*, and also because no account of the little Concord world would be complete which should omit him. He was the son of the distinguished Unitarian moralist, and, I believe, the intimate friend of Thoreau, whom he resembled in having produced literary compositions more esteemed by the few than by the many. He and Hawthorne were both fishermen, and the two used to set themselves afloat in the summer afternoons. "Strange and happy times were those," exclaims the more distinguished of the two writers, "when we cast aside all irksome forms and strait-laced habitudes, and delivered ourselves up to the free air, to live like the Indians or any less conventional race, during one bright semicircle of the sun. Rowing our boat against the current, between wide meadows, we turned aside into the Assabeth. A more lovely stream than this, for a mile above its junction with the Concord, has never flowed on earth—nowhere indeed except to lave the interior regions of a poet's imagination.... It comes flowing softly through the midmost privacy and deepest heart of a wood which whispers it to be quiet; while the stream whispers back again from its sedgy borders, as if river and wood were hushing one another to sleep. Yes; the river sleeps along its course and dreams of the sky and the clustering foliage...." While Hawthorne was looking at these beautiful things, or, for that matter, was writing them, he was well out of the way of a certain class of visitants whom he alludes to in one of the closing passages of this long Introduction. "Never was a poor little country village infested with such a variety of queer, strangely-dressed, oddly-behaved mortals, most of whom took upon themselves to be important agents of the world's destiny, yet were simply bores of a very intense character." "These hobgoblins of flesh and blood," he says in a preceding paragraph, "were attracted thither by the wide-spreading influence of a great original thinker who had his earthly abode at the opposite extremity of our village.... People that had lighted on a new thought or a thought they fancied new, came to Emerson, as the finder of a glittering gem hastens to a lapidary, to ascertain its quality and value." And Hawthorne enumerates some of the categories of pilgrims to the shrine of the mystic counsellor, who as a general thing was probably far from abounding in their own sense (when this sense was perverted), but gave them a due measure of plain practical advice. The whole passage is interesting, and it suggests that little Concord had not been ill-treated by the fates—with "a great original thinker" at one end of the village, an exquisite teller of tales at the other, and the rows of New England elms between. It contains moreover an admirable sentence about Hawthorne's pilgrim-haunted neighbour, with whom, "being happy," as he says, and feeling therefore "as if there were no question to be put," he was not in metaphysical communion. "It was good nevertheless to meet him in the wood-paths, or sometimes in our avenue, with that pure intellectual gleam diffused about his presence, like the garment of a shining one; and he so quiet, so simple, so without pretension, encountering each man alive as if expecting to receive more than he could impart!" One may without indiscretion risk the surmise that Hawthorne's perception, of the "shining" element in his distinguished friend was more intense than his friend's appreciation of whatever luminous property might reside within the somewhat dusky envelope of our hero's identity as a collector of "mosses." Emerson, as a sort of spiritual sun-worshipper, could have attached but a moderate value to Hawthorne's cat-like faculty of seeing in the dark.

"As to the daily coarse of our life," the latter writes in the spring of 1843, "I have written with pretty commendable diligence, averaging from two to four hours a day; and the result is seen in various magazines. I might have written more if it had seemed worth while, but I was content to earn only so much gold as might suffice for our immediate wants, having prospect of official station and emolument which would do away with the necessity of writing for bread. These prospects have not yet had their fulfilment; and we are well content to wait, for an office would inevitably remove us from our present happy home—at least from an outward home; for there is an inner one that will accompany us wherever we go. Meantime, the magazine people do not pay their debts; so that we taste some of the inconveniences of poverty. It is an annoyance, not a trouble." And he goes on to give some account of his usual habits. (The passage is from his Journal, and the account is given to himself, as it were, with that odd, unfamiliar explicitness which marks the tone of this record throughout.) "Every day I trudge through snow and slosh to the village, look into the post-office, and spend an hour at the reading-room; and then return home, generally without having spoken a word to any human being.... In the way of exercise I saw and split wood, and physically I was never in a better condition than now." He adds a mention of an absence he had lately made. "I went alone to Salem, where I resumed all my bachelor habits for nearly a fortnight, leading the same life in which ten years of my youth flitted away like a dream. But how much changed was I! At last I had got hold of a reality which never could be taken from me. It was good thus to get apart from my happiness for the sake of contemplating it."

These compositions, which were so unpunctually paid for, appeared in the *Democratic Review*, a periodical published at Washington, and having, as our author's biographer says, "considerable pretensions to a national character." It is to be regretted that the practice of keeping its creditors waiting should, on the part of the magazine in question, have been thought compatible with these pretensions. The foregoing lines are a description of a very monotonous but a very contented life, and Mr. Lathrop justly remarks upon the dissonance of tone of the tales Hawthorne produced under these happy circumstances. It is indeed not a little of an anomaly. The episode of the Manse was one of the most agreeable he had known, and yet the best of the *Mosses* (though not the greater number of them) are singularly dismal compositions. They are redolent of M. Montégut's pessimism. "The reality of sin, the pervasiveness of evil," says Mr. Lathrop, "had been but slightly insisted upon in the earlier tales: in this series the idea bursts up like a long-buried fire, with earth-shaking strength, and the pits of hell seem yawning beneath us." This is very true (allowing for Mr. Lathrop's rather too emphatic way of putting it); but the anomaly is, I think, on the whole, only superficial. Our writer's imagination, as has been abundantly conceded, was a gloomy one; the old Puritan sense of sin, of penalties to be paid, of the darkness and wickedness of life, had, as I have already suggested, passed into it. It had not passed into the parts of Hawthorne's nature corresponding to those occupied by the same horrible vision of things in his ancestors; but it had still been determined to claim this later comer as its own, and since his heart and his happiness were to escape, it insisted on setting its mark upon his genius—upon his most beautiful organ, his admirable fancy. It may be said that when his fancy was strongest and keenest, when it was most itself, then the dark Puritan tinge showed in it most richly; and there cannot be a better proof that he was not the man of a sombre *parti-pris* whom M. Montégut describes, than the fact that these duskiest flowers of his invention sprang straight from the soil of his happiest days. This surely indicates that there was but little direct connection between the products of his fancy and the state of his affections. When he was lightest at heart, he was most creative, and when he was most creative, the moral picturesqueness of the old secret of mankind in general and of the Puritans in particular, most appealed to him—the secret that we are really not by any means so good as a well-regulated society requires us to appear. It is not too much to say, even, that the very condition of production of some of these unamiable tales would be that they should be superficial, and, as it were, insincere. The magnificent little romance of *Young Goodman Brown*, for instance, evidently means nothing as regards Hawthorne's own state of mind, his conviction of human depravity and his consequent melancholy; for the simple reason that if it meant anything, it would mean too much. Mr. Lathrop speaks of it as a "terrible and lurid parable;" but this, it seems to me, is just what it is not. It is not a parable, but a picture, which is a very different thing. What does M. Montégut make, one would ask, from the point of view of Hawthorne's pessimism, of the singularly objective and unpreoccupied tone of the Introduction to the *Old Manse*, in which the author speaks from himself, and in which the cry of metaphysical despair is not even faintly sounded?

We have seen that when he went into the village he often came home without having spoken a word to a human being. There is a touching entry made a little later, bearing upon his mild taciturnity. "A cloudy veil stretches across the abyss of my nature. I have, however, no love of secrecy and darkness. I am glad to think that God sees through my heart, and if any angel has power to penetrate into it, he is welcome to know everything that is there. Yes, and so may any mortal who is capable of full sympathy, and therefore worthy to come into my depths. But he must find his own way there; I can neither guide nor enlighten him." It must be acknowledged, however, that if he was not able to open the gate of conversation, it was sometimes because he was disposed to slide the bolt himself. "I had a purpose," he writes, shortly before the entry last quoted, "if circumstances would permit, of passing the whole term of my wife's absence without speaking a word to any human being." He beguiled these incommunicative periods by studying German, in Tieck and Bürger, without apparently making much progress; also in reading French, in Voltaire and Rabelais. "Just now," he writes, one October noon, "I heard a sharp tapping at the window of my study, and, looking up from my book (a volume of Rabelais), behold, the head of a little bird, who seemed to demand admittance." It was a quiet life, of course, in which these diminutive incidents seemed noteworthy; and what is noteworthy here to the observer of Hawthorne's contemplative simplicity, is the fact that though he finds a good deal to say about the little bird (he devotes several lines more to it) he makes no remark upon Rabelais. He had other visitors than little birds, however, and their demands were also not Rabelaisian. Thoreau comes to see him, and they talk "upon the spiritual advantages of change of place, and upon the *Dial*, and upon Mr. Alcott, and other kindred or concatenated subjects." Mr. Alcott was an arch-transcendentalist, living in Concord, and the *Dial* was a periodical to which the illuminated spirits of Boston and its neighbourhood used to contribute. Another visitor comes and talks "of Margaret Fuller, who, he says, has risen perceptibly into a higher state since their last meeting." There is probably a great deal of Concord five-and-thirty years ago in that little sentence!

CHAPTER V. THE THREE AMERICAN NOVELS.

The prospect of official station and emolument which Hawthorne mentions in one of those paragraphs from his Journals which I have just quoted, as having offered itself and then passed away, was at last, in the event, confirmed by his receiving from the administration of President Polk the gift of a place in the Custom-house of his native town. The office was a modest one, and "official station" may perhaps appear a magniloquent formula for the functions sketched in the admirable Introduction to The *Scarlet Letter*. Hawthorne's duties were those of Surveyor of the port of Salem, and they had a salary attached, which was the important part; as his biographer tells us that he had received almost nothing for the contributions to the *Democratic Review*. He bade farewell to his ex-parsonage and went back to Salem in 1846, and the immediate effect of his ameliorated fortune was to make him stop writing. None of his Journals of the period from his going to Salem to 1850 have been published; from which I infer that he even ceased to journalise. *The Scarlet Letter* was not written till 1849. In the delightful prologue to that work, entitled *The Custom-house*, he embodies some of the impressions gathered during these years of comparative leisure (I say of leisure because he does not intimate in this sketch of his occupations that his duties were onerous). He intimates, however, that they were not interesting, and that it was a very good thing for him, mentally and morally, when his term of service expired—or rather when he was removed from office by the operation of that wonderful "rotatory" system which his countrymen had invented for the administration of their affairs. This sketch of the Custom-house is, as simple writing, one of the most perfect of Hawthorne's compositions, and one of the most gracefully and humorously autobiographic. It would be interesting to examine it in detail, but I prefer to use my space for making some remarks upon the work which was the ultimate result of this period of Hawthorne's residence in his native town; and I shall, for convenience' sake, say directly afterwards what I have to say about the two companions of *The Scarlet Letter*—*The House of the Seven Gables* and *The Blithedale Romance*. I quoted some passages from the prologue to the first of these novels in the early pages of this essay. There is another passage, however, which bears particularly upon this phase of Hawthorne's career, and which is so happily expressed as to make it a pleasure to transcribe it—the passage in which he says that "for myself, during the whole of my Custom-house experience, moonlight and sunshine, and the glow of the fire-light, were just alike in my regard, and neither of them was of one whit more avail than the twinkle of a tallow candle. An entire class of susceptibilities, and a gift connected with them—of no great richness or value, but the best I had—was gone from me." He goes on to say that he believes that he might have done something if he could have made up his mind to convert the very substance of the commonplace that surrounded him into matter of literature.

"I might, for instance, have contented myself with writing out the narratives of a veteran shipmaster, one of the inspectors, whom I should be most ungrateful not to mention; since scarcely a day passed that he did not stir me to laughter and admiration by his marvellous gift as a story-teller.... Or I might readily have found a more serious task. It was a folly, with the materiality of this daily life pressing so intrusively upon me, to attempt to fling myself back into another age; or to insist on creating a semblance of a world out of airy matter.... The wiser effort would have been, to diffuse thought and imagination through the opaque substance of to-day, and thus make it a bright transparency ... to seek resolutely the true and indestructible value that lay hidden in the petty and wearisome incidents and ordinary characters with which I was now conversant. The fault was mine. The page of life that was spread out before me was dull and commonplace, only because I had not fathomed its deeper import. A better book than I shall ever write was there.... These perceptions came too late.... I had ceased to be a writer of tolerably poor tales and essays, and had become a tolerably good Surveyor of the Customs. That was all. But, nevertheless, it is anything but agreeable to be haunted by a suspicion that one's intellect is dwindling away, or exhaling, without your consciousness, like ether out of phial; so that at every glance you find a smaller and less volatile residuum."

As, however, it was with what was left of his intellect after three years' evaporation, that Hawthorne wrote *The Scarlet Letter*, there is little reason to complain of the injury he suffered in his Surveyorship.

His publisher, Mr. Fields, in a volume entitled *Yesterdays with Authors*, has related the circumstances in which Hawthorne's masterpiece came into the world. "In the winter of 1849, after he had been ejected from the Custom-house, I went down to Salem to see him and inquire after his health, for we heard he had been suffering from illness. He was then living in a modest wooden house.... I found him alone in a chamber over the sitting-room of the dwelling, and as the day was cold he was hovering near a stove. We fell into talk about his future prospects, and he was, as I feared I should find him, in a very desponding mood." His visitor urged him to bethink himself of publishing something, and Hawthorne replied by calling his attention to the small popularity his published productions had yet acquired, and declaring that he had done nothing and had no spirit for doing anything. The narrator of the incident urged upon him the necessity of a more hopeful view of his situation, and proceeded to take leave. He had not reached the street, however, when Hawthorne hurried to overtake him, and, placing a roll of MS. in his hand, bade him take it to Boston, read it, and pronounce upon it. "It is either very good or very bad," said the author; "I don't know which." "On my way back to Boston," says Mr. Fields, "I read the germ of *The Scarlet Letter*; before I slept that night I wrote him a note all aglow with admiration of the marvellous story he had put into my hands, and told him that I would come again to Salem the next day and arrange for its publication. I went on in such an amazing state of excitement, when we met again in the little house, that he would not believe I was really in earnest. He seemed to think I was beside myself, and laughed sadly at my enthusiasm." Hawthorne, however, went on with the book and finished it, but it appeared only a year later. His biographer quotes a passage from a letter which he wrote in February, 1850, to his friend Horatio Bridge. "I finished my book only yesterday; one end being in the press at Boston, while the other was in my head here at Salem, so that, as you see, my story is at least fourteen miles long.... My book, the publisher tells me, will not be out before April. He speaks of it in tremendous terms of approbation, so does Mrs. Hawthorne, to whom I read the conclusion last night. It broke her heart, and sent her to bed with a grievous headache—which I look upon, as a triumphant success. Judging from the effect upon her and the publisher, I may calculate on what bowlers call a ten-strike. But I don't make any such calculation." And Mr. Lathrop calls attention, in regard to this passage, to an allusion in the English Note-Books (September 14, 1855). "Speaking of Thackeray, I cannot but wonder at his coolness in respect to his own pathos, and compare it to my emotions when I read the last scene of *The Scarlet Letter* to my wife, just after writing it—tried to read it rather, for my voice swelled and heaved as if I were tossed up and down on an ocean as it subsides after a storm. But I was in a very nervous state then, having gone through a great diversity of emotion while writing it, for many months."

The work has the tone of the circumstances in which it was produced. If Hawthorne was in a sombre mood, and if his future was painfully vague, *The Scarlet Letter* contains little enough of gaiety or of hopefulness. It is densely dark, with a single spot of vivid colour in it; and it will probably long remain the most consistently gloomy of English novels of the first order. But I just now called it the author's masterpiece, and I imagine it will continue to be, for other generations than ours, his most substantial title to fame. The subject had probably lain a long time in his mind, as his subjects were apt to do; so that he appears completely to possess it, to know it and feel it. It is simpler and more complete than his other novels; it achieves more perfectly what it attempts, and it has about it that charm, very hard to express, which we find in an artist's work the first time he has touched his highest mark—a sort of straightness and naturalness of execution, an unconsciousness of his public, and freshness of interest in his theme. It was a great success, and he immediately found himself famous. The writer of these lines, who was a child at the time, remembers dimly the sensation the book produced, and the little shudder with which people alluded to it, as if a peculiar horror were mixed with its attractions. He was too young to read it himself, but its title, upon which he fixed his eyes as the book lay upon the table, had a mysterious charm. He had a vague belief indeed that the "letter" in question was one of the documents that come by the post, and it was a source of perpetual wonderment to him that it should be of such an unaccustomed hue. Of course it was difficult to explain to a child the significance of poor Hester Prynne's blood-coloured *A*. But the mystery was at last partly dispelled by his being taken to see a collection of pictures (the annual exhibition of the National Academy), where he encountered a representation of a pale, handsome woman, in a quaint black dress and a white coif, holding between her knees an elfish-looking little girl, fantastically dressed and crowned with flowers. Embroidered on the woman's breast was a great crimson *A*, over which the child's fingers, as she glanced strangely out of the picture, were maliciously playing. I was told that this was Hester Prynne and little Pearl, and that when I grew older I might read their interesting history. But the picture remained vividly imprinted on my mind; I had been vaguely frightened and made uneasy by it; and when, years afterwards, I first read the novel, I seemed to myself to have read it before, and to be familiar with its two strange heroines, I mention this incident simply as an indication of the degree to which the success of *The Scarlet Letter* had made the book what is called an actuality. Hawthorne himself was very modest about it; he wrote to his publisher, when there was a question of his undertaking another novel, that what had given the history of Hester Prynne its "vogue" was simply the introductory chapter. In fact, the publication of *The Scarlet Letter* was in the United States a literary event of the first importance. The book was the finest piece of imaginative writing yet put forth in the country. There was a consciousness of this in the welcome that was given it—a satisfaction in the idea of America having produced a novel that belonged to literature, and to the forefront of it. Something might at last be sent to Europe as exquisite in quality as anything that had been received, and the best of it was that the thing was absolutely American; it belonged to the soil, to the air; it came out of the very heart of New England.

It is beautiful, admirable, extraordinary; it has in the highest degree that merit which I have spoken of as the mark of Hawthorne's best things—an indefinable purity and lightness of conception, a quality which in a work of art affects one in the same way as the absence of grossness does in a human being. His fancy, as I just now said, had evidently brooded over the subject for a long time; the situation to be represented had disclosed itself to him in all its phases. When I say in all its phases, the sentence demands modification; for it is to be remembered that if Hawthorne laid his hand upon the well-worn theme, upon the familiar combination of the wife, the lover, and the husband, it was after all but to one period of the history of these three persons that he attached himself. The situation is the situation after the woman's fault has been committed, and the current of expiation and repentance has set in. In spite of the relation between Hester Prynne and Arthur Dimmesdale, no story of love was surely ever less of a "love story." To Hawthorne's imagination the fact that these two persons had loved each other too well was of an interest comparatively vulgar; what appealed to him was the idea of their moral situation in the long years that were to follow. The story indeed is in a secondary degree that of Hester Prynne; she becomes, really, after the first scene, an accessory figure; it is not upon her the *dénoûment* depends. It is upon her guilty lover that the author projects most frequently the cold, thin rays of his fitfully-moving lantern, which makes here and there a little luminous circle, on the edge of which hovers the livid and sinister figure of the injured and retributive husband. The story goes on for the most part between the lover and the husband—the tormented young Puritan minister, who carries the secret of his own lapse from pastoral purity locked up beneath an exterior that commends itself to the reverence of his flock, while he sees the softer partner of his guilt standing in the full glare of exposure and humbling herself to the misery of atonement—between this more wretched and pitiable culprit, to whom dishonour would come as a comfort and the pillory as a relief, and the older, keener, wiser man, who, to obtain satisfaction for the wrong he has suffered, devises the infernally ingenious plan of conjoining himself with his wronger, living with him, living upon him, and while he pretends to minister to his hidden ailment and to sympathise with his pain, revels in his unsuspected knowledge of these things and stimulates them by malignant arts. The attitude of Roger Chillingworth, and the means he takes to compensate himself—these are the highly original elements in the situation that Hawthorne so ingeniously treats. None of his works are so impregnated with that after-sense of the old Puritan consciousness of life to which allusion has so often been made. If, as M. Montégut says, the qualities of his ancestors *filtered* down through generations into his composition, *The Scarlet Letter* was, as it were, the vessel that gathered up the last of the precious drops. And I say this not because the story happens to be of so-called historical cast, to be told of the early days of Massachusetts and of people in steeple-crowned hats and sad coloured garments. The historical colouring is rather weak than otherwise; there is little elaboration of detail, of the modern realism of research; and the author has made no great point of causing his figures to speak the English of their period. Nevertheless, the book is full of the moral presence of the race that invented Hester's penance—diluted and complicated with other things, but still perfectly recognisable. Puritanism, in a word, is there, not only objectively, as Hawthorne tried to place it there, but subjectively as well. Not, I mean, in his judgment of his characters, in any harshness of prejudice, or in the obtrusion of a moral lesson; but in the very quality of his own vision, in the tone of the picture, in a certain coldness and exclusiveness of treatment.

The faults of the book are, to my sense, a want of reality and an abuse of the fanciful element—of a certain superficial symbolism. The people strike me not as characters, but as representatives, very picturesquely arranged, of a single state of mind; and the interest of the story lies, not in them, but in the situation, which is insistently kept before us, with little progression, though with a great deal, as I have said, of a certain stable variation; and to which they, out of their reality, contribute little that helps it to live and move. I was made to feel this want of reality, this over-ingenuity, of *The Scarlet Letter*, by chancing not long since upon a novel which was read fifty years ago much more than to-day, but which is still worth reading—the story of *Adam Blair*, by John Gibson Lockhart. This interesting and powerful little tale has a great deal of analogy with Hawthorne's novel—quite enough, at least, to suggest a comparison between them; and the comparison is a very interesting

115

one to make, for it speedily leads us to larger considerations than simple resemblances and divergences of plot.

Adam Blair, like Arthur Dimmesdale, is a Calvinistic minister who becomes the lover of a married woman, is overwhelmed with remorse at his misdeed, and makes a public confession of it; then expiates it by resigning his pastoral office and becoming a humble tiller of the soil, as his father had been. The two stories are of about the same length, and each is the masterpiece (putting aside of course, as far as Lockhart is concerned, the *Life of Scott*) of the author. They deal alike with the manners of a rigidly theological society, and even in certain details they correspond. In each of them, between the guilty pair, there is a charming little girl; though I hasten to say that Sarah Blair (who is not the daughter of the heroine but the legitimate offspring of the hero, a widower) is far from being as brilliant and graceful an apparition as the admirable little Pearl of *The Scarlet Letter*. The main difference between the two tales is the fact that in the American story the husband plays an all-important part, and in the Scottish plays almost none at all. *Adam Blair* is the history of the passion, and *The Scarlet Letter* the history of its sequel; but nevertheless, if one has read the two books at a short interval, it is impossible to avoid confronting them. I confess that a large portion of the interest of *Adam Blair*, to my mind, when once I had perceived that it would repeat in a great measure the situation of *The Scarlet Letter*, lay in noting its difference of tone. It threw into relief the passionless quality of Hawthorne's novel, its element of cold and ingenious fantasy, its elaborate imaginative delicacy. These things do not precisely constitute a weakness in *The Starlet Letter*; indeed, in a certain way they constitute a great strength; but the absence of a certain something warm and straightforward, a trifle more grossly human and vulgarly natural, which one finds in *Adam Blair*, will always make Hawthorne's tale less touching to a large number of even very intelligent readers, than a love-story told with the robust, synthetic pathos which served Lockhart so well. His novel is not of the first rank (I should call it an excellent second-rate one), but it borrows a charm from the fact that his vigorous, but not strongly imaginative, mind was impregnated with the reality of his subject. He did not always succeed in rendering this reality; the expression is sometimes awkward and poor. But the reader feels that his vision was clear, and his feeling about the matter very strong and rich. Hawthorne's imagination, on the other hand, plays with his theme so incessantly, leads it such a dance through the moonlighted air of his intellect, that the thing cools off, as it were, hardens and stiffens, and, producing effects much more exquisite, leaves the reader with a sense of having handled a splendid piece of silversmith's work. Lockhart, by means much more vulgar, produces at moments a greater illusion, and satisfies our inevitable desire for something, in the people in whom it is sought to interest us, that shall be of the same pitch and the same continuity with ourselves. Above all, it is interesting to see how the same subject appears to two men of a thoroughly different cast of mind and of a different race. Lockhart was struck with the warmth of the subject that offered itself to him, and Hawthorne with its coldness; the one with its glow, its sentimental interest—the other with its shadow, its moral interest. Lockhart's story is as decent, as severely draped, as *The Scarlet Letter*; but the author has a more vivid sense than appears to have imposed itself upon Hawthorne, of some of the incidents of the situation he describes; his tempted man and tempting woman are more actual and personal; his heroine in especial, though not in the least a delicate or a subtle conception, has a sort of credible, visible, palpable property, a vulgar roundness and relief, which are lacking to the dim and chastened image of Hester Prynne. But I am going too far; I am comparing simplicity with subtlety, the usual with the refined. Each man wrote as his turn of mind impelled him, but each expressed something more than himself. Lockhart was a dense, substantial Briton, with a taste for the concrete, and Hawthorne was a thin New Englander, with a miasmatic conscience.

In *The Scarlet Letter* there is a great deal of symbolism; there is, I think, too much. It is overdone at times, and becomes mechanical; it ceases to be impressive, and grazes triviality. The idea of the mystic *A* which the young minister finds imprinted upon his breast and eating into his flesh, in sympathy with the embroidered badge that Hester is condemned to wear, appears to me to be a case in point. This suggestion should, I think, have been just made and dropped; to insist upon it and return to it, is to exaggerate the weak side of the subject. Hawthorne returns to it constantly, plays with it, and seems charmed by it; until at last the reader feels tempted to declare that his enjoyment of it is puerile. In the admirable scene, so superbly conceived and beautifully executed, in which Mr. Dimmesdale, in the stillness of the night, in the middle of the sleeping town, feels impelled to go and stand upon the scaffold where his mistress had formerly enacted her dreadful penance, and then, seeing Hester pass along the street, from watching at a sick-bed, with little Pearl at her side, calls them both to come and stand there beside him— in this masterly episode the effect is almost spoiled by the introduction of one of these superficial conceits. What leads up to it is very fine—so fine that I cannot do better than quote it as a specimen of one of the striking pages of the book.

"But before Mr. Dimmesdale had done speaking, a light gleamed far and wide over all the muffled sky. It was doubtless caused by one of those meteors which the night-watcher may so often observe burning out to waste in the vacant regions of the atmosphere. So powerful was its radiance that it thoroughly illuminated the dense medium of cloud, betwixt the sky and earth. The great vault brightened, like the dome of an immense lamp. It showed the familiar scene of the street with the distinctness of midday, but also with the awfulness that is always imparted to familiar objects by an unaccustomed light. The wooden houses, with their jutting stories and quaint gable-peaks; the doorsteps and thresholds, with the early grass springing up about them; the garden-plots, black with freshly-turned earth; the wheel-track, little worn, and, even in the marketplace, margined with green on either side;—all were visible, but with a singularity of aspect that seemed to give another moral interpretation to the things of this world than they had ever borne before. And there stood the minister, with his hand over his heart; and Hester Prynne, with the embroidered letter glimmering on her bosom; and little Pearl, herself a symbol, and the connecting-link between these two. They stood in the noon of that strange and solemn splendour, as if it were the light that is to reveal all secrets, and the daybreak that shall unite all that belong to one another."

That is imaginative, impressive, poetic; but when, almost immediately afterwards, the author goes on to say that "the minister looking upward to the zenith, beheld there the appearance of an immense letter—the letter *A*—marked out in lines of dull red light," we feel that he goes too far and is in danger of crossing the line that separates the sublime from its intimate neighbour. We are tempted to say that this is not moral tragedy, but physical comedy. In the same way, too much is made of the intimation that Hester's badge had a scorching property, and that if one touched it one would immediately withdraw one's hand. Hawthorne is perpetually looking for images which shall place themselves in picturesque correspondence with the spiritual facts with which he is concerned, and of course the search is of the very essence of poetry. But in such a process discretion is everything, and when the image becomes importunate it is in danger of seeming to stand for nothing more serious than itself. When Hester meets the minister by appointment in the forest, and sits talking with him while little Pearl wanders away and plays by the edge of the brook, the child is represented as at last making her way over to the other side of the woodland stream, and disporting herself there in a manner which makes her mother feel herself, "in some indistinct and tantalising manner, estranged from Pearl; as if the child, in her lonely ramble through the forest, had strayed out of the sphere in which she and her mother dwelt together, and was now vainly seeking to return to it." And Hawthorne devotes a chapter to this idea of the child's having, by putting the brook between Hester and herself, established a kind of spiritual gulf, on the verge of which her little fantastic person innocently mocks at her mother's sense of bereavement. This conception belongs, one would say, quite to the lighter order of a story-teller's devices, and the reader hardly goes with Hawthorne in the large development he gives to it. He hardly goes with him either, I think, in his extreme predilection for a small number of vague ideas which are represented by such terms as "sphere" and "sympathies." Hawthorne makes too liberal a use of these two substantives; it is the solitary defect of his style;

and it counts as a defect partly because the words in question are a sort of specialty with certain writers immeasurably inferior to himself.

I had not meant, however, to expatiate upon his defects, which are of the slenderest and most venial kind. *The Scarlet Letter* has the beauty and harmony of all original and complete conceptions, and its weaker spots, whatever they are, are not of its essence; they are mere light flaws and inequalities of surface. One can often return to it; it supports familiarity and has the inexhaustible charm and mystery of great works of art. It is admirably written. Hawthorne afterwards polished his style to a still higher degree, but in his later productions—it is almost always the case in a writer's later productions—there is a touch of mannerism. In *The Scarlet Letter* there is a high degree of polish, and at the same time a charming freshness; his phrase is less conscious of itself. His biographer very justly calls attention to the fact that his style was excellent from the beginning; that he appeared to have passed through no phase of learning how to write, but was in possession of his means from the first of his handling a pen. His early tales, perhaps, were not of a character to subject his faculty of expression to a very severe test, but a man who had not Hawthorne's natural sense of language would certainly have contrived to write them less well. This natural sense of language—this turn for saying things lightly and yet touchingly, picturesquely yet simply, and for infusing a gently colloquial tone into matter of the most unfamiliar import, he had evidently cultivated with great assiduity. I have spoken of the anomalous character of his Note-Books—of his going to such pains often to make a record of incidents which either were not worth remembering or could be easily remembered without its aid. But it helps us to understand the Note-Books if we regard them as a literary exercise. They were compositions, as school boys say, in which the subject was only the pretext, and the main point was to write a certain amount of excellent English. Hawthorne must at least have written a great many of these things for practice, and he must often have said to himself that it was better practice to write about trifles, because it was a greater tax upon one's skill to make them interesting. And his theory was just, for he has almost always made his trifles interesting. In his novels his art of saying things well is very positively tested, for here he treats of those matters among which it is very easy for a blundering writer to go wrong—the subtleties and mysteries of life, the moral and spiritual maze. In such a passage as one I have marked for quotation from *The Scarlet Letter* there is the stamp of the genius of style.

"Hester Prynne, gazing steadfastly at the clergyman, felt a dreary influence come over her, but wherefore or whence she knew not, unless that he seemed so remote from her own sphere and utterly beyond her reach. One glance of recognition she had imagined must needs pass between them. She thought of the dim forest with its little dell of solitude, and love, and anguish, and the mossy tree-trunk, where, sitting hand in hand, they had mingled their sad and passionate talk with the melancholy murmur of the brook. How deeply had they known each other then! And was this the man? She hardly knew him now! He, moving proudly past, enveloped as it were in the rich music, with the procession of majestic and venerable fathers; he, so unattainable in his worldly position, and still more so in that far vista in his unsympathising thoughts, through which she now beheld him! Her spirit sank with the idea that all must have been a delusion, and that vividly as she had dreamed it, there could be no real bond betwixt the clergyman and herself. And thus much of woman there was in Hester, that she could scarcely forgive him—least of all now, when the heavy footstep of their approaching fate might be heard, nearer, nearer, nearer!—for being able to withdraw himself so completely from their mutual world, while she groped darkly, and stretched forth her cold hands, and found him not!"

The House of the Seven Gables was written at Lenox, among the mountains of Massachusetts, a village nestling, rather loosely, in one of the loveliest corners of New England, to which Hawthorne had betaken himself after the success of *The Scarlet Letter* became conspicuous, in the summer of 1850, and where he occupied for two years an uncomfortable little red house which is now pointed out to the inquiring stranger. The inquiring stranger is now a frequent figure at Lenox, for the place has suffered the process of lionisation. It has become a prosperous watering-place, or at least (as there are no waters), as they say in America, a summer-resort. It is a brilliant and generous landscape, and thirty years ago a man of fancy, desiring to apply himself, might have found both inspiration and tranquillity there. Hawthorne found so much of both that he wrote more during his two years of residence at Lenox than at any period of his career. He began with *The House of the Seven Gables*, which was finished in the early part of 1851. This is the longest of his three American novels, it is the most elaborate, and in the judgment of some persons it is the finest. It is a rich, delightful, imaginative work, larger and more various than its companions, and full of all sorts of deep intentions, of interwoven threads of suggestion But it is not so rounded and complete as *The Scarlet Letter*; it has always seemed to me more like a prologue to a great novel than a great novel itself. I think this is partly owing to the fact that the subject, the *donnée*, as the French say, of the story, does not quite fill it out, and that we get at the same time an impression of certain complicated purposes on the author's part, which seem to reach beyond it. I call it larger and more various than its companions, and it has indeed a greater richness of tone and density of detail. The colour, so to speak, of *The House of the Seven Gables* is admirable. But the story has a sort of expansive quality which never wholly fructifies, and as I lately laid it down, after reading it for the third time, I had a sense of having interested myself in a magnificent fragment. Yet the book has a great fascination, and of all of those of its author's productions which I have read over while writing this sketch, it is perhaps the one that has gained most by re-perusal. If it be true of the others that the pure, natural quality of the imaginative strain is their great merit, this is at least as true of *The House of the Seven Gables*, the charm of which is in a peculiar degree of the kind that we fail to reduce to its grounds—like that of the sweetness of a piece of music, or the softness of fine September weather. It is vague, indefinable, ineffable; but it is the sort of thing we must always point to in justification of the high claim that we make for Hawthorne. In this case of course its vagueness is a drawback, for it is difficult to point to ethereal beauties; and if the reader whom we have wished to inoculate with our admiration inform us after looking a while that he perceives nothing in particular, we can only reply that, in effect, the object is a delicate one.

The House of the Seven Gables comes nearer being a picture of contemporary American life than either of its companions; but on this ground it would be a mistake to make a large claim for it. It cannot be too often repeated that Hawthorne was not a realist. He had a high sense of reality—his Note-Books super-abundantly testify to it; and fond as he was of jotting down the items that make it up, he never attempted to render exactly or closely the actual facts of the society that surrounded him. I have said—I began by saying—that his pages were full of its spirit, and of a certain reflected light that springs from it; but I was careful to add that the reader must look for his local and national quality between the lines of his writing and in the *indirect* testimony of his tone, his accent, his temper, of his very omissions and suppressions. *The House of the Seven Gables* has, however, more literal actuality than the others, and if it were not too fanciful an account of it, I should say that it renders, to an initiated reader, the impression of a summer afternoon in an elm-shadowed New England town. It leaves upon the mind a vague correspondence to some such reminiscence, and in stirring up the association it renders it delightful. The comparison is to the honour of the New England town, which gains in it more than it bestows. The shadows of the elms, in *The House of the Seven Gables*, are exceptionally dense and cool; the summer afternoon is peculiarly still and beautiful; the atmosphere has a delicious warmth, and the long daylight seems to pause and rest. But the mild provincial quality is there, the mixture of shabbiness and freshness, the paucity of ingredients. The end of an old race—this is the situation that Hawthorne has depicted, and he has been admirably inspired in the choice of the figures in whom he seeks to interest us. They are all figures rather than characters— they are all pictures rather than persons. But if their reality is light and vague, it is sufficient, and it is in harmony with the low relief and dimness of outline of the objects that surround them. They are all types, to the author's mind, of something general, of something that is bound up with the history, at large, of families and individuals, and each of them is the centre of a cluster of those ingenious and meditative musings, rather melancholy, as a general thing, than joyous, which melt into the current and texture of the story and give it a kind of moral richness. A grotesque old spinster, simple, childish, penniless, very humble at heart, but rigidly conscious of her pedigree; an amiable bachelor, of an epicurean temperament and an enfeebled intellect, who has passed twenty years of his life in penal confinement for a crime of which he was unjustly pronounced guilty; a sweet-natured and bright-faced young girl from the country, a poor relation of these two ancient decrepitudes, with whose moral mustiness her modern freshness and soundness are contrasted; a young man still more modern, holding the latest opinions, who has sought his fortune up and down the world, and, though he has not found it, takes a genial and enthusiastic view of the future: these, with two or three remarkable accessory figures, are the persons concerned in the little drama. The drama is a small one, but as Hawthorne does not put it before us for its own superficial sake, for the dry facts of the case, but for something in it which he holds to be symbolic and of large application, something that points a moral and that it behoves us to remember, the scenes in the rusty wooden house whose gables give its name to the story, have something of the dignity both of history and of tragedy. Miss Hephzibah Pyncheon, dragging out a disappointed life in her paternal dwelling, finds herself obliged in her old age to open a little shop for the sale of penny toys and gingerbread. This is the central incident of the tale, and, as Hawthorne relates it, it is an incident of the most impressive magnitude and most touching interest. Her dishonoured and vague-minded brother is released from prison at the same moment, and returns to the ancestral roof to deepen her perplexities. But, on the other hand, to alleviate them, and to introduce a breath of the air of the outer world into this long unventilated interior, the little country cousin also arrives, and proves the good angel of the feebly distracted household. All this episode is exquisite— admirably conceived, and executed with a kind of humorous tenderness, an equal sense of everything in it that is picturesque, touching, ridiculous, worthy of the highest praise. Hephzibah Pyncheon, with her near-sighted scowl, her rusty joints, her antique turban, her map of a great territory to the eastward which ought to have belonged to her family, her vain terrors and scruples and resentments, the inaptitude and repugnance of an ancient gentlewoman to the vulgar little commerce which a cruel fate has compelled her to engage in—Hephzibah Pyncheon is a masterly picture. I repeat that she is a picture, as her companions are pictures; she is a charming piece of descriptive writing, rather than a dramatic exhibition. But she is described, like her companions too, so subtly and lovingly that we enter into her virginal old heart and stand with her behind her abominable little counter. Clifford Pyncheon is a still more remarkable conception, though he is perhaps not so vividly depicted. It was a figure needing a much more subtle touch, however, and it was of the essence of his character to be vague and unemphasised. Nothing can be more charming than the manner in which the soft, bright, active presence of Phœbe Pyncheon is indicated, or than the account of her relations with the poor dimly sentient kinsman for whom her light-handed sisterly offices, in the evening of a melancholy life, are a revelation of lost possibilities of happiness. "In her aspect," Hawthorne says of the young girl, "there was a familiar gladness, and a holiness that you could play with, and yet reverence it as much as ever. She was like a prayer offered up in the homeliest beauty of one's mother-tongue. Fresh was Phœbe, moreover, and airy, and sweet in her apparel; as if nothing that she wore—neither her gown, nor her small straw bonnet, nor her little kerchief, any more than her snowy stockings—had ever been put on before; or if worn, were all the fresher for it, and with a fragrance as if they had lain among the rose-buds." Of the influence of her maidenly salubrity upon poor Clifford, Hawthorne gives the prettiest description, and then, breaking off suddenly, renounces the attempt in language which, while pleading its inadequacy, conveys an exquisite satisfaction to the reader. I quote the passage for the sake of its extreme felicity, and of the charming image with which it concludes.

"But we strive in vain to put the idea into words. No adequate expression of the beauty and profound pathos with which it impresses us is attainable. This being, made only for happiness, and heretofore so miserably failing to be happy—his tendencies so hideously thwarted that some unknown time ago, the delicate springs of his character, never morally or intellectually strong, had given way, and he was now imbecile—this poor forlorn voyager from the Islands of the Blest, in a frail bark, on a tempestuous sea, had been flung by the last mountain-wave of his shipwreck, into a quiet harbour. There, as he lay more than half lifeless on the strand, the fragrance of an earthly rose-bud had come to his nostrils, and, as odours will, had summoned up reminiscences or visions of all the living and breathing beauty amid which he should have had his home. With his native susceptibility of happy influences, he inhales the slight ethereal rapture into his soul, and expires!"

I have not mentioned the personage in *The House of the Seven Gables* upon whom Hawthorne evidently bestowed most pains, and whose portrait is the most elaborate in the book; partly because he is, in spite of the space he occupies, an accessory figure, and partly because, even more than the others, he is what I have called a picture rather than a character. Judge Pyncheon is an ironical portrait, very richly and broadly executed, very sagaciously composed and rendered—the portrait of a superb, full blown hypocrite, a large-based, full-nurtured Pharisee, bland, urbane, impressive, diffusing about him a "sultry" warmth of benevolence, as the author calls it again and again, and basking in the noontide of prosperity and the consideration of society; but in reality hard, gross, and ignoble. Judge Pyncheon is an elaborate piece of description, made up of a hundred admirable touches, in which satire is always winged with fancy, and fancy is linked with a deep sense of reality. It is difficult to say whether Hawthorne followed a model in describing Judge Pyncheon; but it is tolerably obvious that the picture is an impression—a copious impression— of an individual. It has evidently a definite starting-point in fact, and the author is able to draw, freely and confidently, after the image established in his mind. Holgrave, the modern young man, who has been a Jack-of-all-trades and is at the period of the story a daguerreotypist, is an attempt to render a kind of national type—that of the young citizen of the United States whose fortune is simply in his lively intelligence, and who stands naked, as it were, unbiased and unencumbered alike, in the centre of the far-stretching level of American life. Holgrave is intended as a contrast; his lack of traditions, his democratic stamp, his condensed experience, are opposed to the desiccated prejudices and exhausted vitality of the race of which poor feebly-scowling, rusty-jointed Hephzibah is the most heroic representative. It is perhaps a pity that Hawthorne should not have proposed to himself to give the old Pyncheon-qualities some embodiment which would help them to balance more fairly with the elastic properties of the young daguerreotypist—should not have painted a lusty conservative to match his strenuous radical. As it is, the mustiness and mouldiness of the tenants of the House of the Seven Gables crumble away rather too easily. Evidently, however, what Hawthorne designed to represent was not the struggle between an old society and a new, for in this case he would have given the old one a better chance; but simply, as I have said, the shrinkage and extinction of a family. This appealed to his imagination; and the idea of long perpetuation and survival always appears to have filled him with a kind of horror and disapproval. Conservative, in a certain degree, as he was himself, and fond of retrospect and quietude and the mellowing influences of time, it is singular how often one encounters in his writings some expression of mistrust of old houses, old institutions, long lines of descent. He was disposed apparently to allow a very moderate measure in these respects, and he condemns the dwelling of the Pyncheons to disappear from the face of the earth because it has been standing a couple of hundred years. In this he was an American of Americans; or rather he was more American than many of his countrymen, who, though they are accustomed to work for the short run rather than the long, have often a lurking esteem for things that show the marks of having lasted. I will add that Holgrave is one of the few figures, among those which Hawthorne created, with regard to which the absence of the realistic mode of treatment is felt as a loss. Holgrave is not sharply enough characterised; he lacks features; he is not an individual, but a type. But my last word about this admirable novel must not be a restrictive one. It is a large and generous production, pervaded with that vague hum, that indefinable echo, of the whole multitudinous life of man, which is the real sign of a great work of fiction.

After the publication of *The House of the Seven Gables*, which brought him great honour, and, I believe, a tolerable share of a more ponderable substance, he composed a couple of little volumes, for children—*The Wonder-Book*, and a small collection of stories entitled *Tanglewood Tales*. They are not among his most serious literary titles, but if I may trust my own early impression of them, they are among the most charming literary services that have been rendered to children in an age (and especially in a country) in which the exactions of the infant mind have exerted much too palpable an influence upon literature. Hawthorne's stories are the old Greek myths, made more vivid to the childish imagination by an infusion of details which both deepen and explain their marvels. I have been careful not to read them over, for I should be very sorry to risk disturbing in any degree a recollection of them that has been at rest since the appreciative period of life to which they are addressed. They seem at that period enchanting, and the ideal of happiness of many American children is to lie upon the carpet and lose themselves in *The Wonder-Book*. It is in its pages that they first make the acquaintance of the heroes and heroines of the antique mythology, and something of the nursery fairy-tale quality of interest which Hawthorne imparts to them always remains.

I have said that Lenox was a very pretty place, and that he was able to work there Hawthorne proved by composing *The House of the Seven Gables* with a good deal of rapidity. But at the close of the year in which this novel was published he wrote to a friend (Mr. Fields, his publisher,) that "to tell you a secret I am sick to death of Berkshire, and hate to think of spending another winter here.... The air and climate do not agree with my health at all, and for the first time since I was a boy I have felt languid and dispirited.... O that Providence would build me the merest little shanty, and mark me out a rood or two of garden ground, near the sea-coast!" He was at this time for a while out of health; and it is proper to remember that though the Massachusetts Berkshire, with its mountains and lakes, was charming during the ardent American summer, there was a reverse to the medal, consisting of December snows prolonged into April and May. Providence failed to provide him with a cottage by the sea; but he betook himself for the winter of 1852 to the little town of West Newton, near Boston, where he brought into the world *The Blithedale Romance*.

This work, as I have said, would not have been written if Hawthorne had not spent a year at Brook Farm, and though it is in no sense of the word an account of the manners or the inmates of that establishment, it will preserve the memory of the ingenious community at West Roxbury for a generation unconscious of other reminders. I hardly know what to say about it save that it is very charming; this vague, unanalytic epithet is the first that comes to one's pen in treating of Hawthorne's novels, for their extreme amenity of form invariably suggests it; but if on the one hand it claims to be uttered, on the other it frankly confesses its inconclusiveness. Perhaps, however, in this case, it fills out the measure of appreciation more completely than in others, for *The Blithedale Romance* is the lightest, the brightest, the liveliest, of this company of unhumorous fictions.

The story is told from a more joyous point of view—from a point of view comparatively humorous—and a number of objects and incidents touched with the light of the profane world—the vulgar, many-coloured world of actuality, as distinguished from the crepuscular realm of the writer's own reveries—are mingled with its course. The book indeed is a mixture of elements, and it leaves in the memory an impression analogous to that of an April day—an alternation of brightness and shadow, of broken sun-patches and sprinkling clouds. Its dénoûment is tragical—there is indeed nothing so tragical in all Hawthorne, unless it be the murder-of Miriam's persecutor by Donatello, in *Transformation*, as the suicide of Zenobia; and yet on the whole the effect of the novel is to make one think more agreeably of life. The standpoint of the narrator has the advantage of being a concrete one; he is no longer, as in the preceding tales, a disembodied spirit, imprisoned in the haunted chamber of his own contemplations, but a particular man, with a certain human grossness.

Of Miles Coverdale I have already spoken, and of its being natural to assume that in so far as we may measure this lightly indicated identity of his, it has a great deal in common with that of its creator. Coverdale is a picture of the contemplative, observant, analytic nature, nursing its fancies, and yet, thanks to an element of strong good sense, not bringing them up to be spoiled children; having little at stake in life, at any given moment, and yet indulging, in imagination, in a good many adventures; a portrait of a man, in a word, whose passions are slender, whose imagination is active, and whose happiness lies, not in doing, but in perceiving—half a poet, half a critic, and all a spectator. He is contrasted, excellently, with the figure of Hollingsworth, the heavily treading Reformer, whose attitude with regard to the world is that of the hammer to the anvil, and who has no patience with his friend's indifferences and neutralities. Coverdale is a gentle sceptic, a mild cynic; he would agree that life is a little worth living—or worth living a little; but would remark that, unfortunately, to live little enough, we have to live a great deal. He confesses to a want of earnestness, but in reality he is evidently an excellent fellow, to whom one might look, not for any personal performance on a great scale, but for a good deal of generosity of detail. "As Hollingsworth once told me, I lack a purpose," he writes, at the close of his story. "How strange! He was ruined, morally, by an over plus of the same ingredient the want of which, I occasionally suspect, has rendered my own life all an emptiness. I by no means wish to die. Yet were there any cause in this whole chaos of human struggle, worth a sane man's dying for, and which my death would benefit, then—provided, however, the effort did not involve an unreasonable amount of trouble—methinks I might be bold to offer up my life. If Kossuth, for example, would pitch the battle-field of Hungarian rights within an easy ride of my abode, and choose a mild sunny morning, after breakfast, for the conflict, Miles Coverdale would gladly be his man, for one brave rush upon the levelled bayonets. Further than that I should be loth to pledge myself."

The finest thing in *The Blithdale Romance* is the character of Zenobia, which I have said elsewhere strikes me as the nearest approach that Hawthorne has made to the complete creation of a *person*. She is more concrete than Hester or Miriam, or Hilda or Phoebe; she is a more definite image, produced by a greater multiplicity of touches. It is idle to inquire too closely whether Hawthorne had Margaret Fuller in his mind in constructing the figure of this brilliant specimen of the strong-minded class and endowing her with the genius of conversation; or, on the assumption that such was the case, to compare the image at all strictly with the model. There is no strictness in the representation by novelists of persons who have struck them in life, and there can in the nature of things be none. From the moment the imagination takes a hand in the game, the inevitable tendency is to divergence, to following what may be called new scents. The original gives hints, but the writer does what he likes with them, and imports new elements into the picture. If there is this amount of reason for referring the wayward heroine of Blithedale to Hawthorne's impression of the most distinguished woman of her day in Boston, that Margaret Fuller was the only literary lady of eminence whom there is any sign of his having known, that she was proud, passionate, and eloquent, that she was much connected with the little world of Transcendentalism out of which the experiment of Brook Farm sprung, and that she had a miserable end and a watery grave—if these are facts to be noted on one side, I say; on the other, the beautiful and sumptuous Zenobia, with her rich and picturesque temperament and physical aspects, offers many points of divergence from the plain and strenuous invalid who represented feminine culture in the suburbs of the New England metropolis. This picturesqueness of Zenobia is very happily indicated and maintained; she is a woman, in all the force of the term, and there is something very vivid and powerful in her large expression of womanly gifts and weaknesses. Hollingsworth is, I think, less successful, though there is much reality in the conception of the type to which he belongs—the strong-willed, narrow-hearted apostle of a special form of redemption for society. There is nothing better in all Hawthorne than the scene between him and Coverdale, when the two men are at work together in the field (piling stones on a dyke), and he gives it to his companion to choose whether he will be with him or against him. It is a pity, perhaps, to have represented him as having begun life as a blacksmith, for one grudges him the advantage of so logical a reason for his roughness and hardness.

"Hollingsworth scarcely said a word, unless when repeatedly and pertinaciously addressed. Then indeed he would glare upon us from the thick shrubbery of his meditations, like a tiger out of a jungle, make the briefest reply possible, and betake himself back into the solitude of his heart and mind.... His heart, I imagine, was never really interested in our socialist scheme, but was for ever busy with his strange, and as most people thought, impracticable plan for the reformation of criminals through an appeal to their higher instincts. Much as I liked Hollingsworth, it cost me many a groan to tolerate him on this point. He ought to have commenced his investigation of the subject by committing some huge sin in his proper person, and examining the condition of his-higher instincts afterwards."

The most touching element in the novel is the history of the grasp that this barbarous fanatic has laid upon the fastidious and high-tempered Zenobia, who, disliking him and shrinking, from him at a hundred points, is drawn into the gulf of his omnivorous egotism. The portion of the story that strikes me as least felicitous is that which deals with Priscilla and with her mysterious relation to Zenobia—with her mesmeric gifts, her clairvoyance, her identity with the Veiled Lady, her divided subjection to Hollingsworth and Westervelt, and her numerous other graceful but fantastic properties— her Sibylline attributes, as the author calls them. Hawthorne is rather too fond of Sibylline attributes—a taste of the same order as his disposition, to which I have already alluded, to talk about spheres and sympathies. As the action advances, in *The Blithdale Romance*, we get too much out of reality, and cease to feel beneath our feet the firm ground of an appeal to our own vision of the world, our observation. I should have liked to see the story concern itself more with the little community in which its earlier scenes are laid, and avail itself of so excellent an opportunity for describing unhackneyed specimens of human nature. I have already spoken of the absence of satire in the novel, of its not aiming in the least at satire, and of its offering no grounds for complaint as an invidious picture. Indeed the brethren of Brook Farm should have held themselves slighted rather than misrepresented, and have regretted that the admirable genius who for a while was numbered among them should have treated their institution mainly as a perch for starting upon an imaginative flight. But when all is said about a certain want of substance and cohesion in the latter portions of *The Blithedale Romance*, the book is still a delightful and beautiful one. Zenobia and Hollingsworth live in the memory, and even Priscilla and Coverdale, who linger there less importunately, have a great deal that touches us and that we believe in. I said just now that Priscilla was infelicitous; but immediately afterwards I open the volume at a page in which the author describes some of the out-of-door amusements at Blithedale, and speaks of a foot-race across the grass, in which some of the slim young girls of the society joined. "Priscilla's peculiar charm in a foot-race was the weakness and irregularity with which she ran. Growing up without exercise, except to her poor little fingers, she had never yet acquired the perfect use of her legs. Setting buoyantly forth therefore, as if no rival less swift than Atalanta could compete with her, she ran falteringly, and often tumbled on the grass. Such an incident—though it seems too slight to think of—was a thing to laugh at, but which brought the water into one's eyes, and lingered in the memory after far greater joys and sorrows were wept out of it, as antiquated trash. Priscilla's life, as I beheld it, was full of trifles that affected me in just this way." That seems to me exquisite, and the book is full of touches as deep and delicate.

After writing it, Hawthorne went back to live in Concord, where he had bought a small house in which, apparently, he expected to spend a large portion of his future. This was in fact the dwelling in which he passed that part of the rest of his days that he spent in his own country. He established himself there before going to Europe, in 1853, and he returned to the Wayside, as he called his house, on coming back to the United States seven years later. Though he actually occupied the place no long time, he had made it his property, and it was more his own home than any of his numerous provisional abodes. I may therefore quote a little account of the house which he wrote to a distinguished friend, Mr. George Curtis.

"As for my old house, you will understand it better after spending a day or two in it. Before Mr. Alcott took it in hand, it was a mean-looking affair, with two peaked gables; no suggestiveness about it, and no venerableness, although from the style of its construction it seems to have survived beyond its first century. He added a porch in front, and a central peak, and a piazza at each end, and painted it a rusty olive hue, and invested the whole with a modest picturesqueness; all which improvements, together with its situation at the foot of a wooded hill, make it a place that one notices and remembers for a few moments after passing. Mr. Alcott expended a good deal of taste and some money (to no great purpose) in forming the hillside behind the house into terraces, and building arbours and summer-houses of rough stems and branches and trees, on a system of his own. They must have been very pretty in their day, and are so still, although much decayed, and shattered more and more by every breeze that blows. The hillside is covered chiefly with locust trees, which come into luxuriant blossom in the month of June, and look and smell very sweetly, intermixed with a few young elms, and white pines and infant oaks—the whole forming rather a thicket than a wood. Nevertheless, there is some very good shade to be found there. I spend delectable hours there in the hottest part of the day, stretched out at my lazy length, with a book in my hand, or some unwritten book in my thoughts. There is almost always a breeze stirring along the sides or brow of the hill. From the hill-top there is a good view along the extensive level surfaces and gentle hilly outlines, covered with wood, that characterise the scenery of Concord.... I know nothing of the history of the house except Thoreau's telling me that it was inhabited, a generation or two ago, by a man who believed he should never die. I believe, however, he is dead; at least, I hope so; else he may probably reappear and dispute my title to his residence."

As Mr. Lathrop points out, this allusion to a man who believed he should never die is "the first intimation of the story of *Septimius Felton*." The scenery of that romance, he adds, "was evidently taken from the Wayside and its hill." *Septimius Felton* is in fact a young man who, at the time of the war of the Revolution, lives in the village of Concord, on the Boston road, at the base of a woody hill which rises abruptly behind his house, and of which the level summit supplies him with a promenade continually mentioned in the course of the tale. Hawthorne used to exercise himself upon this picturesque eminence, and, as he conceived the brooding Septimius to have done before him, to betake himself thither when he found the limits of his dwelling too narrow. But he had an advantage which his imaginary hero lacked; he erected a tower as an adjunct to the house, and it was a jocular tradition among his neighbours, in allusion to his attributive tendency to evade rather than hasten the coming guest, that he used to ascend this structure and scan the road for provocations to retreat.

In so far, however, as Hawthorne suffered the penalties of celebrity at the hands of intrusive fellow-citizens, he was soon to escape from this honourable incommodity. On the 4th of March, 1853, his old college-mate and intimate friend, Franklin Pierce, was installed as President of the United States. He had been the candidate of the Democratic party, and all good Democrats, accordingly, in conformity to the beautiful and rational system under which the affairs of the great Republic were carried on, begun to open their windows to the golden sunshine of Presidential patronage. When General Pierce was put forward by the Democrats, Hawthorne felt a perfectly loyal and natural desire that his good friend should be exalted to so brilliant a position, and he did what was in him to further the good cause, by writing a little book about its hero. His *Life of Franklin Pierce* belongs to that class of literature which is known as the "campaign biography," and which consists of an attempt, more or less successful, to persuade the many-headed monster of universal suffrage that the gentleman on whose behalf it is addressed is a paragon of wisdom and virtue. Of Hawthorne's little book there is nothing particular to say, save that it is in very good taste, that he is a very fairly ingenious advocate, and that if he claimed for the future President qualities which rather faded in the bright light of a high office, this defect of proportion was essential to his undertaking. He dwelt chiefly upon General Pierce's exploits in the war with Mexico (before that, his record, as they say in America, had been mainly that of a successful country lawyer), and exercised his descriptive powers so far as

was possible in describing the advance of the United States troops from Vera
Cruz to the city of the Montezumas. The mouthpieces of the Whig party
spared him, I believe, no reprobation for "prostituting" his exquisite genius;
but I fail to see anything reprehensible in Hawthorne's lending his old friend
the assistance of his graceful quill. He wished him to be President—he held
afterwards that he filled the office with admirable dignity and wisdom—and
as the only thing he could do was to write, he fell to work and wrote for him.
Hawthorne was a good lover and a very sufficient partisan, and I suspect that
if Franklin Pierce had been made even less of the stuff of a statesman, he
would still have found in the force of old associations an injunction to hail
him as a ruler. Our hero was an American of the earlier and simpler type—the
type of which it is doubtless premature to say that it has wholly passed away,
but of which it may at least be said that the circumstances that produced
it have been greatly modified. The generation to which he belonged, that
generation which grew up with the century, witnessed during a period of
fifty years the immense, uninterrupted material development of the young
Republic; and when one thinks of the scale on which it took place, of the
prosperity that walked in its train and waited on its course, of the hopes
it fostered and the blessings it conferred, of the broad morning sunshine,
in a word, in which it all went forward, there seems to be little room for
surprise that it should have implanted a kind of superstitious faith in the
grandeur of the country, its duration, its immunity from the usual troubles
of earthly empires. This faith was a simple and uncritical one, enlivened with
an element of genial optimism, in the light of which it appeared that the
great American state was not as other human institutions are, that a special
Providence watched over it, that it would go on joyously for ever, and that
a country whose vast and blooming bosom offered a refuge to the strugglers
and seekers of all the rest of the world, must come off easily, in the battle
of the ages. From this conception of the American future the sense of its
having problems to solve was blissfully absent; there were no difficulties in
the programme, no looming complications, no rocks ahead. The indefinite
multiplication of the population, and its enjoyment of the benefits of a
common-school education and of unusual facilities for making an income—
this was the form in which, on the whole, the future most vividly presented

itself, and in which the greatness of the country was to be recognised of men. There was indeed a faint shadow in the picture—the shadow projected by the "peculiar institution" of the Southern States; but it was far from sufficient to darken the rosy vision of most good Americans, and above all, of most good Democrats. Hawthorne alludes to it in a passage of his life of Pierce, which I will quote not only as a hint of the trouble that was in store for a cheerful race of men, but as an example of his own easy-going political attitude.

"It was while in the lower house of Congress that Franklin Pierce took that stand on the Slavery question from which he has never since swerved by a hair's breadth. He fully recognised by his votes and his voice, the rights pledged to the South by the Constitution. This, at the period when he declared himself, was an easy thing to do. But when it became more difficult, when the first imperceptible murmur of agitation had grown almost to a convulsion, his course was still the same. Nor did he ever shun the obloquy that sometimes threatened to pursue the Northern man who dared to love that great and sacred reality—his whole united country—better than the mistiness of a philanthropic theory."

This last invidious allusion is to the disposition, not infrequent at the North, but by no means general, to set a decisive limit to further legislation in favour of the cherished idiosyncrasy of the other half of the country. Hawthorne takes the license of a sympathetic biographer in speaking of his hero's having incurred obloquy by his conservative attitude on the question of Slavery. The only class in the American world that suffered in the smallest degree, at this time, from social persecution, was the little band of Northern Abolitionists, who were as unfashionable as they were indiscreet—which is saying much. Like most of his fellow-countrymen, Hawthorne had no idea that the respectable institution which he contemplated in impressive contrast to humanitarian "mistiness," was presently to cost the nation four long years of bloodshed and misery, and a social revolution as complete as any the world has seen. When this event occurred, he was therefore proportionately horrified and depressed by it; it cut from beneath his feet the familiar ground which had long felt so firm, substituting a heaving and quaking medium in which his spirit found no rest. Such was the bewildered sensation of that earlier and simpler generation of which I have spoken; their illusions were rudely dispelled, and they saw the best of all possible republics given over to fratricidal carnage. This affair had no place in their scheme, and nothing was left for them but to hang their heads and close their eyes. The subsidence of that great convulsion has left a different tone from the tone it found, and one may say that the Civil War marks an era in the history of the American mind. It introduced into the national consciousness a certain sense of proportion and relation, of the world being a more complicated place than it had hitherto seemed, the future more treacherous, success more difficult. At the rate at which things are going, it is obvious that good Americana will be more numerous than ever; but the good American, in days to come, will be a more critical person than his complacent and confident grandfather. He has eaten of the tree of knowledge. He will not, I think, be a sceptic, and still less, of course, a cynic; but he will be, without discredit to his well-known capacity for action, an observer. He will remember that the ways of the Lord are inscrutable, and that this is a world in which everything happens; and eventualities, as the late Emperor of the French used to say, will not find him intellectually unprepared. The good American of which Hawthorne was so admirable a specimen was not critical, and it was perhaps for this reason that Franklin Pierce seemed to him a very proper President.

The least that General Pierce could do in exchange for so liberal a confidence was to offer his old friend one of the numerous places in his gift. Hawthorne had a great desire to go abroad and see something of the world, so that a consulate seemed the proper thing. He never stirred in the matter himself, but his friends strongly urged that something should be done; and when he accepted the post of consul at Liverpool there was not a word of reasonable criticism to be offered on the matter. If General Pierce, who was before all things good-natured and obliging, had been guilty of no greater indiscretion than to confer this modest distinction upon the most honourable and discreet of men of letters, he would have made a more brilliant mark in the annals of American statesmanship. Liverpool had not been immediately selected, and Hawthorne had written to his friend and publisher, Mr. Fields, with some humorous vagueness of allusion to his probable expatriation.

"Do make some inquiries about Portugal; as, for instance, in what part of the world it lies, and whether it is an empire, a kingdom, or a republic. Also, and more particularly, the expenses of living there, and whether the Minister would be likely to be much pestered with his own countrymen. Also, any other information about foreign countries would be acceptable to an inquiring mind."

It would seem from this that there had been a question of offering him a small diplomatic post; but the emoluments of the place were justly taken into account, and it is to be supposed that those of the consulate at Liverpool were at least as great as the salary of the American representative at Lisbon. Unfortunately, just after Hawthorne had taken possession of the former post, the salary attached to it was reduced by Congress, in an economical hour, to less than half the sum enjoyed by his predecessors. It was fixed at 7,500 dollars (£1,500); but the consular fees, which were often copious, were an added resource. At midsummer then, in 1853, Hawthorne was established in England.

CHAPTER VI. ENGLAND AND ITALY.

Hawthorne was close upon fifty years of age when he came to Europe—a fact that should be remembered when those impressions which he recorded in five substantial volumes (exclusive of the novel written in Italy), occasionally affect us by the rigidity of their point of view. His Note-Books, kept during his residence in England, his two winters in Rome, his summer in Florence, were published after his death; his impressions of England, sifted, revised, and addressed directly to the public, he gave to the world shortly before this event. The tone of his European Diaries is often so fresh and unsophisticated that we find ourselves thinking of the writer as a young man, and it is only a certain final sense of something reflective and a trifle melancholy that reminds us that the simplicity which is on the whole the leading characteristic of their pages, is, though the simplicity of inexperience, not that of youth. When I say inexperience, I mean that Hawthorne's experience had been narrow. His fifty years had been spent, for much the larger part, in small American towns—Salem, the Boston of forty years ago, Concord, Lenox, West Newton—and he had led exclusively what one may call a village-life. This is evident, not at all directly and superficially, but by implication and between the lines, in his desultory history of his foreign years. In other words, and to call things by their names, he was exquisitely and consistently provincial. I suggest this fact not in the least in condemnation, but, on the contrary, in support of an appreciative view of him. I know nothing more remarkable, more touching, than the sight of this odd, youthful—elderly mind, contending so late in the day with new opportunities for learning old things, and on the whole profiting by them so freely and gracefully. The Note-Books are provincial, and so, in a greatly modified degree, are the sketches of England, in *Our Old Home*; but the beauty and delicacy of this latter work are so interwoven with the author's air of being remotely outside of everything he describes, that they count for more, seem more themselves, and finally give the whole thing the appearance of a triumph, not of initiation, but of the provincial point of view itself.

I shall not attempt to relate in detail the incidents of his residence in England. He appears to have enjoyed it greatly, in spite of the deficiency of charm in the place to which his duties chiefly confined him. His confinement, however, was not unbroken, and his published journals consist largely of minute accounts of little journeys and wanderings, with his wife and his three children, through the rest of the country; together with much mention of numerous visits to London, a city for whose dusky immensity and multitudinous interest he professed the highest relish. His Note-Books are of the same cast as the two volumes of his American Diaries, of which, I have given some account—chiefly occupied with external matters, with the accidents of daily life, with observations made during the long walks (often with his son), which formed his most valued pastime. His office, moreover, though Liverpool was not a delectable home, furnished him with entertainment as well as occupation, and it may almost be said that during these years he saw more of his fellow-countrymen, in the shape of odd wanderers, petitioners, and inquirers of every kind, than he had ever done in his native land. The paper entitled "Consular Experiences," in *Our Old Home*, is an admirable recital of these observations, and a proof that the novelist might have found much material in the opportunities of the consul. On his return to America, in 1860, he drew from his journal a number of pages relating to his observations in England, re-wrote them (with, I should suppose, a good deal of care), and converted them into articles which he published in a magazine. These chapters were afterwards collected, and *Our Old Home* (a rather infelicitous title), was issued in 1863. I prefer to speak of the book now, however, rather than in touching upon the closing years of his life, for it is a kind of deliberate *résumé* of his impressions of the land of his ancestors. "It is not a good or a weighty book," he wrote to his publisher, who had sent him some reviews of it, "nor does it deserve any great amount of praise or censure. I don't care about seeing any more notices of it." Hawthorne's appreciation of his own productions was always extremely just; he had a sense of the relations of things, which some of his admirers have not thought it well to cultivate; and he never exaggerated his own importance as a writer. *Our Old Home* is not a weighty book; it is decidedly a light one. But when he says it is not a good one, I hardly know what he means, and his modesty at this point is in excess of his discretion. Whether good or not, *Our Old Home* is charming—it is most delectable reading. The execution is singularly perfect and ripe; of all his productions it seems to be the best written. The touch, as musicians say, is admirable; the lightness, the fineness, the felicity of characterisation and description, belong to a man who has the advantage of feeling delicately. His judgment is by no means always sound; it often rests on too narrow an observation. But his perception is of the keenest, and though it is frequently partial, incomplete, it is excellent as far as it goes. The book gave but limited satisfaction, I believe, in England, and I am not sure that the failure to enjoy certain manifestations of its sportive irony, has not chilled the appreciation of its singular grace. That English readers, on the whole, should have felt that Hawthorne did the national mind and manners but partial justice, is, I think, conceivable; at the same time that it seems to me remarkable that the tender side of the book, as I may call it, should not have carried it off better. It abounds in passages more delicately appreciative than can easily be found elsewhere, and it contains more charming and affectionate things than, I should suppose, had ever before been written about a country not the writer's own. To say that it is an immeasurably more exquisite and sympathetic work than any of the numerous persons who have related their misadventures in the United States have seen fit to devote to that country, is to say but little, and I imagine that Hawthorne had in mind the array of English voyagers—Mrs. Trollope, Dickens, Marryat, Basil Hall, Miss Martineau, Mr. Grattan—when he reflected that everything is relative and that, as such books go, his own little volume observed the amenities of criticism. He certainly had it in mind when he wrote the phrase in his preface relating to the impression the book might make in England. "Not an Englishman of them all ever spared America for courtesy's sake or kindness; nor, in my opinion, would it contribute in the least to any mutual advantage and comfort if we were to besmear each other all over with butter and honey." I am far from intending to intimate that the vulgar instinct of recrimination had anything to do with the restrictive passages of *Our Old Home*; I mean simply that the author had a prevision that his collection of sketches would in some particulars fail to please his English friends. He professed, after the event, to have discovered that the English are sensitive, and as they say of the Americans, for whose advantage

I believe the term was invented; thin-skinned. "The English critics," he wrote to his publisher, "seem to think me very bitter against their countrymen, and it is perhaps natural that they should, because their self-conceit can accept nothing short of indiscriminate adulation; but I really think that Americans have much more cause than they to complain of me. Looking over the volume I am rather surprised to find that whenever I draw a comparison between the two people, I almost invariably cast the balance against ourselves." And he writes at another time:—"I received several private letters and printed notices of *Our Old Home* from England. It is laughable to see the innocent wonder with which they regard my criticisms, accounting for them by jaundice, insanity, jealousy, hatred, on my part, and never admitting the least suspicion that there may be a particle of truth in them. The monstrosity of their self-conceit is such that anything short of unlimited admiration impresses them as malicious caricature. But they do me great injustice in supposing that I hate them. I would as soon hate my own people." The idea of his hating the English was of course too puerile for discussion; and the book, as I have said, is full of a rich appreciation of the finest characteristics of the country. But it has a serious defect—a defect which impairs its value, though it helps to give consistency to such an image of Hawthorne's personal nature as we may by this time have been able to form. It is the work of an outsider, of a stranger, of a man who remains to the end a mere spectator (something less even than an observer), and always lacks the final initiation into the manners and nature of a people of whom it may most be said, among all the people of the earth, that to know them is to make discoveries. Hawthorne freely confesses to this constant exteriority, and appears to have been perfectly conscious of it. "I remember," he writes in the sketch of "A London Suburb," in *Our Old Home*, "I remember to this day the dreary feeling with which I sat by our first English fireside and watched the chill and rainy twilight of an autumn day darkening down upon the garden, while the preceding occupant of the house (evidently a most unamiable personage in his lifetime), scowled inhospitably from above the mantel-piece, as if indignant that an American should try to make himself at home there. Possibly it may appease his sulky shade to know that I quitted his abode as much a stranger as I entered it." The same note is struck in an entry in his journal, of the date of October 6th, 1854.

"The people, for several days, have been in the utmost anxiety, and latterly in the highest exultation, about Sebastopol—and all England, and Europe to boot, have been fooled by the belief that it had fallen. This, however, now turns out to be incorrect; and the public visage is somewhat grim in consequence. I am glad of it. In spite of his actual sympathies, it is impossible for an American to be otherwise than glad. Success makes an Englishman intolerable, and already, on the mistaken idea that the way was open to a prosperous conclusion of the war, the *Times* had begun to throw out menaces against America. I shall never love England till she sues to us for help, and, in the meantime, the fewer triumphs she obtains, the better for all parties. An Englishman in adversity is a very respectable character; he does not lose his dignity, but merely comes to a proper conception of himself.... I seem to myself like a spy or traitor when I meet their eyes, and am conscious that I neither hope nor fear in sympathy with them, although they look at me in full confidence of sympathy. Their heart 'knoweth its own bitterness,' and as for me, being a stranger and an alien, I 'intermeddle not with their joy.'"

This seems to me to express very well the weak side of Hawthorne's work—his constant mistrust and suspicion of the society that surrounded him, his exaggerated, painful, morbid national consciousness. It is, I think, an indisputable fact that Americans are, as Americans, the most self-conscious people in the world, and the most addicted to the belief that the other nations of the earth are in a conspiracy to undervalue them. They are conscious of being the youngest of the great nations, of not being of the European family, of being placed on the circumference of the circle of civilisation rather than at the centre, of the experimental element not having as yet entirely dropped out of their great political undertaking. The sense of this relativity, in a word, replaces that quiet and comfortable sense of the absolute, as regards its own position in the world, which reigns supreme in the British and in the Gallic genius. Few persons, I think, can have mingled much with Americans in Europe without having made this reflection, and it is in England that their habit of looking askance at foreign institutions—of keeping one eye, as it were, on the American personality, while with the other they contemplate these objects—is most to be observed. Add to this that Hawthorne came to England late in life, when his habits, his tastes, his opinions, were already formed, that he was inclined to look at things in silence and brood over them gently, rather than talk about them, discuss them, grow acquainted with them by action; and it will be possible to form an idea of our writer's detached and critical attitude in the country in which it is easiest, thanks to its aristocratic constitution, to the absence of any considerable public fund of entertainment and diversion, to the degree in which the inexhaustible beauty and interest of the place are private property, demanding constantly a special introduction— in the country in which, I say, it is easiest for a stranger to remain a stranger. For a stranger to cease to be a stranger he must stand ready, as the French say, to pay with his person; and this was an obligation that Hawthorne was indisposed to incur. Our sense, as we read, that his reflections are those of a shy and susceptible man, with nothing at stake, mentally, in his appreciation of the country, is therefore a drawback to our confidence; but it is not a drawback sufficient to make it of no importance that he is at the same time singularly intelligent and discriminating, with a faculty of feeling delicately and justly, which constitutes in itself an illumination. There is a passage in the sketch entitled *About Warwick* which is a very good instance of what was probably his usual state of mind. He is speaking of the aspect of the High Street of the town.

"The street is an emblem of England itself. What seems new in it is chiefly a skilful and fortunate adaptation of what such a people as ourselves would destroy. The new things are based and supported on sturdy old things, and derive a massive strength from their deep and immemorial foundations, though with such limitations and impediments as only an Englishman could endure. But he likes to feel the weight of all the past upon his back; and moreover the antiquity that overburdens him has taken root in his being, and has grown to be rather a hump than a pack, so that there is no getting rid of it without tearing his whole structure to pieces. In my judgment, as he appears to be sufficiently comfortable under the mouldy accretion, he had better stumble on with it as long as he can. He presents a spectacle which is by no means without its charm for a disinterested and unincumbered observer."

There is all Hawthorne, with his enjoyment of the picturesque, his relish of chiaroscuro, of local colour, of the deposit of time, and his still greater enjoyment of his own dissociation from these things, his "disinterested and unincumbered" condition. His want of incumbrances may seem at times to give him a somewhat naked and attenuated appearance, but on the whole he carries it off very well. I have said that *Our Old Home* contains much of his best writing, and on turning over the book at hazard, I am struck with his frequent felicity of phrase. At every step there is something one would like to quote—something excellently well said. These things are often of the lighter sort, but Hawthorne's charming diction lingers in the memory—almost in the ear. I have always remembered a certain admirable characterisation of Doctor Johnson, in the account of the writer's visit to Lichfield—and I will preface it by a paragraph almost as good, commemorating the charms of the hotel in that interesting town.

"At any rate I had the great, dull, dingy, and dreary coffee-room, with its heavy old mahogany chairs and tables, all to myself, and not a soul to exchange a word with except the waiter, who, like most of his class in England, had evidently left his conversational abilities uncultivated. No former practice of solitary living, nor habits of reticence, nor well-tested self-dependence for occupation of mind and amusement, can quite avail, as I now proved, to dissipate the ponderous gloom of an English coffee-room under such circumstances as these, with no book at hand save the county directory, nor any newspaper but a torn local journal of five days ago. So I buried myself, betimes, in a huge heap of ancient feathers (there is no other kind of bed in these old inns), let my head sink into an unsubstantial pillow, and slept a stifled sleep, compounded of the night-troubles of all my predecessors in that same unrestful couch. And when I awoke, the odour of a bygone century was in my nostrils—a faint, elusive smell, of which I never had any conception before crossing the Atlantic."

The whole chapter entitled "Lichfield and Uttoxeter" is a sort of graceful tribute to Samuel Johnson, who certainly has nowhere else been more tenderly spoken of.

"Beyond all question I might have had a wiser friend than he. The atmosphere in which alone he breathed was dense; his awful dread of death showed how much muddy imperfection was to be cleansed out of him, before he could be capable of spiritual existence; he meddled only with the surface of life, and never cared to penetrate further than to ploughshare depth; his very sense and sagacity were but a one-eyed clear-sightedness. I laughed at him, sometimes standing beside his knee. And yet, considering that my native propensities were toward Fairy Land, and also how much yeast is generally mixed up with the mental sustenance of a New Englander, it may not have been altogether amiss, in those childish and boyish days, to keep pace with this heavy-footed traveller and feed on the gross diet that he carried in his knapsack. It is wholesome food even now! And then, how English! Many of the latent sympathies that enabled me to enjoy the Old Country so well, and that so readily amalgamated themselves with the American ideas that seemed most adverse to them, may have been derived from, or fostered and kept alive by, the great English moralist. Never was a descriptive epithet more nicely appropriate than that! Doctor Johnson's morality was as English an article as a beef-steak."

And for mere beauty of expression I cannot forbear quoting this passage about the days in a fine English summer:—

"For each day seemed endless, though never wearisome. As far as your actual experience is concerned, the English summer day has positively no beginning and no end. When you awake, at any reasonable hour, the sun is already shining through the curtains; you live through unnumbered hours of Sabbath quietude, with a calm variety of incident softly etched upon their tranquil lapse; and at length you become conscious that it is bedtime again, while there is still enough daylight in the sky to make the pages of your book distinctly legible. Night, if there be any such season, hangs down a transparent veil through which the bygone day beholds its successor; or if not quite true of the latitude of London, it may be soberly affirmed of the more northern parts of the island that To-morrow is born before its Yesterday is dead. They exist together in the golden twilight, where the decrepit old day dimly discerns the face of the ominous infant; and you, though a mere mortal, may simultaneously touch them both, with one finger of recollection and another of prophecy."

The Note-Books, as I have said, deal chiefly with, the superficial aspect of English life, and describe the material objects with which the author was surrounded. They often describe them admirably, and the rural beauty of the country has never been more happily expressed. But there are inevitably a great many reflections and incidental judgments, characterisations of people he met, fragments of psychology and social criticism, and it is here that Hawthorne's mixture of subtlety and simplicity, his interfusion of genius with what I have ventured to call the provincial quality, is most apparent. To an American reader this later quality, which is never grossly manifested, but pervades the Journals like a vague natural perfume, an odour of purity and kindness and integrity, must always, for a reason that I will touch upon, have a considerable charm; and such a reader will accordingly take an even greater satisfaction in the Diaries kept during the two years Hawthorne spent in Italy; for in these volumes the element I speak of is especially striking. He resigned his consulate at Liverpool towards the close of 1857—whether because he was weary of his manner of life there and of the place itself, as may well have been, or because he wished to anticipate supersession by the new government (Mr. Buchanan's) which was just establishing itself at Washington, is not apparent from the slender sources of information from which these pages have been compiled. In the month of January of the following year he betook himself with his family to the Continent, and, as promptly as possible, made the best of his way to Rome. He spent the remainder of the winter and the spring there, and then went to Florence for the summer and autumn; after which he returned to Rome and passed a second season. His Italian Note-Books are very pleasant reading, but they are of less interest than the others, for his contact with the life of the country, its people and its manners, was simply that of the ordinary tourist—which amounts to saying that it was extremely superficial. He appears to have suffered a great deal of discomfort and depression in Rome, and not to have been on the whole in the best mood for enjoying the place and its resources. That he did, at one time and another, enjoy these things keenly is proved by his beautiful romance, *Transformation*, which could never have been written by a man who had not had many hours of exquisite appreciation of the lovely land of Italy. But he took It hard, as it were, and suffered himself to be painfully discomposed by the usual accidents of Italian life, as foreigners learn to know it. His future was again uncertain, and during his second winter in Rome he was in danger of losing his elder daughter by a malady which he speaks of as a trouble "that pierced to my very vitals." I may mention, with regard to this painful episode, that Franklin Pierce, whose presidential days were over, and who, like other ex-presidents, was travelling in Europe, came to Rome at the time, and that the Note-Books contain some singularly beautiful and touching allusions to his old friend's gratitude for his sympathy, and enjoyment of his society. The sentiment of friendship has on the whole been so much less commemorated in literature than might have been expected from the place it is supposed to hold in life, that there is always something striking in any frank and ardent expression of it. It occupied, in so far as Pierce was the object of it, a large place in Hawthorne's mind, and it is impossible not to feel the manly tenderness of such lines as these:—

"I have found him here in Rome, the whole of my early friend, and even better than I used to know him; a heart as true and affectionate, a mind much widened and deepened by the experience of life. We hold just the same relation to one another as of yore, and we have passed all the turning-off places, and may hope to go on together, still the same dear friends, as long as we live. I do not love him one whit the less for having been President, nor for having done me the greatest good in his power; a fact that speaks eloquently in his favour, and perhaps says a little for myself. If he had been merely a benefactor, perhaps I might not have borne it so well; but each did his best for the other, as friend for friend."

The Note-Books are chiefly taken up with descriptions of the regular sights and "objects of interest," which we often feel to be rather perfunctory and a little in the style of the traditional tourist's diary. They abound in charming touches, and every reader of *Transformation* will remember the delightful colouring of the numerous pages in that novel, which are devoted to the pictorial aspects of Rome. But we are unable to rid ourselves of the impression that Hawthorne was a good deal bored by the importunity of Italian art, for which his taste, naturally not keen, had never been cultivated. Occasionally, indeed, he breaks out into explicit sighs and groans, and frankly declares that he washes his hands of it. Already, in England, he had made the discovery that he could, easily feel overdosed with such things. "Yesterday," he wrote in 1856, "I went out at about twelve and visited the British Museum; an exceedingly tiresome affair. It quite crushes a person to see so much at once, and I wandered from hall to hall with a weary and heavy heart, wishing (Heaven forgive me!) that the Elgin marbles and the frieze of the Parthenon were all burnt into lime, and that the granite Egyptian statues were hewn and squared into building stones."

The plastic sense was not strong in Hawthorne; there can be no better proof of it than his curious aversion to the representation of the nude in sculpture. This aversion was deep-seated; he constantly returns to it, exclaiming upon the incongruity of modern artists making naked figures. He apparently quite failed to see that nudity is not an incident, or accident, of sculpture, but its very essence and principle; and his jealousy of undressed images strikes the reader as a strange, vague, long-dormant heritage of his straight-laced Puritan ancestry. Whenever he talks of statues he makes a great point of the smoothness and whiteness of the marble—speaks of the surface of the marble as if it were half the beauty of the image; and when he discourses of pictures, one feels that the brightness or dinginess of the frame is an essential part of his impression of the work—as he indeed somewhere distinctly affirms. Like a good American, he took more pleasure in the productions of Mr. Thompson and Mr. Brown, Mr. Powers and Mr. Hart, American artists who were plying their trade in Italy, than in the works which adorned the ancient museums of the country. He suffered greatly from the cold, and found little charm in the climate, and during the weeks of winter that followed his arrival in Rome, he sat shivering by his fire and wondering why he had come to such a land of misery. Before he left Italy he wrote to his publisher—"I bitterly detest Rome, and shall rejoice to bid it farewell for ever; and I fully acquiesce in all the mischief and ruin that has happened to it, from Nero's conflagration downward. In fact, I wish the very site had been obliterated before I ever saw it." Hawthorne presents himself to the reader of these pages as the last of the old-fashioned Americans—and this is the interest which I just now said that his compatriots would find in his very limitations. I do not mean by this that there are not still many of his fellow-countrymen (as there are many natives of every land under the sun,) who are more susceptible of being irritated than of being soothed by the influences of the Eternal City. What I mean is that an American of equal value with Hawthorne, an American of equal genius, imagination, and, as our forefathers said, sensibility, would at present inevitably accommodate himself more easily to the idiosyncrasies of foreign lands. An American as cultivated as Hawthorne, is now almost inevitably more cultivated, and, as a matter of course, more Europeanised in advance, more cosmopolitan. It is very possible that in becoming so, he has lost something of his occidental savour, the quality which excites the goodwill of the American reader of our author's Journals for the dislocated, depressed, even slightly bewildered diarist. Absolutely the last of the earlier race of Americans Hawthorne was, fortunately, probably far from being. But I think of him as the last specimen of the more primitive type of men of letters; and when it comes to measuring what he succeeded in being, in his unadulterated form, against what he failed of being, the positive side of the image quite extinguishes the negative. I must be on my guard, however, against incurring the charge of cherishing a national consciousness as acute as I have ventured to pronounce his own.

Out of his mingled sensations, his pleasure and his weariness, his discomforts and his reveries, there sprang another beautiful work. During the summer of 1858, he hired a picturesque old villa on the hill of Bellosguardo, near Florence, a curious structure with a crenelated tower, which, after having in the course of its career suffered many vicissitudes and played many parts, now finds its most vivid identity in being pointed out to strangers as the sometime residence of the celebrated American romancer. Hawthorne took a fancy to the place, as well he might, for it is one of the loveliest spots on earth, and the great view that stretched itself before him contains every element of beauty. Florence lay at his feet with her memories and treasures; the olive-covered hills bloomed around him, studded with villas as picturesque as his own; the Apennines, perfect in form and colour, disposed themselves opposite, and in the distance, along its fertile valley, the Arno wandered to Pisa and the sea. Soon after coming hither he wrote to a friend in a strain of high satisfaction:—

"It is pleasant to feel at last that I am really away from America—a satisfaction that I never really enjoyed as long as I stayed in Liverpool, where it seemed to be that the quintessence of nasal and hand-shaking Yankeedom was gradually filtered and sublimated through my consulate, on the way outward and homeward. I first got acquainted with my own countrymen there. At Rome too it was not much better. But here in Florence, and in the summer-time, and in this secluded villa, I have escaped out of all my old tracks, and am really remote. I like my present residence immensely. The house stands on a hill, overlooking Florence, and is big enough to quarter a regiment, insomuch that each member of the family, including servants, has a separate suite of apartments, and there are vast wildernesses of upper rooms into which we have never yet sent exploring expeditions. At one end of the house there is a moss-grown tower, haunted by owls and by the ghost of a monk who was confined there in the thirteenth century, previous to being burnt at the stake in the principal square of Florence. I hire this villa, tower and all, at twenty-eight dollars a month; but I mean to take it away bodily and clap it into a romance, which I have in my head, ready to be written out."

This romance was *Transformation*, which he wrote out during the following winter in Rome, and re-wrote during the several months that he spent in England, chiefly at Leamington, before returning to America. The Villa Montauto figures, in fact, in this tale as the castle of Monte-Beni, the patrimonial dwelling of the hero. "I take some credit to myself," he wrote to the same friend, on returning to Rome, "for having sternly shut myself up for an hour or two every day, and come to close grips with a romance which I have been trying to tear out of my mind." And later in the same winter he says—"I shall go home, I fear, with a heavy heart, not expecting to be very well contented there.... If I were but a hundred times richer than I am, how very comfortable I could be! I consider it a great piece of good fortune that I have had experience of the discomforts and miseries of Italy, and did not go directly home from England. Anything will seem like a Paradise after a Roman winter." But he got away at last, late in the spring, carrying his novel with him, and the book was published, after, as I say, he had worked it over, mainly during some weeks that he passed at the little watering-place of Redcar, on the Yorkshire coast, in February of the following year. It was issued primarily in England; the American edition immediately followed. It is an odd fact that in the two countries the book came out under different titles. The title that the author had bestowed upon it did not satisfy the English publishers, who requested him to provide it with another; so that it is only in America that the work bears the name of *The Marble Fawn*. Hawthorne's choice of this appellation is, by the way, rather singular, for it completely fails to characterise the story, the subject of which is the living faun, the faun of flesh and blood, the unfortunate Donatello. His marble counterpart is mentioned only in the opening chapter. On the other hand Hawthorne complained that *Transformation* "gives one the idea of Harlequin in a pantomime." Under either name, however, the book was a great success, and it has probably become the most popular of Hawthorne's four novels. It is part of the intellectual equipment of the Anglo-Saxon visitor to Rome, and is read by every English-speaking traveller who arrives there, who has been there, or who expects to go.

It has a great deal of beauty, of interest and grace; but it has to my sense a slighter value than its companions, and I am far from regarding it as the masterpiece of the author, a position to which we sometimes hear it assigned. The subject is admirable, and so are many of the details; but the whole thing is less simple and complete than either of the three tales of American life, and Hawthorne forfeited a precious advantage in ceasing to tread his native soil. Half the virtue of *The Scarlet Letter* and *The House of the Seven Gables* is in their local quality; they are impregnated with the New England air. It is very true that Hawthorne had no pretension to pourtray actualities and to cultivate that literal exactitude which is now the fashion. Had this been the case, he would probably have made a still graver mistake in transporting the scene of his story to a country which he knew only superficially. His tales all go on more or less "in the vague," as the French say, and of course the vague may as well be placed in Tuscany as in Massachusetts. It may also very well be urged in Hawthorne's favour here, that in *Transformation* he has attempted to deal with actualities more than he did in either of his earlier novels. He has described the streets and monuments of Rome with a closeness which forms no part of his reference to those of Boston and Salem. But for all this he incurs that penalty of seeming factitious and unauthoritative, which is always the result of an artist's attempt to project himself into an atmosphere in which he has not a transmitted and inherited property. An English or a German writer (I put poets aside) may love Italy well enough, and know her well enough, to write delightful fictions about her; the thing has often been done. But the productions in question will, as novels, always have about them something second-rate and imperfect. There is in *Transformation* enough beautiful perception of the interesting character of Rome, enough rich and eloquent expression of it, to save the book, if the book could be saved; but the style, what the French call the *genre*, is an inferior one, and the thing remains a charming romance with intrinsic weaknesses.

Allowing for this, however, some of the finest pages in all Hawthorne are to be found in it. The subject, as I have said, is a particularly happy one, and there is a great deal of interest in the simple combination and opposition of the four actors. It is noticeable that in spite of the considerable length of the story, there are no accessory figures; Donatello and Miriam, Kenyon and Hilda, exclusively occupy the scene. This is the more noticeable as the scene is very large, and the great Roman background is constantly presented to us. The relations of these four people are full of that moral picturesqueness which Hawthorne was always looking for; he found it in perfection in the history of Donatello. As I have said, the novel is the most popular of his works, and every one will remember the figure of the simple, joyous, sensuous young Italian, who is not so much a man as a child, and not so much a child as a charming, innocent animal, and how he is brought to self-knowledge and to a miserable conscious manhood, by the commission of a crime. Donatello is rather vague and impalpable; he says too little in the book, shows himself too little, and falls short, I think, of being a creation. But he is enough of a creation to make us enter into the situation, and the whole history of his rise, or fall, whichever one chooses to call it—his tasting of the tree of knowledge and finding existence complicated with a regret—is unfolded with a thousand ingenious and exquisite touches. Of course, to make the interest complete, there is a woman in the affair, and Hawthorne has done few things more beautiful than the picture of the unequal complicity of guilt between his immature and dimly-puzzled hero, with his clinging, unquestioning, unexacting devotion, and the dark, powerful, more widely-seeing feminine nature of Miriam. Deeply touching is the representation of the manner in which these two essentially different persons—the woman intelligent, passionate, acquainted with life, and with a tragic element in her own career; the youth ignorant, gentle, unworldly, brightly and harmlessly natural—are equalised and bound together by their common secret, which insulates them, morally, from the rest of mankind. The character of Hilda has always struck me as an admirable invention—one of those things that mark the man of genius. It needed a man of genius and of Hawthorne's imaginative delicacy, to feel the propriety of such a figure as Hilda's and to perceive the relief it would both give and borrow. This pure and somewhat rigid New England girl, following the vocation of a copyist of pictures in Rome, unacquainted with evil and untouched by impurity, has been accidentally the witness, unknown and unsuspected, of the dark deed by which her friends, Miriam and Donatello, are knit together. This is *her* revelation of evil, her loss of perfect innocence. She has done no wrong, and yet wrongdoing has become a part of her experience, and she carries the weight of her detested knowledge upon her heart. She carries it a long time, saddened and oppressed by it, till at last she can bear it no longer. If I have called the whole idea of the presence and effect of Hilda in the story a trait of genius, the purest touch of inspiration is the episode in which the poor girl deposits her burden. She has passed the whole lonely summer in Rome, and one day, at the end of it, finding herself in St. Peter's, she enters a confessional, strenuous daughter of the Puritans as she is, and pours out her dark knowledge into the bosom of the Church—then comes away with her conscience lightened, not a whit the less a Puritan than before. If the book contained nothing else noteworthy but this admirable scene, and the pages describing the murder committed by Donatello under Miriam's eyes, and the ecstatic wandering, afterwards, of the guilty couple, through the "blood-stained streets of Rome," it would still deserve to rank high among the imaginative productions of our day.

Like all of Hawthorne's things, it contains a great many light threads of symbolism, which shimmer in the texture of the tale, but which are apt to break and remain in our fingers if we attempt to handle them. These things are part of Hawthorne's very manner—almost, as one might say, of his vocabulary; they belong much more to the surface of his work than to its stronger interest. The fault of *Transformation* is that the element of the unreal is pushed too far, and that the book is neither positively of one category nor of another. His "moonshiny romance," he calls it in a letter; and, in truth, the lunar element is a little too pervasive. The action wavers between the streets of Rome, whose literal features the author perpetually sketches, and a vague realm of fancy, in which quite a different verisimilitude prevails. This is the trouble with Donatello himself. His companions are intended to be real—if they fail to be so, it is not for want of intention; whereas he is intended to be real or not, as you please. He is of a different substance from them; it is as if a painter, in composing a picture, should try to give you an impression of one of his figures by a strain of music. The idea of the modern faun was a charming one; but I think it a pity that the author should not have made him more definitely modern, without reverting so much to his mythological properties and antecedents, which are very gracefully touched upon, but which belong to the region of picturesque conceits, much more than to that of real psychology. Among the young Italians of to-day there are still plenty of models for such an image as Hawthorne appears to have wished to present in the easy and natural Donatello. And since I am speaking critically, I may go on to say that the art of narration, in *Transformation*, seems to me more at fault than in the author's other novels. The story straggles and wanders, is dropped and taken up again, and towards the close lapses into an almost fatal vagueness.

CHAPTER VII. LAST YEARS.

Of the four last years of Hawthorne's life there is not much to tell that I have not already told. He returned to America in the summer of 1860, and took up his abode in the house he had bought at Concord before going to Europe, and of which his occupancy had as yet been brief. He was to occupy it only four years. I have insisted upon the fact of his being an intense American, and of his looking at all things, during his residence in Europe, from the standpoint of that little clod of western earth which he carried about with him as the good Mohammedan carries the strip of carpet on which he kneels down to face towards Mecca. But it does not appear, nevertheless, that he found himself treading with any great exhilaration the larger section of his native soil upon which, on his return, he disembarked. Indeed, the closing part of his life was a period of dejection, the more acute that it followed directly upon seven years of the happiest opportunities he was to have known. And his European residence had been brightest at the last; he had broken almost completely with those habits of extreme seclusion into which he was to relapse on his return to Concord. "You would be stricken dumb," he wrote from London, shortly before leaving it for the last time, "to see how quietly I accept a whole string of invitations, and, what is more, perform my engagements without a murmur.... The stir of this London life, somehow or other," he adds in the same letter, "has done me a wonderful deal of good, and I feel better than for months past. This is strange, for if I had my choice I should leave undone almost all the things I do." "When he found himself once more on the old ground," writes Mr. Lathrop, "with the old struggle for subsistence staring him in the face again, it is not difficult to conceive how a certain degree of depression would follow." There is indeed not a little sadness in the thought of Hawthorne's literary gift, light, delicate, exquisite, capricious, never too abundant, being charged with the heavy burden of the maintenance of a family. We feel that it was not intended for such grossness, and that in a world ideally constituted he would have enjoyed a liberal pension, an assured subsistence, and have been able to produce his charming prose only when the fancy took him.

The brightness of the outlook at home was not made greater by the explosion of the Civil War in the spring of 1861. These months, and the three years that followed them, were not a cheerful time for any persons but army-contractors; but over Hawthorne the war-cloud appears to have dropped a permanent shadow. The whole affair was a bitter disappointment to him, and a fatal blow to that happy faith in the uninterruptedness of American prosperity which I have spoken of as the religion of the old-fashioned American in general, and the old-fashioned Democrat in particular. It was not a propitious time for cultivating the Muse; when history herself is so hard at work, fiction has little left to say. To fiction, directly, Hawthorne did not address himself; he composed first, chiefly during the year 1862, the chapters of which our *Our Old Home* was afterwards made up. I have said that, though this work has less value than his purely imaginative things, the writing is singularly good, and it is well to remember, to its greater honour, that it was produced at a time when it was painfully hard for a man of Hawthorne's cast of mind to fix his attention. The air was full of battle-smoke, and the poet's vision was not easily clear. Hawthorne was irritated, too, by the sense of being to a certain extent, politically considered, in a false position. A large section of the Democratic party was not in good odour at the North; its loyalty was not perceived to be of that clear strain which public opinion required. To this wing of the party Franklin Pierce had, with reason or without, the credit of belonging; and our author was conscious of some sharpness of responsibility in defending the illustrious friend of whom he had already made himself the advocate. He defended him manfully, without a grain of concession, and described the ex-President to the public (and to himself), if not as he was, then as he ought to be. *Our Old Home* is dedicated to him, and about this dedication there was some little difficulty. It was represented to Hawthorne that as General Pierce was rather out of fashion, it might injure the success, and, in plain terms, the sale of his book. His answer (to his publisher), was much to the point.

"I find that it would be a piece of poltroonery in me to withdraw either the dedication or the dedicatory letter. My long and intimate personal relations with Pierce render the dedication altogether proper, especially as regards this book, which would have had no existence without his kindness; and if he is so exceedingly unpopular that his name ought to sink the volume, there is so much the more need that an old friend should stand by him. I cannot, merely on account of pecuniary profit or literary reputation, go back from what I have deliberately felt and thought it right to do; and if I were to tear out the dedication I should never look at the volume again without remorse and shame. As for the literary public, it must accept my book precisely as I think fit to give it, or let it alone. Nevertheless I have no fancy for making myself a martyr when it is honourably and conscientiously possible to avoid it; and I always measure out heroism very accurately according to the exigencies of the occasion, and should be the last man in the world to throw away a bit of it needlessly. So I have looked over the concluding paragraph and have amended it in such a way that, while doing what I know to be justice to my friend, it contains not a word that ought to be objectionable to any set of readers. If the public of the North see fit to ostracise me for this, I can only say that I would gladly sacrifice a thousand or two dollars, rather than retain the goodwill of such a herd of dolts and mean-spirited scoundrels."

The dedication was published, the book was eminently successful, and Hawthorne was not ostracised. The paragraph under discussion stands as follows:—"Only this let me say, that, with the record of your life in my memory, and with a sense of your character in my deeper consciousness, as among the few things that time has left as it found them, I need no assurance that you continue faithful for ever to that grand idea of an irrevocable Union which, as you once told me, was the earliest that your brave father taught you. For other men there may be a choice of paths—for you but one; and it rests among my certainties that no man's loyalty is more steadfast, no man's hopes or apprehensions on behalf of our national existence more deeply heartfelt, or more closely intertwined with his possibilities of personal happiness, than those of Franklin Pierce." I know not how well the ex-President liked these lines, but the public thought them admirable, for they served as a kind of formal profession of faith, on the question of the hour, by a loved and honoured writer. That some of his friends thought such a profession needed is apparent from the numerous editorial ejaculations and protests appended to an article describing a visit he had just paid to Washington, which Hawthorne contributed to the *Atlantic Monthly* for July, 1862, and which, singularly enough, has not been reprinted. The article has all the usual merit of such sketches on Hawthorne's part—the merit of delicate, sportive feeling, expressed with consummate grace—but the editor of the periodical appears to have thought that he must give the antidote with the poison, and the paper is accompanied with several little notes disclaiming all sympathy with the writer's political heresies. The heresies strike the reader of to-day as extremely mild, and what excites his emotion, rather, is the questionable taste of the editorial commentary, with which it is strange that Hawthorne should have allowed his article to be encumbered. He had not been an Abolitionist before the War, and that he should not pretend to be one at the eleventh hour, was, for instance, surely a piece of consistency that might have been allowed to pass. "I shall not pretend to be an admirer of old John Brown," he says, in a page worth quoting, "any further than sympathy with Whittier's excellent ballad about him may go; nor did I expect ever to shrink so unutterably from any apophthegm of a sage whose happy lips have uttered a hundred golden sentences"—the allusion here, I suppose, is to Mr. Emerson—"as from that saying (perhaps falsely attributed to so honoured a name), that the death of this blood-stained fanatic has 'made the Gallows as venerable as the Cross!' Nobody was ever more justly hanged. He won his martyrdom fairly, and took it fairly. He himself, I am persuaded (such was his natural integrity), would have acknowledged that Virginia had a right to take the life which he had staked and lost; although it would have been better for her, in the hour that is fast coming, if she could generously have forgotten the criminality of his attempt in its enormous folly. On the other hand, any common-sensible man, looking at the matter unsentimentally, must have felt a certain intellectual satisfaction in seeing him hanged, if it were only in requital of his preposterous miscalculation of possibilities." Now that the heat of that great conflict has passed away, this is a capital expression of the saner estimate, in the United States, of the dauntless and deluded old man who proposed to solve a complex political problem by stirring up a servile insurrection. There is much of the same sound sense, interfused with light, just appreciable irony, in such a passage as the following:—

"I tried to imagine how very disagreeable the presence of a Southern army would be in a sober town of Massachusetts; and the thought considerably lessened my wonder at the cold and shy regards that are cast upon our troops, the gloom, the sullen demeanour, the declared, or scarcely hidden, sympathy with rebellion, which are so frequent here. It is a strange thing in human life that the greatest errors both of men and women often spring from their sweetest and most generous qualities; and so, undoubtedly, thousands of warmhearted, generous, and impulsive persons have joined the Rebels, not from any real zeal for the cause, but because, between two conflicting loyalties, they chose that which necessarily lay nearest the heart. There never existed any other Government against which treason was so easy, and could defend itself by such plausible arguments, as against that of the United States. The anomaly of two allegiances, (of which that of the State comes nearest home to a man's feelings, and includes the altar and the hearth, while the General Government claims his devotion only to an airy mode of law, and has no symbol but a flag,) is exceedingly mischievous in this point of view; for it has converted crowds of honest people into traitors, who seem to themselves not merely innocent but patriotic, and who die for a bad cause with a quiet conscience as if it were the best. In the vast extent of our country— too vast by far to be taken into one small human heart—we inevitably limit to our own State, or at farthest, to our own little section, that sentiment of physical love for the soil which renders an Englishman, for example, so intensely sensitive to the dignity and well-being of his little island, that one hostile foot, treading anywhere upon it, would make a bruise on each individual breast. If a man loves his own State, therefore, and is content to be ruined with her, let us shoot him, if we can, but allow him an honourable burial in the soil he fights for."

To this paragraph a line of deprecation from the editor is attached; and indeed from the point of view of a vigorous prosecution of the war it was doubtless not particularly pertinent. But it is interesting as an example of the way an imaginative man judges current events—trying to see the other side as well as his own, to feel what his adversary feels, and present his view of the case.

But he had other occupations for his imagination than putting himself into the shoes of unappreciative Southerners. He began at this time two novels, neither of which he lived to finish, but both of which were published, as fragments, after his death. The shorter of these fragments, to which he had given the name of *The Dolliver Romance*, is so very brief that little can be said of it. The author strikes, with all his usual sweetness, the opening notes of a story of New England life, and the few pages which have been given to the world contain a charming picture of an old man and a child.

The other rough sketch—it is hardly more—is in a manner complete; it was unfortunately deemed complete enough to be brought out in a magazine as a serial novel. This was to do it a great wrong, and I do not go too far in saying that poor Hawthorne would probably not have enjoyed the very bright light that has been projected upon this essentially crude piece of work. I am at a loss to know how to speak of *Septimius Felton, or the Elixir of Life*; I have purposely reserved but a small space for doing so, for the part of discretion seems to be to pass it by lightly. I differ therefore widely from the author's biographer and son-in-law in thinking it a work of the greatest weight and value, offering striking analogies with Goethe's *Faust*; and still more widely from a critic whom Mr. Lathrop quotes, who regards a certain portion of it as "one of the very greatest triumphs in all literature." It seems to me almost cruel to pitch in this exalted key one's estimate of the rough first draught of a tale in regard to which the author's premature death operates, virtually, as a complete renunciation of pretensions. It is plain to any reader that *Septimius Felton*, as it stands, with its roughness, its gaps, its mere allusiveness and slightness of treatment, gives us but a very partial measure of Hawthorne's full intention; and it is equally easy to believe that this intention was much finer than anything we find in the book. Even if we possessed the novel in its complete form, however, I incline to think that we should regard it as very much the weakest of Hawthorne's productions. The idea itself seems a failure, and the best that might have come of it would have been very much below *The Scarlet Letter* or *The House of the Seven Gables*. The appeal to our interest is not felicitously made, and the fancy of a potion, to assure eternity of existence, being made from the flowers which spring from the grave of a man whom the distiller of the potion has deprived of life, though it might figure with advantage in a short story of the pattern of the *Twice-Told Tales*, appears too slender to carry the weight of a novel. Indeed, this whole matter of elixirs and potions belongs to the fairy-tale period of taste, and the idea of a young man enabling himself to live forever by concocting and imbibing a magic draught, has the misfortune of not appealing to our sense of reality or even to our sympathy. The weakness of *Septimius Felton* is that the reader cannot take the hero seriously—a fact of which there can be no better proof than the element of the ridiculous which inevitably mingles itself in the scene in which he entertains his lady-love with a prophetic sketch of his occupations during the successive centuries of his earthly immortality. I suppose the answer to my criticism is that this is allegorical, symbolic, ideal; but we feel that it symbolises nothing substantial, and that the truth—whatever it may be—that it illustrates, is as moonshiny, to use Hawthorne's own expression, as the allegory itself. Another fault of the story is that a great historical event—the war of the Revolution—is introduced in the first few pages, in order to supply the hero with a pretext for killing the young man from whose grave the flower of immortality is to sprout, and then drops out of the narrative altogether, not even forming a background to the sequel. It seems to me that Hawthorne should either have invented some other occasion for the death of his young officer, or else, having struck the note of the great public agitation which overhung his little group of characters, have been careful to sound it through the rest of his tale. I do wrong, however, to insist upon these things, for I fall thereby into the error of treating the work as if it had been cast into its ultimate form and acknowledged by the author. To avoid this error I shall make no other criticism of details, but content myself with saying that the idea and intention of the book appear, relatively speaking, feeble, and that even had it been finished it would have occupied a very different place in the public esteem from the writer's masterpieces.

The year 1864 brought with it for Hawthorne a sense of weakness and depression from which he had little relief during the four or five months that were left him of life. He had his engagement to produce *The Dolliver Romance*, which had been promised to the subscribers of the *Atlantic Monthly* (it was the first time he had undertaken to publish a work of fiction in monthly parts), but he was unable to write, and his consciousness of an unperformed task weighed upon him, and did little to dissipate his physical inertness. "I have not yet had courage to read the Dolliver proof-sheet," he wrote to his publisher in December, 1863; "but will set about it soon, though with terrible reluctance, such as I never felt before. I am most grateful to you," he went on, "for protecting me from that visitation of the elephant and his cub. If you happen to see Mr.——, of L——, a young man who was here last summer, pray tell him anything that your conscience will let you, to induce him to spare me another visit, which I know he intended. I really am not well, and cannot be disturbed by strangers, without more suffering than it is worth while to endure." A month later he was obliged to ask for a further postponement. "I am not quite up to writing yet, but shall make an effort as soon as I see any hope of success. You ought to be thankful that (like most other broken-down authors) I do not pester you with decrepit pages, and insist upon your accepting them as full of the old spirit and vigour. That trouble perhaps still awaits you, after I shall have reached a further stage of decay. Seriously, my mind has, for the time, lost its temper and its fine edge, and I have an instinct that I had better keep quiet. Perhaps I shall have a new spirit of vigour if I wait quietly for it; perhaps not." The winter passed away, but the "new spirit of vigour" remained absent, and at the end of February he wrote to Mr. Fields that his novel had simply broken down, and that he should never finish it. "I hardly know what to say to the public about this abortive romance, though I know pretty well what the case will be. I shall never finish it. Yet it is not quite pleasant for an author to announce himself, or to be announced, as finally broken down as to his literary faculty.... I cannot finish it unless a great change comes over me; and if I make too great an effort to do so, it will be my death; not that I should care much for that, if I could fight the battle through and win it, thus ending a life of much smoulder and a scanty fire, in a blaze of glory. But I should smother myself in mud of my own making.... I am not low-spirited, nor fanciful, nor freakish, but look what seem to me realities in the face, and am ready to take whatever may come. If I could but go to England now, I think that the sea-voyage and the 'old Home' might set me all right."

But he was not to go to England; he started three months later upon a briefer journey, from which he never returned. His health was seriously disordered, and in April, according to a letter from Mrs. Hawthorne, printed by Mr. Fields, he had been "miserably ill." His feebleness was complete; he appears to have had no definite malady, but he was, according to the common phrase, failing. General Pierce proposed to him that they should make a little tour together among the mountains of New Hampshire, and Hawthorne consented, in the hope of getting some profit from the change of air. The northern New England spring is not the most genial season in the world, and this was an indifferent substitute for the resource for which his wife had, on his behalf, expressed a wish—a visit to "some island in the Gulf Stream." He was not to go far; he only reached a little place called Plymouth, one of the stations of approach to the beautiful mountain scenery of New Hampshire, when, on the 18th of May, 1864, death overtook him. His companion, General Pierce, going into his room in the early morning, found that he had breathed his last during the night—had passed away, tranquilly, comfortably, without a sign or a sound, in his sleep. This happened at the hotel of the place—a vast white edifice, adjacent to the railway station, and entitled the Pemigiwasset House. He was buried at Concord, and many of the most distinguished men in the country stood by his grave.

He was a beautiful, natural, original genius, and his life had been singularly exempt from worldly preoccupations and vulgar efforts. It had been as pure, as simple, as unsophisticated, as his work. He had lived primarily in his domestic affections, which were of the tenderest kind; and then—without eagerness, without pretension, but with a great deal of quiet devotion—in his charming art. His work will remain; it is too original and exquisite to pass away; among the men of imagination he will always have his niche. No one has had just that vision of life, and no one has had a literary form that more successfully expressed his vision. He was not a moralist, and he was not simply a poet. The moralists are weightier, denser, richer, in a sense; the poets are more purely inconclusive and irresponsible. He combined in a singular degree the spontaneity of the imagination with a haunting care for moral problems. Man's conscience was his theme, but he saw it in the light of a creative fancy which added, out of its own substance, an interest, and, I may almost say, an importance.

THE END.

About Author

Henry James OM (15 April 1843 – 28 February 1916) was an American-British author regarded as a key transitional figure between literary realism and literary modernism, and is considered by many to be among the greatest novelists in the English language. He was the son of Henry James Sr. and the brother of renowned philosopher and psychologist William James and diarist Alice James.

He is best known for a number of novels dealing with the social and marital interplay between émigré Americans, English people, and continental Europeans. Examples of such novels include The Portrait of a Lady, The Ambassadors, and The Wings of the Dove. His later works were increasingly experimental. In describing the internal states of mind and social dynamics of his characters, James often made use of a style in which ambiguous or contradictory motives and impressions were overlaid or juxtaposed in the discussion of a character's psyche. For their unique ambiguity, as well as for other aspects of their composition, his late works have been compared to impressionist painting.

His novella The Turn of the Screw has garnered a reputation as the most analysed and ambiguous ghost story in the English language and remains his most widely adapted work in other media. He also wrote a number of other highly regarded ghost stories and is considered one of the greatest masters of the field.

James published articles and books of criticism, travel, biography, autobiography, and plays. Born in the United States, James largely relocated to Europe as a young man and eventually settled in England, becoming a British subject in 1915, one year before his death. James was nominated for the Nobel Prize in Literature in 1911, 1912 and 1916.

Life

Early years, 1843–1883

James was born at 2 Washington Place in New York City on 15 April 1843. His parents were Mary Walsh and Henry James Sr. His father was intelligent and steadfastly congenial. He was a lecturer and philosopher who had inherited independent means from his father, an Albany banker and investor. Mary came from a wealthy family long settled in New York City. Her sister Katherine lived with her adult family for an extended period of time. Henry Jr. had three brothers, William, who was one year his senior, and younger brothers Wilkinson (Wilkie) and Robertson. His younger sister was Alice. Both of his parents were of Irish and Scottish descent.

The family first lived in Albany, at 70 N. Pearl St., and then moved to Fourteenth Street in New York City when James was still a young boy. His education was calculated by his father to expose him to many influences, primarily scientific and philosophical; it was described by Percy Lubbock, the editor of his selected letters, as "extraordinarily haphazard and promiscuous." James did not share the usual education in Latin and Greek classics. Between 1855 and 1860, the James' household traveled to London, Paris, Geneva, Boulogne-sur-Mer and Newport, Rhode Island, according to the father's current interests and publishing ventures, retreating to the United States when funds were low. Henry studied primarily with tutors and briefly attended schools while the family traveled in Europe. Their longest stays were in France, where Henry began to feel at home and became fluent in French. He was afflicted with a stutter, which seems to have manifested itself only when he spoke English; in French, he did not stutter.

In 1860 the family returned to Newport. There Henry became a friend of the painter John La Farge, who introduced him to French literature, and in particular, to Balzac. James later called Balzac his "greatest master," and said that he had learned more about the craft of fiction from him than from anyone else.

In the autumn of 1861 Henry received an injury, probably to his back, while fighting a fire. This injury, which resurfaced at times throughout his life, made him unfit for military service in the American Civil War.

170

In 1864 the James family moved to Boston, Massachusetts to be near William, who had enrolled first in the Lawrence Scientific School at Harvard and then in the medical school. In 1862 Henry attended Harvard Law School, but realised that he was not interested in studying law. He pursued his interest in literature and associated with authors and critics William Dean Howells and Charles Eliot Norton in Boston and Cambridge, formed lifelong friendships with Oliver Wendell Holmes Jr., the future Supreme Court Justice, and with James and Annie Fields, his first professional mentors.

His first published work was a review of a stage performance, "Miss Maggie Mitchell in Fanchon the Cricket," published in 1863. About a year later, A Tragedy of Error, his first short story, was published anonymously. James's first payment was for an appreciation of Sir Walter Scott's novels, written for the North American Review. He wrote fiction and non-fiction pieces for The Nation and Atlantic Monthly, where Fields was editor. In 1871 he published his first novel, Watch and Ward, in serial form in the Atlantic Monthly. The novel was later published in book form in 1878.

During a 14-month trip through Europe in 1869–70 he met Ruskin, Dickens, Matthew Arnold, William Morris, and George Eliot. Rome impressed him profoundly. "Here I am then in the Eternal City," he wrote to his brother William. "At last—for the first time—I live!" He attempted to support himself as a freelance writer in Rome, then secured a position as Paris correspondent for the New York Tribune, through the influence of its editor John Hay. When these efforts failed he returned to New York City. During 1874 and 1875 he published Transatlantic Sketches, A Passionate Pilgrim, and Roderick Hudson. During this early period in his career he was influenced by Nathaniel Hawthorne.

In 1869 he settled in London. There he established relationships with Macmillan and other publishers, who paid for serial installments that they would later publish in book form. The audience for these serialized novels was largely made up of middle-class women, and James struggled to fashion serious literary work within the strictures imposed by editors' and publishers' notions of what was suitable for young women to read. He lived in rented rooms but was able to join gentlemen's clubs that had libraries and where he could entertain male friends. He was introduced to English society by Henry Adams and Charles Milnes Gaskell, the latter introducing him to the Travellers' and the Reform Clubs.

In the fall of 1875 he moved to the Latin Quarter of Paris. Aside from two trips to America, he spent the next three decades—the rest of his life—in Europe. In Paris he met Zola, Alphonse Daudet, Maupassant, Turgenev, and others. He stayed in Paris only a year before moving to London.

In England he met the leading figures of politics and culture. He continued to be a prolific writer, producing The American (1877), The Europeans (1878), a revision of Watch and Ward (1878), French Poets and Novelists (1878), Hawthorne (1879), and several shorter works of fiction. In 1878 Daisy Miller established his fame on both sides of the Atlantic. It drew notice perhaps mostly because it depicted a woman whose behavior is outside the social norms of Europe. He also began his first masterpiece, The Portrait of a Lady, which would appear in 1881.

In 1877 he first visited Wenlock Abbey in Shropshire, home of his friend Charles Milnes Gaskell whom he had met through Henry Adams. He was much inspired by the darkly romantic Abbey and the surrounding countryside, which features in his essay Abbeys and Castles. In particular the gloomy monastic fishponds behind the Abbey are said to have inspired the lake in The Turn of the Screw.

While living in London, James continued to follow the careers of the "French realists", Émile Zola in particular. Their stylistic methods influenced his own work in the years to come. Hawthorne's influence on him faded during this period, replaced by George Eliot and Ivan Turgenev. 1879–1882 saw the publication of The Europeans, Washington Square, Confidence, and The Portrait of a Lady. He visited America in 1882–1883, then returned to London.

The period from 1881 to 1883 was marked by several losses. His mother died in 1881, followed by his father a few months later, and then by his brother Wilkie. Emerson, an old family friend, died in 1882. His friend Turgenev died in 1883.

Middle years, 1884–1897

In 1884 James made another visit to Paris. There he met again with Zola, Daudet, and Goncourt. He had been following the careers of the French "realist" or "naturalist" writers, and was increasingly influenced by them. In 1886, he published The Bostonians and The Princess Casamassima, both influenced by the French writers he'd studied assiduously. Critical reaction and sales were poor. He wrote to Howells that the books had hurt his career rather than helped because they had "reduced the desire, and demand, for my productions to zero". During this time he became friends with Robert Louis Stevenson, John Singer Sargent, Edmund Gosse, George du Maurier, Paul Bourget, and Constance Fenimore Woolson. His third novel from the 1880s was The Tragic Muse. Although he was following the precepts of Zola in his novels of the '80s, their tone and attitude are closer to the fiction of Alphonse Daudet. The lack of critical and financial success for his novels during this period led him to try writing for the theatre. (His dramatic works and his experiences with theatre are discussed below.)

In the last quarter of 1889, he started translating "for pure and copious lucre" Port Tarascon, the third volume of Alphonse Daudet adventures of Tartarin de Tarascon. Serialized in Harper's Monthly Magazine from June 1890, this translation praised as "clever" by The Spectator was published in January 1891 by Sampson Low, Marston, Searle & Rivington.

After the stage failure of Guy Domville in 1895, James was near despair and thoughts of death plagued him. The years spent on dramatic works were not entirely a loss. As he moved into the last phase of his career he found ways to adapt dramatic techniques into the novel form.

In the late 1880s and throughout the 1890s James made several trips through Europe. He spent a long stay in Italy in 1887. In that year the short novel The Aspern Papers and The Reverberator were published.

Late years, 1898–1916

In 1897–1898 he moved to Rye, Sussex, and wrote The Turn of the Screw. 1899–1900 saw the publication of The Awkward Age and The Sacred

Fount. During 1902–1904 he wrote The Ambassadors, The Wings of the Dove, and The Golden Bowl.

In 1904 he revisited America and lectured on Balzac. In 1906–1910 he published The American Scene and edited the "New York Edition", a 24-volume collection of his works. In 1910 his brother William died; Henry had just joined William from an unsuccessful search for relief in Europe on what then turned out to be his (Henry's) last visit to the United States (from summer 1910 to July 1911), and was near him, according to a letter he wrote, when he died.

In 1913 he wrote his autobiographies, A Small Boy and Others, and Notes of a Son and Brother. After the outbreak of the First World War in 1914 he did war work. In 1915 he became a British subject and was awarded the Order of Merit the following year. He died on 28 February 1916, in Chelsea, London. As he requested, his ashes were buried in Cambridge Cemetery in Massachusetts.

Biographers

James regularly rejected suggestions that he should marry, and after settling in London proclaimed himself "a bachelor". F. W. Dupee, in several volumes on the James family, originated the theory that he had been in love with his cousin Mary ("Minnie") Temple, but that a neurotic fear of sex kept him from admitting such affections: "James's invalidism ... was itself the symptom of some fear of or scruple against sexual love on his part." Dupee used an episode from James's memoir A Small Boy and Others, recounting a dream of a Napoleonic image in the Louvre, to exemplify James's romanticism about Europe, a Napoleonic fantasy into which he fled.

Dupee had not had access to the James family papers and worked principally from James's published memoir of his older brother, William, and the limited collection of letters edited by Percy Lubbock, heavily weighted toward James's last years. His account therefore moved directly from James's childhood, when he trailed after his older brother, to elderly invalidism. As more material became available to scholars, including the diaries of contemporaries and hundreds of affectionate and sometimes erotic letters written by James to younger men, the picture of neurotic celibacy gave way to a portrait of a closeted homosexual.

Between 1953 and 1972, Leon Edel authored a major five-volume biography of James, which accessed unpublished letters and documents after Edel gained the permission of James's family. Edel's portrayal of James included the suggestion he was celibate. It was a view first propounded by critic Saul Rosenzweig in 1943. In 1996 Sheldon M. Novick published Henry James: The Young Master, followed by Henry James: The Mature Master (2007). The first book "caused something of an uproar in Jamesian circles" as it challenged the previous received notion of celibacy, a once-familiar paradigm in biographies of homosexuals when direct evidence was non-existent. Novick also criticised Edel for following the discounted Freudian interpretation of homosexuality "as a kind of failure." The difference of opinion erupted in a series of exchanges between Edel and Novick which were published by the online magazine Slate, with the latter arguing that even the suggestion of celibacy went against James's own injunction "live!"—not "fantasize!"

A letter James wrote in old age to Hugh Walpole has been cited as an explicit statement of this. Walpole confessed to him of indulging in "high jinks", and James wrote a reply endorsing it: "We must know, as much as possible, in our beautiful art, yours & mine, what we are talking about — & the only way to know it is to have lived & loved & cursed & floundered & enjoyed & suffered — I don't think I regret a single 'excess' of my responsive youth".

The interpretation of James as living a less austere emotional life has been subsequently explored by other scholars. The often intense politics of Jamesian scholarship has also been the subject of studies. Author Colm Tóibín has said that Eve Kosofsky Sedgwick's Epistemology of the Closet made a landmark difference to Jamesian scholarship by arguing that he be read as a homosexual writer whose desire to keep his sexuality a secret shaped his layered style and dramatic artistry. According to Tóibín such a reading "removed James from the realm of dead white males who wrote about posh people. He became our contemporary."

175

James's letters to expatriate American sculptor Hendrik Christian Andersen have attracted particular attention. James met the 27-year-old Andersen in Rome in 1899, when James was 56, and wrote letters to Andersen that are intensely emotional: "I hold you, dearest boy, in my innermost love, & count on your feeling me—in every throb of your soul". In a letter of 6 May 1904, to his brother William, James referred to himself as "always your hopelessly celibate even though sexagenarian Henry". How accurate that description might have been is the subject of contention among James's biographers, but the letters to Andersen were occasionally quasi-erotic: "I put, my dear boy, my arm around you, & feel the pulsation, thereby, as it were, of our excellent future & your admirable endowment." To his homosexual friend Howard Sturgis, James could write: "I repeat, almost to indiscretion, that I could live with you. Meanwhile I can only try to live without you."

His numerous letters to the many young gay men among his close male friends are more forthcoming. In a letter to Howard Sturgis, following a long visit, James refers jocularly to their "happy little congress of two" and in letters to Hugh Walpole he pursues convoluted jokes and puns about their relationship, referring to himself as an elephant who "paws you oh so benevolently" and winds about Walpole his "well meaning old trunk". His letters to Walter Berry printed by the Black Sun Press have long been celebrated for their lightly veiled eroticism.

He corresponded in almost equally extravagant language with his many female friends, writing, for example, to fellow novelist Lucy Clifford: "Dearest Lucy! What shall I say? when I love you so very, very much, and see you nine times for once that I see Others! Therefore I think that—if you want it made clear to the meanest intelligence—I love you more than I love Others." To his New York friend Mary Cadwalader Jones: "Dearest Mary Cadwalader. I yearn over you, but I yearn in vain; & your long silence really breaks my heart, mystifies, depresses, almost alarms me, to the point even of making me wonder if poor unconscious & doting old Célimare [Jones's pet name for James] has 'done' anything, in some dark somnambulism of the spirit, which has ... given you a bad moment, or a wrong impression, or a 'colourable pretext' ... However these things may be, he loves you as tenderly as ever;

nothing, to the end of time, will ever detach him from you, & he remembers those Eleventh St. matutinal intimes hours, those telephonic matinées, as the most romantic of his life ..." His long friendship with American novelist Constance Fenimore Woolson, in whose house he lived for a number of weeks in Italy in 1887, and his shock and grief over her suicide in 1894, are discussed in detail in Edel's biography and play a central role in a study by Lyndall Gordon. (Edel conjectured that Woolson was in love with James and killed herself in part because of his coldness, but Woolson's biographers have objected to Edel's account.)

Works

Style and themes

James is one of the major figures of trans-Atlantic literature. His works frequently juxtapose characters from the Old World (Europe), embodying a feudal civilisation that is beautiful, often corrupt, and alluring, and from the New World (United States), where people are often brash, open, and assertive and embody the virtues—freedom and a more highly evolved moral character—of the new American society. James explores this clash of personalities and cultures, in stories of personal relationships in which power is exercised well or badly. His protagonists were often young American women facing oppression or abuse, and as his secretary Theodora Bosanquet remarked in her monograph Henry James at Work:

> When he walked out of the refuge of his study and into the world and looked around him, he saw a place of torment, where creatures of prey perpetually thrust their claws into the quivering flesh of doomed, defenseless children of light ... His novels are a repeated exposure of this wickedness, a reiterated and passionate plea for the fullest freedom of development, unimperiled by reckless and barbarous stupidity.

Critics have jokingly described three phases in the development of James's prose: "James I, James II, and The Old Pretender." He wrote short stories and plays. Finally, in his third and last period he returned to the long, serialised novel. Beginning in the second period, but most noticeably in the third, he increasingly abandoned direct statement in favour of frequent

177

double negatives, and complex descriptive imagery. Single paragraphs began to run for page after page, in which an initial noun would be succeeded by pronouns surrounded by clouds of adjectives and prepositional clauses, far from their original referents, and verbs would be deferred and then preceded by a series of adverbs. The overall effect could be a vivid evocation of a scene as perceived by a sensitive observer. It has been debated whether this change of style was engendered by James's shifting from writing to dictating to a typist, a change made during the composition of What Maisie Knew.

In its intense focus on the consciousness of his major characters, James's later work foreshadows extensive developments in 20th century fiction. Indeed, he might have influenced stream-of-consciousness writers such as Virginia Woolf, who not only read some of his novels but also wrote essays about them. Both contemporary and modern readers have found the late style difficult and unnecessary; his friend Edith Wharton, who admired him greatly, said that there were passages in his work that were all but incomprehensible. James was harshly portrayed by H. G. Wells as a hippopotamus laboriously attempting to pick up a pea that had got into a corner of its cage. The "late James" style was ably parodied by Max Beerbohm in "The Mote in the Middle Distance".

More important for his work overall may have been his position as an expatriate, and in other ways an outsider, living in Europe. While he came from middle-class and provincial beginnings (seen from the perspective of European polite society) he worked very hard to gain access to all levels of society, and the settings of his fiction range from working class to aristocratic, and often describe the efforts of middle-class Americans to make their way in European capitals. He confessed he got some of his best story ideas from gossip at the dinner table or at country house weekends. He worked for a living, however, and lacked the experiences of select schools, university, and army service, the common bonds of masculine society. He was furthermore a man whose tastes and interests were, according to the prevailing standards of Victorian era Anglo-American culture, rather feminine, and who was shadowed by the cloud of prejudice that then and later accompanied suspicions of his homosexuality. Edmund Wilson famously compared James's objectivity to Shakespeare's:

One would be in a position to appreciate James better if one compared him with the dramatists of the seventeenth century—Racine and Molière, whom he resembles in form as well as in point of view, and even Shakespeare, when allowances are made for the most extreme differences in subject and form. These poets are not, like Dickens and Hardy, writers of melodrama—either humorous or pessimistic, nor secretaries of society like Balzac, nor prophets like Tolstoy: they are occupied simply with the presentation of conflicts of moral character, which they do not concern themselves about softening or averting. They do not indict society for these situations: they regard them as universal and inevitable. They do not even blame God for allowing them: they accept them as the conditions of life.

It is also possible to see many of James's stories as psychological thought-experiments. In his preface to the New York edition of The American he describes the development of the story in his mind as exactly such: the "situation" of an American, "some robust but insidiously beguiled and betrayed, some cruelly wronged, compatriot..." with the focus of the story being on the response of this wronged man. The Portrait of a Lady may be an experiment to see what happens when an idealistic young woman suddenly becomes very rich. In many of his tales, characters seem to exemplify alternative futures and possibilities, as most markedly in "The Jolly Corner", in which the protagonist and a ghost-doppelganger live alternative American and European lives; and in others, like The Ambassadors, an older James seems fondly to regard his own younger self facing a crucial moment.

Major novels

The first period of James's fiction, usually considered to have culminated in The Portrait of a Lady, concentrated on the contrast between Europe and America. The style of these novels is generally straightforward and, though personally characteristic, well within the norms of 19th-century fiction. Roderick Hudson (1875) is a Künstlerroman that traces the development of the title character, an extremely talented sculptor. Although the book shows some signs of immaturity—this was James's first serious attempt at a full-length novel—it has attracted favourable comment due to the vivid realisation of the three major characters: Roderick Hudson, superbly gifted but unstable and unreliable; Rowland Mallet, Roderick's limited but much more mature friend and patron; and Christina Light, one of James's most enchanting and maddening femmes fatales. The pair of Hudson and Mallet has been seen as representing the two sides of James's own nature: the wildly imaginative artist and the brooding conscientious mentor.

In The Portrait of a Lady (1881) James concluded the first phase of his career with a novel that remains his most popular piece of long fiction. The story is of a spirited young American woman, Isabel Archer, who "affronts her destiny" and finds it overwhelming. She inherits a large amount of money and subsequently becomes the victim of Machiavellian scheming by two American expatriates. The narrative is set mainly in Europe, especially in England and Italy. Generally regarded as the masterpiece of his early phase, The Portrait of a Lady is described as a psychological novel, exploring the minds of his characters, and almost a work of social science, exploring the differences between Europeans and Americans, the old and the new worlds.

The second period of James's career, which extends from the publication of The Portrait of a Lady through the end of the nineteenth century, features less popular novels including The Princess Casamassima, published serially in The Atlantic Monthly in 1885–1886, and The Bostonians, published serially in The Century Magazine during the same period. This period also featured James's celebrated Gothic novella, The Turn of the Screw.

The third period of James's career reached its most significant achievement in three novels published just around the start of the 20th century: The Wings of the Dove (1902), The Ambassadors (1903), and The Golden Bowl (1904). Critic F. O. Matthiessen called this "trilogy" James's major phase, and these novels have certainly received intense critical study. It was the second-written of the books, The Wings of the Dove (1902) that was the first published because it attracted no serialization. This novel tells the story of Milly Theale, an American heiress stricken with a serious disease, and her impact on the people around her. Some of these people befriend Milly with honourable motives, while others are more self-interested. James stated in his autobiographical books that Milly was based on Minny Temple, his beloved cousin who died at an early age of tuberculosis. He said that he attempted in the novel to wrap her memory in the "beauty and dignity of art".

Shorter narratives

James was particularly interested in what he called the "beautiful and blest nouvelle", or the longer form of short narrative. Still, he produced a number of very short stories in which he achieved notable compression of sometimes complex subjects. The following narratives are representative of James's achievement in the shorter forms of fiction.

- "A Tragedy of Error" (1864), short story
- "The Story of a Year" (1865), short story
- A Passionate Pilgrim (1871), novella
- Madame de Mauves (1874), novella
- Daisy Miller (1878), novella
- The Aspern Papers (1888), novella
- The Lesson of the Master (1888), novella
- The Pupil (1891), short story
- "The Figure in the Carpet" (1896), short story
- The Beast in the Jungle (1903), novella
- An International Episode (1878)
- Picture and Text
- Four Meetings (1885)
- A London Life, and Other Tales (1889)
- The Spoils of Poynton (1896)

- Embarrassments (1896)

- The Two Magics: The Turn of the Screw, Covering End (1898)

- A Little Tour of France (1900)

- The Sacred Fount (1901)

- Views and Reviews (1908)

- The Wings of the Dove, Volume I (1902)

- The Wings of the Dove, Volume II (1909)

- The Finer Grain (1910)

- The Outcry (1911)

- Lady Barbarina: The Siege of London, An International Episode and Other Tales (1922)

- The Birthplace (1922)

Plays

At several points in his career James wrote plays, beginning with one-act plays written for periodicals in 1869 and 1871 and a dramatisation of his popular novella Daisy Miller in 1882. From 1890 to 1892, having received a bequest that freed him from magazine publication, he made a strenuous effort to succeed on the London stage, writing a half-dozen plays of which only one, a dramatisation of his novel The American, was produced. This play was performed for several years by a touring repertory company and had a respectable run in London, but did not earn very much money for James. His other plays written at this time were not produced.

In 1893, however, he responded to a request from actor-manager George Alexander for a serious play for the opening of his renovated St. James's Theatre, and wrote a long drama, Guy Domville, which Alexander produced. There was a noisy uproar on the opening night, 5 January 1895, with hissing from the gallery when James took his bow after the final curtain, and the author was upset. The play received moderately good reviews and had a modest run of four weeks before being taken off to make way for Oscar Wilde's The Importance of Being Earnest, which Alexander thought would have better prospects for the coming season.

After the stresses and disappointment of these efforts James insisted that he would write no more for the theatre, but within weeks had agreed to write a curtain-raiser for Ellen Terry. This became the one-act "Summersoft", which he later rewrote into a short story, "Covering End", and then expanded into a full-length play, The High Bid, which had a brief run in London in 1907, when James made another concerted effort to write for the stage. He wrote three new plays, two of which were in production when the death of Edward VII on 6 May 1910 plunged London into mourning and theatres closed. Discouraged by failing health and the stresses of theatrical work, James did not renew his efforts in the theatre, but recycled his plays as successful novels. The Outcry was a best-seller in the United States when it was published in 1911. During the years 1890–1893 when he was most engaged with the theatre, James wrote a good deal of theatrical criticism and assisted Elizabeth Robins and others in translating and producing Henrik Ibsen for the first time in London.

Leon Edel argued in his psychoanalytic biography that James was traumatised by the opening night uproar that greeted Guy Domville, and that it plunged him into a prolonged depression. The successful later novels, in Edel's view, were the result of a kind of self-analysis, expressed in fiction, which partly freed him from his fears. Other biographers and scholars have not accepted this account, however; the more common view being that of F.O. Matthiessen, who wrote: "Instead of being crushed by the collapse of his hopes [for the theatre]... he felt a resurgence of new energy."

Non-fiction

Beyond his fiction, James was one of the more important literary critics in the history of the novel. In his classic essay The Art of Fiction (1884), he argued against rigid prescriptions on the novelist's choice of subject and method of treatment. He maintained that the widest possible freedom in content and approach would help ensure narrative fiction's continued vitality.

James wrote many valuable critical articles on other novelists; typical is his book-length study of Nathaniel Hawthorne, which has been the subject of critical debate. Richard Brodhead has suggested that the study was emblematic of James's struggle with Hawthorne's influence, and constituted an effort to place the elder writer "at a disadvantage." Gordon Fraser, meanwhile, has suggested that the study was part of a more commercial effort by James to introduce himself to British readers as Hawthorne's natural successor.

When James assembled the New York Edition of his fiction in his final years, he wrote a series of prefaces that subjected his own work to searching, occasionally harsh criticism.

At 22 James wrote The Noble School of Fiction for The Nation's first issue in 1865. He would write, in all, over 200 essays and book, art, and theatre reviews for the magazine.

For most of his life James harboured ambitions for success as a playwright. He converted his novel The American into a play that enjoyed modest returns in the early 1890s. In all he wrote about a dozen plays, most of which went unproduced. His costume drama Guy Domville failed disastrously on its opening night in 1895. James then largely abandoned his efforts to conquer the stage and returned to his fiction. In his Notebooks he maintained that his theatrical experiment benefited his novels and tales by helping him dramatise his characters' thoughts and emotions. James produced a small but valuable amount of theatrical criticism, including perceptive appreciations of Henrik Ibsen.

With his wide-ranging artistic interests, James occasionally wrote on the visual arts. Perhaps his most valuable contribution was his favourable assessment of fellow expatriate John Singer Sargent, a painter whose critical status has improved markedly in recent decades. James also wrote sometimes charming, sometimes brooding articles about various places he visited and lived in. His most famous books of travel writing include Italian Hours (an example of the charming approach) and The American Scene (most definitely on the brooding side).

James was one of the great letter-writers of any era. More than ten thousand of his personal letters are extant, and over three thousand have been published in a large number of collections. A complete edition of James's letters began publication in 2006, edited by Pierre Walker and Greg Zacharias. As of 2014, eight volumes have been published, covering the period from 1855 to 1880. James's correspondents included celebrated contemporaries like Robert Louis Stevenson, Edith Wharton and Joseph Conrad, along with many others in his wide circle of friends and acquaintances. The letters range from the "mere twaddle of graciousness" to serious discussions of artistic, social and personal issues.

Very late in life James began a series of autobiographical works: A Small Boy and Others, Notes of a Son and Brother, and the unfinished The Middle Years. These books portray the development of a classic observer who was passionately interested in artistic creation but was somewhat reticent about participating fully in the life around him.

Reception

Criticism, biographies and fictional treatments

James's work has remained steadily popular with the limited audience of educated readers to whom he spoke during his lifetime, and has remained firmly in the canon, but, after his death, some American critics, such as Van Wyck Brooks, expressed hostility towards James for his long expatriation and eventual naturalisation as a British subject. Other critics such as E. M. Forster complained about what they saw as James's squeamishness in the treatment of sex and other possibly controversial material, or dismissed his late style as difficult and obscure, relying heavily on extremely long sentences and excessively latinate language. Similarly Oscar Wilde criticised him for writing "fiction as if it were a painful duty". Vernon Parrington, composing a canon of American literature, condemned James for having cut himself off from America. Jorge Luis Borges wrote about him, "Despite the scruples and delicate complexities of James, his work suffers from a major defect: the absence of life." And Virginia Woolf, writing to Lytton Strachey, asked, "Please tell me what you find in Henry James. ... we have his works here, and

I read, and I can't find anything but faintly tinged rose water, urbane and sleek, but vulgar and pale as Walter Lamb. Is there really any sense in it?" The novelist W. Somerset Maugham wrote, "He did not know the English as an Englishman instinctively knows them and so his English characters never to my mind quite ring true," and argued "The great novelists, even in seclusion, have lived life passionately. Henry James was content to observe it from a window." Maugham nevertheless wrote, "The fact remains that those last novels of his, notwithstanding their unreality, make all other novels, except the very best, unreadable." Colm Tóibín observed that James "never really wrote about the English very well. His English characters don't work for me."

Despite these criticisms, James is now valued for his psychological and moral realism, his masterful creation of character, his low-key but playful humour, and his assured command of the language. In his 1983 book, The Novels of Henry James, Edward Wagenknecht offers an assessment that echoes Theodora Bosanquet's:

> "To be completely great," Henry James wrote in an early review, "a work of art must lift up the heart," and his own novels do this to an outstanding degree ... More than sixty years after his death, the great novelist who sometimes professed to have no opinions stands foursquare in the great Christian humanistic and democratic tradition. The men and women who, at the height of World War II, raided the secondhand shops for his out-of-print books knew what they were about. For no writer ever raised a braver banner to which all who love freedom might adhere.

William Dean Howells saw James as a representative of a new realist school of literary art which broke with the English romantic tradition epitomised by the works of Charles Dickens and William Makepeace Thackeray. Howells wrote that realism found "its chief exemplar in Mr. James... A novelist he is not, after the old fashion, or after any fashion but his own." F.R. Leavis championed Henry James as a novelist of "established pre-eminence" in The Great Tradition (1948), asserting that The Portrait of a Lady and The Bostonians were "the two most brilliant novels in the language." James is now prized as a master of point of view who moved literary fiction forward by insisting in showing, not telling, his stories to the reader. (Source: Wikipedia)

NOTABLE WORKS

NOVELS

Watch and Ward (1871)

Roderick Hudson (1875)

The American (1877)

The Europeans (1878)

Confidence (1879)

Washington Square (1880)

The Portrait of a Lady (1881)

The Bostonians (1886)

The Princess Casamassima (1886)

The Reverberator (1888)

The Tragic Muse (1890)

The Other House (1896)

The Spoils of Poynton (1897)

What Maisie Knew (1897)

The Awkward Age (1899)

The Sacred Fount (1901)

The Wings of the Dove (1902)

The Ambassadors (1903)

The Golden Bowl (1904)

The Whole Family (collaborative novel with eleven other authors, 1908)

The Outcry (1911)

The Ivory Tower (unfinished, published posthumously 1917)

The Sense of the Past (unfinished, published posthumously 1917)

SHORT STORIES AND NOVELLAS

A Tragedy of Error (1864)

The Story of a Year (1865)

A Landscape Painter (1866)

A Day of Days (1866)

My Friend Bingham (1867)

Poor Richard (1867)

The Story of a Masterpiece (1868)

A Most Extraordinary Case (1868)

A Problem (1868)

De Grey: A Romance (1868)

Osborne's Revenge (1868)

The Romance of Certain Old Clothes (1868)

A Light Man (1869)

Gabrielle de Bergerac (1869)

Travelling Companions (1870)

A Passionate Pilgrim (1871)

At Isella (1871)

Master Eustace (1871)

Guest's Confession (1872)

The Madonna of the Future (1873)

The Sweetheart of M. Briseux (1873)

The Last of the Valerii (1874)

Madame de Mauves (1874)

Adina (1874)

Professor Fargo (1874)

Eugene Pickering (1874)

Benvolio (1875)

Crawford's Consistency (1876)

The Ghostly Rental (1876)

Four Meetings (1877)

Rose-Agathe (1878, as Théodolinde)

Daisy Miller (1878)

Longstaff's Marriage (1878)

An International Episode (1878)

The Pension Beaurepas (1879)

A Diary of a Man of Fifty (1879)

A Bundle of Letters (1879)

The Point of View (1882)

The Siege of London (1883)

Impressions of a Cousin (1883)

Lady Barberina (1884)

Pandora (1884)

The Author of Beltraffio (1884)

Georgina's Reasons (1884)

A New England Winter (1884)

The Path of Duty (1884)

Mrs. Temperly (1887)

Louisa Pallant (1888)

The Aspern Papers (1888)

The Liar (1888)

The Modern Warning (1888, originally published as The Two Countries)

A London Life (1888)

The Patagonia (1888)

The Lesson of the Master (1888)

The Solution (1888)

The Pupil (1891)

Brooksmith (1891)

The Marriages (1891)

The Chaperon (1891)

Sir Edmund Orme (1891)

Nona Vincent (1892)

The Real Thing (1892)

The Private Life (1892)

Lord Beaupré (1892)

The Visits (1892)

Sir Dominick Ferrand (1892)

Greville Fane (1892)

Collaboration (1892)

Owen Wingrave (1892)

The Wheel of Time (1892)

The Middle Years (1893)

The Death of the Lion (1894)

The Coxon Fund (1894)

The Next Time (1895)

Glasses (1896)

The Altar of the Dead (1895)

The Figure in the Carpet (1896)

The Way It Came (1896, also published as The Friends of the Friends)

The Turn of the Screw (1898)

Covering End (1898)

In the Cage (1898)

John Delavoy (1898)

The Given Case (1898)

Europe (1899)

The Great Condition (1899)

The Real Right Thing (1899)

Paste (1899)

The Great Good Place (1900)

Maud-Evelyn (1900)

Miss Gunton of Poughkeepsie (1900)

The Tree of Knowledge (1900)

The Abasement of the Northmores (1900)

The Third Person (1900)

The Special Type (1900)

The Tone of Time (1900)

Broken Wings (1900)

The Two Faces (1900)

Mrs. Medwin (1901)

The Beldonald Holbein (1901)

The Story in It (1902)

Flickerbridge (1902)

The Birthplace (1903)

The Beast in the Jungle (1903)

The Papers (1903)

Fordham Castle (1904)

Julia Bride (1908)

The Jolly Corner (1908)

The Velvet Glove (1909)

Mora Montravers (1909)

Crapy Cornelia (1909)

The Bench of Desolation (1909)

A Round of Visits (1910)

OTHER

Transatlantic Sketches (1875)

French Poets and Novelists (1878)

Hawthorne (1879)

Portraits of Places (1883)

A Little Tour in France (1884)

Partial Portraits (1888)

Essays in London and Elsewhere (1893)

Picture and Text (1893)

Terminations (1893)

Theatricals (1894)

Theatricals: Second Series (1895)

Guy Domville (1895)

The Soft Side (1900)

William Wetmore Story and His Friends (1903)

The Better Sort (1903)

English Hours (1905)

The Question of our Speech; The Lesson of Balzac. Two Lectures (1905)

The American Scene (1907)

Views and Reviews (1908)

Italian Hours (1909)

A Small Boy and Others (1913)

Notes on Novelists (1914)

Notes of a Son and Brother (1914)

Within the Rim (1918)

Travelling Companions (1919)

Notebooks (various, published posthumously)

The Middle Years (unfinished, published posthumously 1917)

A Most Unholy Trade (1925, published posthumously)

The Art of the Novel : Critical Prefaces (1934)

CPSIA information can be obtained
at www.ICGtesting.com
Printed in the USA
LVHW091915261020
669864LV00002B/19

9 781662 715631